Praise for

Were Chronicles

I think Max was the right mix of sexy, protective and emotionally wounded. He was smart and caring and I loved how easily he fell for Cassie. Their romance was tender and sweet with an underlying fiery chemistry that neither could ignore.
~ *Ramblings from a Chaotic Mind*

Max was such a great character. He wasn't so broken that I felt he was irredeemable but he had just enough baggage that showed he was human (well shifter) and relatable. Cassie has such a kind spirit and is generous with those she loves. When the two meet there is an instant attraction but they keep their hormones in check and get to know each other first. ~ *Jeep Diva*

Totally Bound Publishing books by Crissy Smith:

Seduced by the Neighbour
Lacey's Seduction
Eternal
Bid High
Fated Love
Vamps in the City

Were Chronicles Volume One
Pack Alpha
Pack Enforcer
Pack Territory

Were Chronicles Volume Two
Pack Rogue
Pack Community
Pack Mates

Were Chronicles Volume Three
Pack Daughter
Pack Hunter
Pack Council

Were Chronicles Volume Four
Pack Security
Pack Beta
Pack Secrets

Corporate Wolves
The Favour
Losing Control

Secrets
The Shifter and the Dreamer

Shifter Chronicles
Birds of Prey
Bear Claw

Anthologies
Caught in theMiddle: Magical Ménage

Collections
Bite Me!: Savage Love
Summer Seductions: Summers' Girl
Cloaks and Daggers: Vampire Hunter

What's her Secret?
Last Call

WERE CHRONICLES
Volume Four

Pack Security

Pack Beta

Pack Secrets

CRISSY SMITH

Were Chronicles Volume Four
ISBN # 978-1-78430-453-9
©Copyright Crissy Smith 2015
Cover Art by Posh Gosh ©Copyright 2015
Interior text design by Claire Siemaszkiewicz
Totally Bound Publishing

Published in 2015 by Totally Bound Publishing, Newland House, The Point, Weaver Road, Lincoln, LN6 3QN, United Kingdom.

PACK SECURITY

Dedication

For my girl — always believe.

Chapter One

Cassandra Wilson pushed open the bedroom balcony doors and stepped out into the cool morning air. She was still reeling from the events of the night before. Someone had actually broken into her studio and destroyed...everything. It had been like a bad dream, really.

After she'd eaten dinner with her brothers, sister-in-law and nephews, they'd taken the horses for a ride. The journey through the canyon had been freeing and she'd enjoyed the time with her family.

The glorious sunset and warm sensations she'd had after their ride had vanished when she'd opened her studio door and had seen the destruction. Her canvases had been torn and ripped, paint scattered over the floor and walls and every brush had been broken in half.

She had a security system and cameras, but had forgotten to set them that evening. Everything that had been ruined was really her fault. It wasn't just the loss of months of work that bothered her. She felt violated. And scared.

A knock on her bedroom door interrupted her, but she ignored it. She just wanted to be alone. Was that too much to ask? She didn't want to go to her workspace nor did she want to talk to anyone.

The police, her family, her assistant, even some of the Pack had shown up the night before. While she appreciated their support and concern, they just didn't understand.

Someone had been in her house. Since her studio was located in her residence, there was no place that seemed untouched. A stranger could have gone through her things before tearing apart her creations.

She just didn't know what to do. Her first instinct had been to hide, covers over her head, and cry, but she knew that wouldn't solve anything. So she'd gotten up and showered. But that was as far as she'd made it. She just couldn't force herself to go into her studio yet.

The rapping on her door grew louder and more persistent. She suspected it was her older brother. When the door opened and Alex called her name, she sighed.

"Hey," he said as he joined her on the balcony.

Cassie glanced over her shoulder. "Hi."

"You okay?"

She nodded, turning back to look at the sun rising above the canyon. They were lucky. The Wilson ranch was one of the few privately owned properties that shared the public canyon land. The estate had belonged to their family long before the government had come in and sectioned off acreage for a national park.

The government had tried to claim their property too, but years of legal battles had insured that the Wilson land would stay in the family.

So Cassie got to rouse every morning to one of the most beautiful views in the world. Even after the night of heartbreak she'd experienced, there was nothing like standing outside and watching the earth wake up.

"I just got off the phone with the Alpha," Alex told her. "We have a meeting with him this morning about how to handle this situation."

Knowing that she couldn't avoid the issue any longer, she turned and gave her brother her full attention. He stood at the sliding glass door with two mugs in his hand.

She smiled and relieved him of one of the cups. The scent of fresh, strong coffee drifted up and she was grateful. She was extremely dependent on coffee and having caffeine to carry her through long days.

"What time?" she asked before taking a long drink. Flavor burst over her tongue — she knew her sister-in-law must have made the coffee that morning. Alex tended to make his more sludge.

"An hour," he replied. He walked toward her and tilted his head. "Are you really okay?"

To have time to phrase her answer correctly, she took another long drink. Her brother always worried. He said it was because as the eldest he was responsible for her and their younger brother Jacob. Cassie just thought he was a worry wart.

"I'll be fine," she assured him. "I just don't understand why someone would break in and destroy my stuff."

"Hopefully we'll find out. Alpha Shawn is concerned about the publicity you've gotten lately. That's one of the reasons he wants to meet."

Publicity? She snorted. All artists wanted to receive credit for their work. All Cassie had ever needed was to paint. Her parents had supported her through the beginning stages and after their death, Alex had continued with encouragement. She'd made a good living, then the shifters had announced their presence and became public. There had been a surprising demand for her work after that.

The strangest part to her was that the Pack hadn't gone public with the others. Alpha Shawn had decided to remain in secret. So the fact that her art was being considered as an authentic representative of the shifter world, by both the human and shifters, was surprising.

And a little uncomfortable.

The press constantly pressured her about her knowledge of shifters. She'd gotten to where she didn't even do interviews anymore. She just wanted to paint. She didn't really care about the rest of it.

"I never meant to draw attention to us," she told Alex.

"Ah, honey" — he hugged her — "there's nothing to be done about it. I'm proud of you. We'll get to the bottom of this and it'll all work out. I promise."

She wanted to believe him, but the wound was too fresh. She hoped Alpha Shawn had some ideas. He was one of the smartest men she knew and just a tad devious.

"I spoke to James also," Alex said. "He's going to bring over everything we have in storage and order more supplies for you. We'll have you back to work before you know it."

Cassie always had back-up supplies. She lived in the guesthouse and her studio was one of the rooms. But in the main house, where Alex lived, he kept a supply room for her.

"I'm almost ready for the show anyway." She was supposed to having a showing in less than a month. "If we even still have it."

"We'll have it," Alex said. "I told you not to worry about it."

She nodded and stopped herself from telling him she was going to worry anyway. The threat they'd received in the mail to stop the show or else, still weighed on her mind. Even though everyone told her it wasn't her fault, she knew it was. The crazy church that had been after the shifters for months now had narrowed in on her town.

"We'll talk about it with Alpha Shawn. He is aware of the threat and has Chase looking into it."

"Okay," she relented. It was never worth arguing with Alex. He would eventually get his way, by wearing her down. Hopefully Shawn could talk some sense into him. He was one of the few people Alex listened to.

"Let's go then." Her brother motioned her back inside.

Cassie followed him through her bedroom and into the hallway. Her house consisted of four bedrooms, a living room, kitchen and a small fenced in area for a backyard. The guesthouse was just yards away from the main residence where Alex lived. She loved her place.

Jacob and Peyton resided a couple of miles down the hill in their own home. They had a nice six-bedroom dwelling that fit their family perfectly. Jacob worked for the Parks and Wildlife Department stationed in the canyon. Peyton stayed home and took care of their boys, one four and one six. Cassie enjoyed having her family so close to her most of the time. However, she would've preferred a little more distance right then.

Alex strolled through her place like he belonged there. She didn't comment as she followed him. Normally Alex tried to show her that he respected her space, although every once in a while he went overprotective on her.

Since she'd found the destruction the night before, Alex was in full Alpha male mode. She would never admit it to him, but his protectiveness was easing some of her fear.

His truck was parked in front of the entrance and she climbed into the passenger seat. Alex opened the driver's door and took his seat. He started the vehicle and drove off once she had her seatbelt fastened.

The drive to the Alpha compound took thirty minutes. Shawn lived deeper in the canyon. If they'd taken the horses, it would have only been ten minutes.

Not all of the pack lived inside the canyon. Most had houses and businesses in town. Only the oldest families had claim to any canyon land.

As he drove, Alex talked about the horses and his upcoming plans for the ranch. Cassie had heard it all before, so she was able to tune him out and respond with some sounds.

By the time they arrived at the large Alpha cabin, she'd almost fallen asleep. She'd barely slept at all the previous night and was bone-tired. The winding roads that led to the house had just about put her down for the night.

Her brother stopped the truck and patted her knee. "Let's get this over with, then you can get some real sleep. I can tell you didn't get a wink."

"Yeah, okay," she agreed and pushed her door open.

There were other vehicles parked nearby, but that wasn't a surprise. She'd never been to Alpha Shawn's when the house didn't have several guests. All those

Pack members around would drive her crazy. She couldn't stand to have people constantly around. It was one of the reasons she lived in the guesthouse instead of the main home. Alex worked from home, and Cassie couldn't handle all the people who came in and out to do business with Alex.

The door opened before they reached it and her Alpha stepped out. Shawn Mathewson stood on the porch and opened his arms. He was an attractive man, dark skin and hair, his eyes and smile dazzling her. The power that rolled off him could be quite intimidating, but he was truly a good man. A great leader.

She grinned and walked up the stairs where her Alpha engulfed her. He held her tightly then patted her shoulder.

Taking a step back, she peered up at the impressive man in front of her. Just being in his presence helped calm the wolf inside her which had been agitated since she'd found the break-in.

"Let's go inside," he said, placing his arm around her shoulder.

They entered his home and traveled through the entry to the living room. Cassie saw the Beta of the pack, Chase Lawson. She inclined her head toward him in respect.

"Hey, sweetie," he greeted. "You doing okay?"

Cassie nodded. "As well as can be expected."

"We'll find out who did this."

A promise that she knew Chase would do his best to keep. The Lawson family had been part of the Pack as long as hers had. Chase owned the local diner and was one of the best cooks in the area. She made a point of stopping by for some home-cooked meals as often as possible.

He always greeted her with a smile and a kind word. He was Alex's age and the two had grown up together as the best of friends since they'd started school.

Chase welcomed Alex with a hug and a manly slap on the back while Alpha Shawn moved Cassie to the couch, taking a seat with her. Alex sat across from her in one of the chairs and, after making four mugs of coffee, Chase passed them around before he joined them.

Cassie placed both hands on the large cup as she settled back in the corner of the couch. She felt protected and secure with the three men. If she closed her eyes, she had no doubt she would be fine.

Their voices flowed over her as they discussed who could have been responsible and why. Cassie just couldn't imagine anyone who would have wanted to destroy her work. Even with the shifter controversy, she was only an artist.

"We're just guessing here," Alpha Shawn's words drew her out of her thoughts. "And until we get to the bottom of this, the entire Pack will be on high alert. I don't want anyone alone. I'll double the guards around town and here."

"Cassie can stay at the main house," Alex added.

"Wait!" She sat up straight. "I'm not moving out of my house."

Three sets of eyes turned to her.

"No." She shook her head. "I have to work hard to make up for the canvases that I lost."

"It's just temporary," Alex assured her.

"I'll set the alarm. I'm sorry I forget. And we have the cameras."

"Cass." Alex leaned forward and braced his forearms on his knees. "It's more than that. We don't know who or why someone did this. Luckily, you weren't home but…"

Cassie saw the struggle on his face. He was concerned about her.

She set her mug down and spoke directly to him. "But if I just move to the main house, then they win."

"This isn't about winning! This is about keeping you safe!"

Cassie ignored the rise of Alex's voice. "I'm not giving up my house."

"Yes, you are!"

"Hold on!" Alpha Shawn tried to interrupt.

"No, I'm not. I'm a big girl and I can take care of myself."

Alex rose and towered over her. "You…are…staying in the main house." Each word was clipped.

She seldom argued with him. But she just couldn't give in this time. She'd worked hard to gain her independence after their parent's death. She was thirty years old and refused to be treated like she was five.

"No."

Alex stepped forward, but Chase stood and got between them. "How about a compromise?"

Both she and Alex turned to him.

Chase motioned Alex back down and waited until he had settled again before taking his own seat.

"What's your idea?" Alpha Shawn asked.

"Well, you know Max is back. He's working in the diner right now, but we can use him as Cassie's personal security."

Max Lawson, Cassie mused. She hadn't seen Chase's elder brother in a long time. He was older than both Alex and Chase so Cassie had never really been around him much growing up. By the time Max had left the Pack at seventeen to join the Navy, she was only seven. She knew about him because he was the Pack's only non-shifter.

Max was a shifter. He carried the DNA that made them different from humans. However, Max was unable to shift into his animal. Cassie didn't know much about non-shifters, but Alpha Shawn had never allowed Max to be treated any differently.

There were rumors about Max being part of one of the elite Navy Seal teams in the military, but she wasn't even sure that it wasn't all talk.

Alpha Shawn was smiling. "I like that idea."

Cassie wasn't so sure. "I don't really think I need personal security. I hardly even leave the property." She just didn't feel right about having someone follow her around all the time. Yes, the situation was scary, but assigning a bodyguard? It was just a little too much.

"I disagree," her Alpha said. "The break-in was at your residence. Max would be able to keep an eye on you and look into who might have been responsible."

She knew the expression on his face. Alpha Shawn had made up his mind.

"I'll spend most of my time in the studio anyway," she argued. "He'll be in my way."

Chase chuckled. "I promise he won't."

Knowing she was coming up against a wall, she sighed. "This is stupid."

Alpha Shawn reached over and patted her knee. "Then just humor me. I want you safe."

"Fine." She rolled her eyes. She would make the best of the situation, she always did. Besides, how bad could it be? Chase was a good guy, so she doubted that Max was much different.

Chapter Two

Max Lawson pulled the skillets off the stove then dropped them into the sink full of soapy water. He stretched his arms over his head and rolled his neck. He liked working at the Canyon Café with his brother, even if it was dissimilar from what he had always done before. The most important thing was that he had something to do. He could concentrate on a task and not have to think or remember.

Not having enough to do worried him, made him nervous, so he was glad for the hard work.

"Hey, Max!"

He glanced over his shoulder and saw his brother in the doorway. "Hey, bro."

His brother had been summoned to the Alpha house earlier that morning so Max had been handling the breakfast rush for him.

"Got a minute?" Chase tilted his head indicating that Max join him out front.

"Sure." Max turned and followed him out of the kitchen into the dining area.

The rush was over. Only a few customers were still eating. Sue Ellen was manning the patrons, so Max didn't have to worry about them. He always liked being in the back more than waiting tables.

He'd only been home about six months, so when the Pack members saw him, they always wanted to know about his time away. And Max honestly couldn't talk about it. Too much of what he'd done was still classified.

Chase took a seat on one of the chairs in front of the counter next to another man. Max followed but remained back where the scarred countertop separated them. He still didn't like to be too close to people.

Once he reached the two, he recognized Alex Wilson. Chase and Alex still remained tight even as the years had passed and they'd found different interests. Max grinned at Alex and offered his hand. "Nice to see you again, Alex."

They shook and Alex smiled.

"You too. Glad you made it back safe."

Max nodded but didn't say anything. Yes, he had returned safely, but... No, he couldn't think about that now. Instead, he noticed his brother's obvious worry.

The Wilson family was one of the oldest members of the Pack. Alex, of course, was closer to them living as a Pack, but Max still had a connection with the family. He'd been out of the country when he'd received word that both of the Wilson parents had been killed in an accident.

Chase was devastated and had told him how hard it had been on the kids. It seemed Alex had stepped up and done a good job getting his siblings through the grief process.

"Coffee?" Max picked up the pot from under the counter.

Chase and Alex nodded.

He poured three cups then slid the first two across to them. "So what's going on?"

They exchanged a look that stood the hair up on the back of Max's neck. "What?"

"We need your help," Alex said.

"Of course," he offered. He would do whatever he could to help any of the Pack members. Even though he hadn't quite fit in with the kids growing up, they had never been mean to him. Their Alpha would not have allowed it.

Max didn't understand why he was different from everyone else. What had gone wrong to make him unable to shift? But it was what it was and there was nothing he could do about it.

"Good." Chase drew his attention. "Do you remember Cassandra?"

"Your younger sister?" he asked Alex. He could picture the freckled-face girl with skinned knees, running around in shorts. She had always been tagging behind Alex and Chase as the boys had grown up. "Sort of."

Alex nodded. "We need security for her."

"Why?"

As Alex and Chase filled him in on what was going on, Max found himself growing angry. He knew he had to get a handle on his reaction, though. After his last mission, he had gone through a debriefing and had been shown several techniques to control himself. The military did not want him to go off on civilians.

But the thought of anyone threatening a member of his Pack made his blood boil. He listened intently as Alex explained the entire situation.

"What do you need from me?" he asked when the man was finished.

"Cassie won't agree to move into the main house. She wants to stay in her residence and studio. I'm not comfortable with her being alone."

"You want me to watch over her?" he asked, surprised. He wasn't a guard. He didn't actually have a position with the Pack. His brother was the Alpha's second, his Beta, but after Max had left for the Navy, he'd given up any rank within the Pack.

"Yes," Chase answered. "Alpha Shawn agreed. We are doubling all security for the Pack, but we want Cassie to have someone with her full time."

Max owed his Alpha a lot for always supporting him. Hell, he owed his brother too. Chase had welcomed him back with open arms. His brother let Max stay in his house and had given him a job. "Okay, when do you want me to start?"

Alex sighed heavily and dropped his head. "Thank you."

Max wasn't a touchy-feely kind of guy. Normally he did everything he could to avoid contact with others, but he found himself reaching over and patting Alex's shoulder. "Sure, I'm glad to help."

"I knew you would," Chase said proudly.

Max warmed to his brother's praise.

"Chase can go over everything with you." Alex stood. "I need to get back to the house. Cassie is with Jacob right now, but he has to work today."

Max nodded and waited until Alex was out the door before turning to his brother. "What else?"

Chase rubbed his hands roughly over his face. "Alpha Shawn is concerned with the publicity the gallery is getting. Several of the artists, Cassie in particular, have gotten a lot of attention. Last week we received a threat that if we didn't cancel the upcoming show, we would regret it. It was from the Church for Humanity, the people the wolves have had problems with ever since we went public. Our Pack didn't go public, and Shawn isn't sure how much longer he can hide us if the church has targeted us."

"Is that really a big concern? From what I've seen, there have only been a few issues since the shifters announced their presence."

"It's a concern," Chase told him. "The Coalition between all the shifter species is brand new. We're hoping that will protect all shifters, but until we know for sure, we still want to remain secret. Some of the human lawmakers are talking about forcing shifters to register."

"Register?"

"Yeah, so they can have a database on all of us."

"That's not right," Max said in disgust.

"I know. Shawn is talking with the council on what we can do, but he's worried."

"Well, I'll do what I can," Max promised.

"Good. How are you doing?"

He knew his brother was concerned. Chase might not know everything that had gone down with his last mission, but his brother knew him well. Chase had also witnessed some of his nightmares.

"I'm fine."

Chase didn't look like he believed him but didn't push. "Scott's coming in. I thought we could grab your stuff, then I'll follow you over to the Wilson ranch."

"Sure." Max picked up the empty coffee cups. "Let me just finish cleaning up real quick."

"Okay, I have to grab a few things from the office anyway."

Max went back into the kitchen to wash the last of the pans he'd used earlier. He didn't like leaving a mess. His brother might own the diner, but Max always pulled his own weight. He hoped he would be an asset for the Wilson family. He remembered they had always had been so happy. Very similar to his own. They never treated him any different either.

He was scrubbing the last pan when Scott Little walked in the back door.

"Hey, man!" Scott waved at him.

Max inclined his head since his hands were still in the water. "Thanks for coming."

"No problem," Scott assured him. "Didn't have anything planned today anyway."

Scott attended the community college in the next town over and was an okay kid. Max enjoyed their shifts together as well as Scott's quirky humor.

"You about ready?" Chase called from the front of the diner.

Max rinsed off the pan then placed it in the strainer. "Yeah."

He waved to Scott as he joined his brother out front. He grabbed his jacket and keys from under the counter. Together, they walked out.

One of his first purchases when he'd returned to the states had been his Harley. Chase had tried to get him to use one of the Alpha's many vehicles, but Max enjoyed riding the bike. He craved the freedom that the motorcycle provided him.

He'd found that the best time to ride down the canyon was just before sunset. The gorgeous views on the back of his Harley could not be seen the same way in a truck or SUV. Max threw his leg over the bike and turned the key. The machine came alive under him. He couldn't suppress his grin. Yes, motorcycles were dangerous, and he loved every single second he was on his.

Chase waved at him as he climbed inside his truck.

Chase's house was just outside the city limits. He needed to be close to the Alpha in case any problems arose. The fifteen-minute ride was smooth and without a lot of traffic. Max could see his brother ahead of him as they both drove in the same direction.

The Wilson ranch was farther inside the canyon lands. He would be able to take his bike there and hopefully would have time to ride some of the private roads.

Plus there was good hiking around the Wilson place. He didn't know if Cassie Wilson hiked, but he sure hoped so. It would be nice to be able to get some fresh air and just be away from everyone and everything.

He pulled up beside his brother's truck then turned the engine off. Chase's abode was small compared to a lot of the other Packs' houses. But the three-bedroom structure was enough for them. Chase had welcomed the company when Max had come back to town. Their parents had offered to let Max stay with them. However, he was glad Chase had suggested they live together. He loved his mom and dad, but at forty, he didn't want to live with them again.

"I'm going to take a shower while you get your things together," Chase informed him.

Max nodded and made his way to his bedroom. He didn't have a lot. Just clothes and a few things he'd kept in storage. Even the furniture in the bedroom was his brother's.

Finally, Max felt like he was putting roots down. Eventually he would buy his own home and concentrate on discovering what he wanted to do with the rest of his life. Whether he'd stay in Canyon or move on, he wasn't sure. He had time to decide.

He grabbed two duffels out of his closet then started to pack. He didn't know how long he would be needed at the Wilson ranch. It was better to have too much stuff than to have to leave Cassandra to go pick up what he needed.

He threw in jeans, T-shirts, boxers, socks and a light jacket. Back at his closet, he reached up to the top shelf and brought down the lock box. Max carried the box to the bed and sat.

It had been six months since he'd opened it.

He removed the keys from his pocket and carefully unlocked then lifted the lid. Inside was his favorite gun. A .45 Desert Eagle.

He ran his fingers over the stainless-steel barrel and sighed. He hadn't held a weapon in his hand since he'd left the Navy. He wasn't sure he would even be able to fire it again.

As he sat on the bed, he could still smell the smoke from the last gunfight. He hadn't been shooting his Desert Eagle that day. The M4 that he'd had on his shoulder had run out of ammo and Max had looked down in horror when he'd realized the entire team had used all the bullets they'd brought with them.

The house they'd been hiding in was small. Evan Cruise laid at Max's feet, wounded and crying out in pain.

Deep down, he'd feared that was it. They were all going to die over in some god-awful place and no one would know all they had wanted to do was rescue the captured aid workers.

The mission would be classified and Max wondered if Evan's family would even be given his body.

The guerilla fighters who had gotten the jump on them had still been shooting into the house. Max had knelt beside his friend and gripped Evan's hand. He was supposed to have been in charge of his five-man team. It'd been up to him to get them out.

"You okay?"

Max started at Chase's voice. He slammed the lid closed on the gun box and stood. Quickly, he stuffed the container at the top of one of the duffels and faced his brother. "Yeah, just about done."

Concern was evident on Chase's face. Max had to ignore it. He wasn't ready to talk about what he'd been through. Actually, he couldn't speak to anyone about anything. He rushed into the bathroom then quickly packed everything he would need for the next several days.

When he returned to the bedroom, Chase was zipping up one of the bags. Max dumped his toiletries into the other then closed it. They each grabbed one as they headed out of the door. Max was relieved that Chase wasn't pushing him. He knew that he would have to eventually share something with Chase. Luckily, his brother was giving him time.

"I'll take your bags over for you," Chase offered.

"Thanks." He passed the second duffle to his brother. Ready to go, he strode to the bike.

He could probably find the Wilson ranch on his own, but any time he had a flashback he was always a little shaky. He needed a few minutes to get his bearings. Although he would have to follow Chase closely so he wouldn't get lost.

Chase backed out slowly and Max waited until the dust settled then followed. He was happy to have something to keep his mind off what he'd been through.

Hopefully this new job would help him clear his mind.

It took longer than he expected to reach the Wilson property. He slowed at the large gate where Chase was waiting. His brother waved him through and Max drove on. He pulled off to the side as Chase closed and locked the gate again.

Max was glad to see that they were indeed taking precautions on security.

Chase climbed back into his truck and started south. Max followed using his senses to get familiar with the area. The main house loomed in the distance, a strong, solid structure that appeared inviting. Max could remember the barbeques that he and his family attended there when he was younger.

Even with the passing of their parents, it looked like the Wilson children had kept the property up. Green grass filled both sides of the paved road. As he pulled next to his brother and turned off his motorcycle, he could hear horses not far from him.

He turned his head to see if he could spot them and couldn't. He hadn't ridden in over a decade. His family didn't keep animals, and in the service he hadn't had the opportunity. Excitement had him swinging off his bike. He'd always enjoyed the freedom of being on the back of one of the large animals. Luckily, even though the horses could sense the predator in a shifter, as long as a mount was treated with respect it didn't have any problems accepting shifters as riders or caregivers. The stallions and mares sure were trusting. In that regard, Max was envious of them.

"They still have horses?"

Chase nodded. "Yeah, Alex puts a lot of time into them."

"I thought he worked in the gallery."

Chase waved his hand. "He does. But his love will always be the horses first."

The front door opened and the subject of their conversation stepped out. "Hey, guys."

Alex stomped down the stairs to greet them. Smiling widely, he'd changed out of his slacks into jeans. Max was relieved to see Alex more relaxed. Max was glad he had agreed to help. It was great to be needed again.

They shook hands, then Alex motioned toward the house. "Cassie's inside. Let's talk here before you go over to the house."

Max nodded and followed Alex and his brother.

The cool air hit him as soon as he walked inside. Max hadn't noticed just how hot he was until the air conditioner blew over him.

He must have made a sound because Alex glanced back at him. "Cassie keeps the air on frigid. She can't stand being hot."

Since Max had spent way too much time in deserts and jungles, he agreed with her. "Feels good."

Alex grinned. "You'll fit in just fine."

He hung back, taking in the homey feel of the ranch house. The Wilsons had money, but he wasn't uncomfortable walking through the hall. The simple touches around the place were welcoming, not intimidating.

The hall opened into a large living room with beautiful wood flooring. Dark-brown leather couches dominated the space, a huge flat-screen television was placed over the stone hearth. In the corner, standing by of the curved bar, was the most gorgeous woman he'd ever seen.

She smiled wide when their gazes met. "Wow! You grew up."

Max opened his mouth to respond then closed it again quickly. There was no way this sexy creature in front of him was Cassie Wilson. Gone were the braids and the crooked teeth. Instead, she had a pixie cut of short brown hair with streaks of blond. She had to be only five foot five or so. She was tanned and had a body built for a man's hands. He actually had to clench his teeth to keep from reaching out for her.

He groaned mentally. Not what he had expected.

Cassie Wilson was an attractive woman. Her soft, chocolate eyes sparkled with amusement as she licked her lips.

Fuck! His cock hardened painfully. Max struggled to push aside his carnal needs and remember there were two other people in the room.

Chapter Three

Max's reaction shot a thrill through her. The way his gaze traveled up and down her body pushed a strong tingle of lust through her. Heat flushed into her face as she watched his eyes lighten with arousal. His appraisal of her also gave her the opportunity to stare back at him. She'd suspected Max would be good-looking since Chase and their dad were both attractive. Still, the hot, heavily muscled man across from her was *not* what she'd been expecting.

He was taller than both her brother and his, so that had to put him a few inches above six feet. His short black hair was a reminder that he'd just gotten out of the military. Wide hazel eyes stared into hers and his massive chest expanded with each breath. A tight black T-shirt, faded jeans and heavy boots made up his wardrobe. She wanted to see what was underneath those garments.

The tattoos covering both arms intrigued her. She wondered how he would respond if she ran her tongue along them — and wherever else he might have ink. How much of him *was* covered in ink?

She flushed and had to tear her gaze away from his body. She turned back to the mini fridge. "So...a beer?"

Alex chuckled and she wanted to sink into the floor. Of course her brother had caught her attraction to Max. There would be no living with him now.

Alex was always trying to get her to step away from her studio and date. But until she'd gotten a look at Max, dating hadn't been a high priority. She'd grown up in a small town. Sure, she'd gone out with a few of the guys, but she had never been serious about any of them.

She popped the tops to four beers and strolled around the bar.

Max had settled on one of the couches and Alex and Chase took the one closer to her. So she was going to have to take a seat next to Max.

Her heart pounded frantically as she moved farther into the middle of the room.

She passed the bottles to Chase and Alex, ignoring the gleam in her brother's gaze. She walked over and held out another beer to Max. Their fingers brushed as he took it from her and she barely held in a gasp at the electricity that sparked between them. A glance at his lap showed he was indeed as attracted to her as she was to him. The heavy aroma of arousal and need surrounded them. His erection pushed at the zipper of his jeans. A nice-sized package, she believed.

Since dropping to her knees to help him out probably wouldn't go over well with the other two men in the room, she backed away slowly.

When she'd agreed to have Max hang around as security, she'd had no idea what she was getting herself into.

"Thank you."

His deep voice sent a thrill down her spine. Cassie managed a smile and nodded. She sat gently on the edge of the couch as Max took a long pull on his beer. She watched his throat work. Who knew a throat could be so damn sexy?

She caught herself staring and quickly looked away. Her gaze passed over Alex, who still smirked. She needed to get control over herself and stop fantasizing about what Max's large hands would feel like on her body.

Especially under the watchful attention of her brother.

"Shall we get started?" Alex asked with amusement.

She shrugged.

Alex, Chase and Max started going over the plan to beef up security on the property. Since she wasn't hearing anything that she objected to, she just listened. Listened and watched.

Max reclined back with the bottle held loosely between his fingers. He was a big guy but appeared comfortable. He had a certain amount of power surrounding him. The wolf inside her recognized it and wanted to present herself for him. The only other person she'd ever felt that kind of radiating dominance from was her Alpha.

The inner strength that she was picking up on could very well be why she was so attracted to him. Constantly surrounded by such domineering men, she had found herself more and more comfortable around the type. Although her reaction to Max was very unique from anyone else she'd ever met.

Across from her, she studied her brother as his voice rose and fell in a calming manner. Alex was leaning forward, speaking directly to Max about the alarm system. She'd grown up in a loving home. Every day she had known she was loved and her parents had doted on each of their children. Alex had become her parent after their real parents' deaths in a car accident on an icy road. He'd just graduated from college and had returned to care for her and their younger brother Jacob.

While he had a business degree and did in fact make a lot of money at the gallery, she knew that it was the ranch, the horses that Alex truly loved.

The money that the family had, that Alex had made, always went to the animals first. Alex put everything he had, every free minute into the horses. Back when he'd first returned, Alex had been involved with a woman in college. Cassie had met her once. Right after the funeral of their parents.

She didn't know what had happened between Alex and the woman, but she'd never seen her again and Alex refused to talk about it.

Instead, Alex spent his time trying to get her to settle down like Jacob. So far Cassie had managed to turn the tables on him about settling down, but now she wasn't sure she would be able to anymore.

Chase picked up where Alex trailed off, getting into the security cameras and how more should be added.

At the moment, they only had cameras outside the house and stables. Chase wanted some installed in the interior of the buildings too.

"I don't want cameras in my studio," Cassie spoke up.

The three men turned to her.

"The studio was the target," Chase responded. "It makes the most sense to cover that area."

Cassie shook her head. "No, I can't work knowing someone is watching me."

"They will only be there for your protection. It's not like we'll be watching them all the time," Alex assured her.

There was no way she could handle even that. "No, please."

Alex opened his mouth, but beside her, Max held up his hand. "Let's wait. We can go ahead and order some more cameras. If Cassie doesn't want them inside maybe we'll place them over the entry doors. We can work it out so everyone is comfortable."

Relief washed over her. She was glad that Max seemed to understand. She nodded in acceptance.

"Let me look though the houses and I'll make a map of where I think the new cameras should go. I assume we'll do both the main house and Cassie's?"

"Jacob's too," Alex added. "I want them covered."

Max inclined his head. "I agree."

Chase stood. "It seems like you all have everything under control. I need to stop back by the Alpha's place and make sure the new shifts in town have been sorted out. I'll update him on the situation here."

Alex and Max both rose with him.

"I expect you'll hear from the Alpha soon anyway. He'll want to check on things himself."

"I'll walk you out," Alex offered.

"If you're ready to take me over, I'd like to see the studio." Max turned to her.

Cassie placed her beer on the side table then wiped her hands down the legs of her jeans. Suddenly she was very nervous about having Max in her personal space. She spent the majority of her time in the studio. It was her heart and soul. Only a few people had ever been there.

"Yeah, sure." She climbed to her feet. "Uh, thanks, Chase. We'll see you later, Alex."

She waited while Chase hugged his brother and he followed Alex out before she turned to Max.

"Ready?"

He nodded.

She led the way out the patio door and down the steps. Alex hadn't wanted her to leave the ranch so he had been the one who had suggested that she take the guesthouse and make it her home. She'd been thinking about getting her own place.

He'd offered to have a house built like he'd done for Jacob and Peyton, but that hadn't made sense since the guesthouse sat empty. Instead, they'd remodeled it to fit her needs.

It was only a few yards from the main house's porch to the front of her place. Since the break-in she had been better at locking and setting the alarm whenever she left.

Alex still hadn't forgiven her for forgetting the night before. But in all honesty, she was never the best at remembering.

She'd never been worried about someone breaking in. They would have to get into the canyon, go through the property then get in and out without anyone seeing them. And why would anyone want to destroy her art anyway?

All the questions that she just couldn't answer, no matter how much she thought about it, weren't really helping her not to worry either.

She unlocked the front door with Max staying close behind her. Her hand shook slightly, but she didn't think he noticed.

After she pushed the door open, the long beep from the alarm alerted her it was still armed. She punched in the four-number code and turned to face Max.

"Who all has the code?"

"Me, Alex, Jacob and Peyton. Oh, and James."

"James?"

"He's been working as my assistant He just graduated and is trying to get his own showing. He's very talented."

"How long has he been working for you?"

"About six months or so. He applied at the gallery and Alex hired him for the reception desk. We met and started talking, and he now works part-time for Alex and part-time for me."

"Last name?"

Cassie frowned at him. "James wasn't involved."

Max lifted a brow.

"Strut. His last name is Strut."

"Is he part of the pack?"

"No, he's not a shifter."

Max nodded, but Cassie couldn't let it go. "He's a good kid. There is no way he was involved."

The look Max sent her said he wasn't convinced. "Then he has nothing to worry about."

She sighed and figured he was right. She knew James was too dedicated to art for him to ever get involved in something like the break-in.

Max was glancing around and Cassie wondered what he saw. The entryway was open and painted a bright white. There were three wide archways that led farther into the residence.

"Through there is the kitchen." Cassie waved a hand. He would be able to see the stainless-steel appliances from where they stood. She pointed behind her. "Living room and patio door." Then she faced the hallway opening. "Back here are the rooms."

He motioned for her to go ahead, so she stepped around him.

"The first door is the second bedroom," she told him as she turned the knob. The room was sparse with only a bed, dresser and nightstand. "So I guess this is where you'll be staying."

Max walked in and placed his two bags on the bed. He spun in a circle. "Okay, show me the rest."

Cassie didn't respond right away. It had just dawned on her that she would have a man staying in her house with her. A very attractive man who she wouldn't mind seeing naked. And just a couple of doors down from her bedroom.

When her palms started to sweat, she rubbed her hands down her thighs again.

Max's presence was a big deal in her life. He would see everything she was. There was no way she could hide her quirks from him.

"Cassie?"

She jumped, not realizing he had moved so close. She tilted her head back to look up at him. Damn, he was tall.

"It'll be all right," he assured her with that deep tremble.

Cassie found herself shivering. She wanted to reach for him, have Max pull her into his arms. Have the press of his lips against hers. She swallowed and took a step back.

"Uh, I'm…uh…"

He smiled, his hazel eyes bright.

She was losing her mind. She whirled back around into the hallway and took several deep breaths to calm her racing heart.

"Okay," she said. "Next door is the bathroom. Then the office." She moved forward as she spoke. Then paused again. "My bedroom."

That took care of the three doors that were on the east side of the house and left her standing in front of the large door to the studio.

She hadn't been back inside since she'd first discovered the incident. Cassie placed her hand on the wood. "The studio," she whispered.

"Has it been cleaned up?" Max asked behind her.

She nodded. "Alex took care of it."

Max's chest pressed into her back and she felt him lift his hand. "Deep breath," he spoke softly, his mouth close to her ear.

She inhaled through her nose then let the air out.

"Good," he said and opened the door.

In her mind, she could see the ripped canvases, the paint spilled over the floor and walls and her brushes in pieces.

Max held his hand down on her shoulder and she blinked.

None of that was there.

Alex had come through like always. The walls had been repainted the mint green that she'd had before. The hardwood floors were glistening and clean. The room was also restocked.

Slowly, she stepped forward, one foot in front of the other. Her easels stood with blank sheets, her paints were lined up in their holders along the walls and her desk held a variety of brand new brushes.

She made it to the middle of the room as tears filled her eyes.

It looked good, but it also reminded her of what had been taken from her. Months of work ruined. She'd put her entire being into each piece. Now there was nothing to show for it.

Cassie sobbed and Max wrapped his arms around her.

"Shh," he cooed. "It will be okay."

Sure, she knew it could have been worse, but her heart ached. She clung to Max, allowing him to rock her gently. He felt good pressed to her body. As she soaked up the comfort he offered, peace filled her. Closing her eyes, she rested her cheek against his chest and just breathed in Max's spicy scent.

Her body started to respond and it was with regret that she forced herself to pull away. "I'm going to lie down for a little bit."

He released her. Their gazes locked, causing her breath to catch. His sparkling eyes were kind and called to both the woman and wolf inside her.

She spun on her heel, escaping into her bedroom. She had a lot to think about, because all signs were pointing to Max being more than just a bodyguard or security for her. The connection was so strong between the two of them that Cassie was unsure how she would let him go when everything was resolved.

Chapter Four

Max woke up with sweat pouring off him and his heart beating frantically. He had been back in that house, the room where he'd thought he was going to die, where his best friend hadn't made it out alive.

He clenched his eyes closed and tried to get control of himself and regulate his breathing.

Once his heart rate had slowed to almost normal, he knew he wouldn't be able to get back to sleep, so he swung his legs over the side of the bed. A glance at the clock on the nightstand told him it was two in the morning.

It had been so long since he'd gotten a full night's sleep. He should probably take one of the sleeping pills that the doctor had given him, but he didn't like how they made him feel the next day. Needing to keep an eye out for Cassie and the Wilson family, he couldn't very well be stoned during the day.

Max pushed himself off the bed then pulled on the jeans from earlier. He would get a bottle of water from the kitchen and look over the plans for the Wilson ranch. He'd already gone over everything with Alex the night before, but another look wouldn't hurt.

He opened his bedroom door quietly, not wanting to wake Cassie, who slept only a few doors down.

There was no doubt he'd been shocked when he'd first seen her again. He wasn't sure why he'd still pictured the young girl from his memories, but Cassandra Wilson was in no way a little girl.

She was a beautiful woman.

It had thrown him off balance when she'd looked at him with those expressive chocolate eyes. He hadn't been prepared for the punch he'd felt from the pixie woman.

She was much smaller than his big frame. And every single part of him had wanted to wrap her up and protect her.

It had just about killed him when they'd entered her studio and he'd seen the devastation on her face. Yes, the room had been cleaned, but he could see that she was picturing the way she'd found it before.

With her in his arms, he'd wanted to kill whoever had hurt her. His normal quiet and calm wolf had not been any happier. The itch under his skin had been an experience he had only felt a few times in his life.

Since he couldn't actually shift into his animal, he could sometimes pretend it wasn't even there. But sometimes, when he was stressed or emotional, there was an extra awareness of his wolf.

Just as he'd started to wonder about his wolf's response to Cassie, she had shut down.

She'd excused herself from the room and told him she was tired and wanted to lie down. A door inside the studio apparently led to the bathroom that then connected to Cassie's bedroom.

Alex had shown up about thirty minutes after Cassie left him. When he asked about Cassie, Max explained what had happened. Alex had finished the tour and told him about the adjoining doors to Cassie's rooms.

While Alex went and checked on his sister, Max had started drawing a map of where he wanted the extra cameras installed.

Cassie's studio had a balcony door that linked to the sliding glass door of her bedroom. He made a note that both of those exits needed a camera above them. Cassie would still be able to open them when she wanted, but they would be able to see if anyone tried to enter that way.

He didn't turn on any lights until he reached the kitchen. There, he flicked on the switch and saw a half-empty bottle of wine on the marble counter. So Cassie must have gotten up in the three hours he'd managed to sleep.

He pulled a cold bottle of water from the fridge and drank half of it down. He was starting to calm and felt better already.

Thoughts of the woman replaced the aftershocks of the nightmare.

Since Cassie had been holed up in her room, he'd had a simple meal of a burger and some chips with Alex earlier in the night. He wished he could offer the family more reassurance, but he still didn't know what was going on.

The worry Alex had for his sister had been evident as they'd talked over dinner.

Max had vowed that he would get to the bottom of the break-in. And he would keep that promise.

His laptop still sat on the island top. He checked the alarm and cameras Alex had given him access to.

The blinking red light showed him that one of the balcony doors was open. He frowned. He grabbed his water and hurried down the hall. All of the interior doors were still closed. Not wanting to go into Cassie's bedroom without invitation, he paused at the studio door.

He listened but couldn't hear any sound coming from inside.

Slowly, he turned the knob and, as silently as he could, pushed the door open. The first things he spotted were several large canvases tossed on the ground half-completed. One of the easels held a blank sheet and paint lay scattered around on the wheeled table.

He peered further in the room and spotted her.

She did, indeed, have the balcony doors open as she sat on the deck leaning against one of them.

Max stepped into the room. He hadn't expected to really find her there. He'd thought she'd left the door open by mistake. Now he wasn't entirely sure he should disturb her.

"Couldn't sleep?" she asked quietly, not even turning her head.

"No," he replied. Since she'd spoken first, he decided to take a chance. He walked closer. "I see you started working."

She snorted. "It was all shit."

The anger in her tone surprised him. He strolled forward then paused in the doorway. She looked a little lost holding an empty wineglass and staring out into the night.

"I'm sure it will take a bit to get back into the rhythm."

She shook her head. "Fucking sucks."

Max wondered if she was drunk. He crouched down beside her. "What?"

She turned her head to look at him.

He saw frustration in her eyes. "I can't reproduce what I lost, never have been able to. I paint...what I feel at the time. And right now I feel nothing, so all that" — she waved a hand back into the studio — "was just a waste of time."

Unable to offer much in words, Max decided just to listen to her talk. He didn't know much about art. However, even he had heard about Cassie's work. She'd been scared, but if he were honest, he preferred the fury he now heard. He stretched his legs out and mirrored her position against the second door.

"I wonder if they knew," she continued. "Whoever did this shit — did they know that I would never be able to make up what I lost?"

"I don't know."

"Yeah." She sighed. "I guess it doesn't matter anyway."

When she didn't say anything else, he racked his brain on what he could do to help. "Tell me about your favorite painting."

Her eyebrows drew together. "Favorite?"

He nodded. "Yeah, out of everything you've ever done, what's your favorite?"

She smiled. "Jacob and Peyton's wedding present."

"Tell me about it."

"About six months until the wedding, Peyton and I went for a run. She was getting nervous about everything left to do for the wedding and I'd just finished my first showing and was exhausted."

She paused and looked at him. He inclined his head for her to continue.

"We drove farther into the canyon where no one else would be. We shifted and... God, I still remember it. It had been so long since I'd transformed into my wolf. The freedom... I remember thinking that if I never turned back it would be okay."

She laughed then. "But Peyton was still all tied up inside, so we ran. It must have been for hours. It was still early when we'd first started out, and even when it got dark, we didn't stop. We chased turkey and a few small critters, but we weren't after any of them. We just needed to let loose."

Max could see it. He could picture it perfectly as she shared her memory. He'd never experienced for himself what she spoke about. Although listening to her, he felt closer to another shifter than he ever had in his life.

"Alex and Jacob must have gotten worried. They followed our trail and found us. I knew Alex was mad, so I shifted back. But Jacob just went over to Peyton and buried his muzzle into her neck."

Her voice softened. "It was then that I realized how much they really loved each other. Watching Jacob and Peyton together, I could feel my fingers wanting to reconstruct that moment. Alex and I left the two of them alone and I came straight here. I painted the two of them in a couple of days. Didn't eat, didn't sleep, I just had to get it down on a canvas."

Cassie met his gaze with tears in her eyes. "It was perfect. The moment that I saw, and I gave it to them. They both cried they loved it so much."

Max wished he could see the painting she was talking about so passionately.

"That was my favorite."

Since she was smiling, he was glad he had asked.

"Can I ask you a question?" she said.

"Sure," he said easily.

"You don't have to answer if you don't want. I'm just curious."

He couldn't imagine anything that he wouldn't want to tell her. "Go ahead."

"You can't shift, right? Like at all?"

Surprised, Max jerked. Everyone in the pack knew he was a non-shifter. "No."

She pressed her lips together. "Sorry, I shouldn't have asked."

He hadn't meant to snap. "No, it's okay. It's just been a long time since anyone has asked."

She nodded but didn't look at him.

"Why do you ask?" He wasn't sure why he wanted to know but he couldn't see Cassie being cruel. There must have been a reason she was curious.

"I was sitting out here thinking," she said quietly. "I haven't shifted in a few weeks and was getting restless. I just wondered if you felt like that. If it bothered you?"

Max took a long drink, finishing his water. "It bothers me," he confessed.

Her head turned back to him.

"When you spoke about what it felt like... The freedom? I want to know that."

"I'm sorry," she started.

He held up a hand. "I always felt left out when the pack shifted together. At first, when I was young, one of my parents would have to stay with me. Then as I got older I could be left on my own. Don't get me wrong, everyone tried to include me, but it wasn't the same."

"That had to be terrible."

Grunting, he nodded.

"Is that why you left?"

No one had ever asked him that. He was sure his parents and Chase knew, even suspected Alpha Shawn had a good idea, but no one had ever said the words out loud. "Yes."

"But you can feel him? Your wolf?"

"Sometimes," he admitted. "I don't think it's the same like you or Chase, but there have been times I'm uneasy or the animal fighting to get out. I've dealt with him long enough that I can ignore it but..." He wasn't really wanting to share how much he had despised his wolf at one time.

It sucked to be different. Growing up, he had just wanted to fit in.

They sat for a few moments in silence.

"I bet he's fucking beautiful."

He'd been staring out into the dark night and jerked his face to hers. She was blushing, her fingers twined together, legs moving slightly.

"Yeah?" he asked, pleased.

She peeked up at him through her bangs and nodded.

"How would you describe him?" he questioned.

She bit her lip and searched his face. He didn't know what she was looking for, but whatever it was, she must have found it.

"Black, he would be pure black. Chase has some white and gray in his coat, but you would be solid black."

He was charmed by her. Wanting, maybe even needing more, he moved closer. "And?"

"Powerful." She scooted the few inches that separated them "Strong and dominant, but not pushy. He'd have broad shoulders and a wide chest."

He wasn't sure he should find the conversation about his inner animal so arousing but it was. His cock was half hard and getting fuller by the minute.

"A born leader." She spoke softly. "I'd follow you."

Their thighs were touching, and he was close enough to catch that her breathing had picked up. He turned his upper body toward hers as she angled her head back to look him in the eye.

"Anything else?" he asked as he raised his hand to her throat. He ran his thumb under her chin.

"Sexy, so damn sexy. Just like you are in human form."

There was no way he could have denied the attraction that was sparking between them. He slowly inched forward, keeping his gaze locked with hers.

Cassie didn't back away. Their lips met with the slightest touch. He backed his head a little and watched her eyelids flutter then close.

She was the sexy one. He pressed their mouths together with more force and was rewarded with a moan from her. She gripped the back of his neck while their lips moved against one another.

He teased her bottom lip until she opened for him. Max threaded his fingers through Cassie's hair and held her head tightly, plundering her mouth. She arched into him, opening even more.

It had been so long since he had been with anyone and never had he felt this fierce so quickly. He wanted to claim and control her.

Cassie's fingers dug into his arms as she pushed into his hold. She wanted this just as bad as he did. It would be so easy to just roll on top of her and let them sate their hunger for passion.

But it was too soon. They still had a lot to learn about each other. Plus he really was starting to believe that Cassie was the type of woman he'd always searched for. The mate he would find himself settling down with someday. First, he had to make sure he would be able to take care of whomever he chose to mate with. He'd somehow lost himself along the way and he needed to get back the man he once was.

He pulled back slowly and with regret.

She was still reeling from the events of the night before and he wasn't exactly a catch with his current emotion mess.

But it was so hard to back away when she stared up at him with need written clearly across her face.

"We shouldn't do this," he said to her.

She frowned but loosened her hold.

"We have time. We don't have to rush into anything." He barely got the words out before he was on his feet and stalking away. He had to put some distance between them. He was not strong enough to resist Cassie Wilson. If he didn't get away, he would end up claiming her for his own. And she had no idea who he really was.

Max closed his bedroom door firmly and leaned against the cool wood. For the second time in a day, he'd felt his wolf inside clawing to get out. He knew it was impossible, although if he could shift, he had no doubt he would be on four furry paws.

Running his palm over his heart, he closed his eyes, not that it would help. He could picture Cassie's desire then her confusion. He had screwed up royally.

He slammed his hand on the door.

It wouldn't be fair to Cassie to start something. He was still trying to deal with what had happened to him and his team. He grabbed the bottom of his shirt and whipped it over his head. Then, with determination, he walked to the mirror above the dresser.

He ran his shaking finger lightly around the tattoo over his heart.

A name and date was scrawled in black. The day that he'd lost his best friend in that hellhole.

Not being able to stop the dreams, unable to understand what had gone wrong, he wasn't able to offer himself to Cassie. He couldn't give her what he wasn't sure still existed.

Chapter Five

Max managed to fall back asleep, but it hadn't been easy. In addition to being trapped in that rundown house with his team, now the dream had Cassie there as well.

He had been trying to protect her right as the explosion had gone off.

Then he woke up.

Sweating and shaking, he stumbled to the bathroom to try to wash the dream away. The other doors in the hall were all closed, so he didn't know if Cassie was awake yet or not.

His head might not be on straight in regards to relationships, but he would make sure that Cassie was safe so they would be able to explore the strong connection between them. Lying in bed the night before with her scent still surrounding him, he'd been happy for the first time in longer than he could remember.

Not wanting to disturb her if she was still asleep, Max quietly strolled down the hall and into the bathroom. He turned the shower knob on hot and closed the door to warm up the glass stall. He bent over to the sink to peer at himself in the mirror.

The dark circles that he had been carrying around the last couple of months were worse. His skin was too pale, plus the weight loss he'd suffered was more obvious.

He needed to take better care of himself. He couldn't figure out why Cassie would even be attracted to him in his current state. But there was something about her. Whenever they were in the same room, he felt a pull in her direction.

There were some decisions that he needed to make. He didn't like the person he was becoming. Now, if he could just figure out how to get back everything he'd lost in himself, he would have something to offer Cassie. He needed to be his own man again.

Determination pulsing inside him, he pushed away from his image and climbed into the shower. The almost scorching water pelted down on him and he sighed deeply as his muscles relaxed.

He grabbed the shower gel off the shelf then poured a good amount into his palm. With his other hand, he used a washcloth to scrub himself clean. He felt better and the fog from the nightmare lifted.

Max rolled his shoulders and rinsed the soap from his body before shampooing his hair. Still keeping the buzz cut from his Navy days saved him time.

Body freshened up, he fisted his half-hard cock, sliding his hand up and down slowly. He'd been somewhat hard since he'd first laid eyes on Cassie. Since he'd returned to the States, it had only been his hand he'd had as company. And that was when he could even get it up. But all of that was changing.

He tightened his hold and, stroking himself faster, called up the memory of the kisses they'd shared the night before. Cassie's soft lips beneath his played through his mind, and the pressure of her body heightened his arousal.

He groaned and his cum squirted, painting the shower wall. It had been a long time since he'd gone over the edge so quickly. With a lighter air, he rinsed once more, making sure to clean his spunk off the wall then turned the water off. He grabbed one of the towels from the rod next to him and dried himself just as a knock came from the front of the house.

Max wrapped the cloth around his hips and rushed to his room. He pulled on a clean pair of jeans before grabbing a short-sleeved T-shirt. He dragged the top on as he headed toward the front entrance.

"Coming!" he called when the knock came again.

Just as he reached for the handle, he caught the scent of his Alpha outside. Max took a deep breath and opened the door.

Alpha Shawn stood on the porch holding a takeout container with three cups and a bakery bag. He held them up in offering.

Max grinned and waved the man inside. "Hey."

"Max, I hope I'm not disturbing you."

"Of course not. Please come in."

Alpha Shawn walked through the entry and into the kitchen. Max followed behind, both pleased to see his Alpha again and nervous at the same time. Alpha Shawn had a way of making Max confess things he would rather keep hidden. He'd been doing his best to avoid his Alpha since he'd returned home.

It figured that as soon as he was starting to pull his head out of his ass he'd actually not be able to steer clear of Alpha Shawn. While his Alpha set the coffees on the island countertop between them, Max walked to the cabinet to pull out some plates.

"I don't know if Cassie is awake yet, but I can check."

Alpha Shawn shook his head. "No, it's okay. I'd like a few minutes with you anyway."

Max nodded. His Alpha didn't just stop by for no reason. Everyone in the Pack knew that their leader was always looking out for them. Even Max knew that he could only hide for so long.

"So how are you doing?"

"I'm fine," he assured his Alpha.

Shawn leaned against the counter and lifted an eyebrow. "You sleeping okay?"

"Sure," he lied. "Some nights are better than others, but I'm handling everything."

Instead of calling him on his lie, Shawn just shook his head. "I have no doubt that you're handling everything, but that doesn't mean you can't ask for help if you need it. It takes a strong man to lean on others."

He sighed. "I know... I just need to figure things out." There was no use pretending. His Alpha had that stoic look on his face whenever he was determined to get through to one of the Pack members. "I just need more time."

"Okay." Shawn smiled. "I won't push right now. You know you can always talk to me, don't you?"

"Of course."

"All right." Shawn lifted the lid off one of the cups and Max followed suit. The smell of the fresh coffee was good and his stomach growled. "I brought some of muffins too."

"Thanks, man." He dug into the bag and chose one of the banana-nut muffins. He bit into it and moaned. God, those were so damn good.

"How are things going here?"

He chewed and took a long sip of his coffee. Alpha Shawn wouldn't know what had taken place between him and Cassie the night before, but Max still found himself shifting his feet nervously. "I...uh...well...we..."

"Max?"

As he took another drink, he mentally cursed himself. "Everything is okay. I've only just really started. I have some ideas on how to increase security and add a few more cameras without being too intrusive."

"Good, good. After this mess is over, I hope to talk you about the rest of the Pack."

That sounded like his Alpha wanted more than just a favor. "Well, you know that I'm happy to help in any way that I can, but I'm not a security expert or anything. Don't you have people for that?"

"Yes, but they're not Pack. I want someone who I can trust to oversee them."

"You want me to do it?" Max asked in disbelief. That was a major responsibility. He wanted to contribute to his community, but he wasn't sure he could handle such a large job.

"Absolutely."

"I'm not sure I'm the right person," he said honestly.

His Alpha didn't know everything that was going on in his head. If he did, there was no way Shawn would want him.

"You're the perfect person. You're a strong leader, smart, dedicated, loyal and compassionate."

He felt himself blush at the compliments. Even though he knew he wasn't those things, at least not anymore. "I'm not sure."

"It's something that I want you to think about. Take care of things here and see if you can find out who broke in to Cassie's studio, then make sure your sole focus is to protect her. The rest will work itself out."

He sure as hell hoped so. He nodded.

"I knew I could depend on you." Shawn patted his back as he passed Max. "I'll show myself out. I want to stop by and have a quick word with Alex while I'm here."

Max stood speechless as Shawn did, in fact, leave on his own. He wanted to be polite and at least walk the man to the door, but he couldn't seem to make his feet work. His Alpha's words were still bouncing around in his head.

Shawn believed in him. He wished he was as sure as his Alpha. Before his last mission had gone to shit, he'd had the confidence that Shawn was showing in him. He'd even been a little bit cocky. It was weird how one day could change all of that.

All he'd ever wanted to do was make a difference. To help people. When he'd left Canyon, he'd been a young man determined to show the world what he'd been made of. He'd joined the Navy and had known just weeks into boot camp that he'd found his place in the world.

He thrived at the physical part of training. He enjoyed pushing his body to its limits. The brothers he'd connected with were like an extension of his Pack. He'd been overseas and still thought he would spend his entire life in the service.

Eight years after he'd first joined, he'd applied to the Special Forces Units. It had taken everything he had to make it mentally and physically. Even so, he had never felt better in his life. The first several missions had been simple gathering of intel. He hadn't really been in danger. Then he'd been transferred to his new team and everything had changed.

Under the cover of night, he'd found himself in some very fucked-up situations. Still, every time he'd made it back home, he'd been proud. When he'd been promoted and given his own squad, he'd vowed to bring each member home with him every time.

In the end, he hadn't been able to keep that promise to his fellow soldiers. He might have brought Evan's body back, but it had been under his command that the man had died.

He closed his eyes, fighting back the memories, but they still bombarded him.

They'd dropped inside the enemy lines in the pitch blackness of night. The coordinates that they'd been given had just been a rough estimate. It hadn't been known whether or not the hostages were dead or alive.

But they'd had to try. That's what they did.

So he'd led his small band of men deep into the jungle to complete their task.

It had been sickening-hot. The air so thick it had been hard to breathe. Sounds they'd only heard a few times had followed them as they'd traveled farther and farther into danger.

Even when their boots had hit the ground, he hadn't felt good about the mission. Something, some small part of him, had known there was just something off. He'd ignored the feeling and followed orders. He would always regret that.

They'd walked for two hours before they'd started to hear signs of life from humans instead of just the jungle animals. Max had stopped his team's forward movement with a fist in the air. He'd been well known for his above average hearing. No one had known he was a shifter. They'd just teased him that it was his gut instinct, but they'd always followed him. Max had let them believe that.

* * * *

Max took point and methodically moved his men into position. They were just south of a small group of tents. One old, beat-up Jeep was parked to the side and it was filled with guns and ammo. They would need to secure that vehicle first. But that was a sure sign that the rebels were very well armed.

A few rough-looking men sat around a fire smoking and talking. He motioned to his team to drop and wait.

One by one their targets went into one of the sleeping areas. A large tent on the far side looked like their best bet of where to find the hostages.

He crawled over to Evan and the youngest member Jon Banks. He gave the hand signal for them to approach, and after receiving nods of affirmation, he crept back retaking his position.

Waiting until all was calm, he blew out a breath, and sent his unit in.

Jose Sanchez guarded the vehicle while he and Matt Wallace covered Evan and Banks.

The shouts from the large tent alerted not only his team but also the enemy.

All hell broke loose, but Max had a clear view of the hostages running with Evan and Banks, so he motioned Sanchez to set the explosive and take out the extra guns and ammo they'd taken. There wasn't enough time to secure the weapons on the bodies, but they needed to ensure that they couldn't be turned against them.

He and Wallace used their own rifles in the firefight and before he knew it, the huge explosion rocked the night.

"Move! Move!" he screamed. Max kept close bringing up the rear as they disappeared into the darkness.

* * * *

If only things had ended there.

Max shook himself out of his thoughts. He knew he had to let go of what had happened. It wasn't easy. He relived that day over and over.

Pushing himself away from the counter, his stomach was in knots. The first part of their mission had been a success. The rest had been one fuck up after another. He had to keep himself busy to prevent himself from thinking about where things had gone wrong.

He picked up the extra coffee Alpha Shawn had brought then started down the hall.

If Cassie was awake, he'd give it to her. If not, he would check to make sure everything was secure.

He tapped softly on her studio door, hoping if she wasn't awake he wouldn't bother her. He heard movement in the room and cracked the door.

The patio door was closed and the room was much the same as it had been the night before. Except for one thing.

Sitting in the middle of the room on the easel was a painting. It wasn't one of the half-finished pieces he'd seen earlier. No, this was amazing...just amazing.

He pushed the door all the way open so he could get a better look.

He recognized the canyon cliffs of their home. The colors blended together so seamlessly it was almost like he could reach out and stroke the hard ridges of the cliffs.

Standing strong and powerful in the center of the canvas was a huge black wolf.

He nearly dropped the Styrofoam cup as he felt compelled to get closer.

It was the most astounding thing he'd ever seen. Inside his body, his wolf stretched in need. He hadn't been lying when he'd told Cassie he sensed the animal inside. But it was like she'd been able to peer deep inside him and paint how he pictured his wolf.

"Do you like it?"

He heard Cassie behind him yet couldn't look away from the wolf staring back at him. He even recognized the gaze that met his in the mirror. "Yes."

She moved closer, bringing the heat from her body next to his.

"After you left, all I could think about was showing you my vision. It was like I could see him and I wanted you to be able view your wolf through my eyes," she said quietly.

Max nodded. "It's remarkable." He turned suddenly and grabbed her to yank her forward. He slammed his mouth down on hers and kissed her hungrily.

Chapter Six

Cassie had been so scared about showing her newest piece to Max. She hadn't expected such a passionate response when he did see it. She found herself pressed to Max as he ravaged her mouth. God, it felt so good. She'd never experienced such an overwhelming need for another person like she did with Max.

She gripped his shirt with her fists to keep him from stopping. They'd touched on some sensitive subjects, but she knew there was more going on with him other than his non-shifter status. She wanted to know everything that made him tick. She'd realized that the night before. Max was everything she had always desired in a mate. They weren't ready to declare their love for each another, but she thought they might get there one day. There was a pull between them. And needed him more every minute she spent with him.

He had one arm around her waist anchoring her, but she wanted his full body not just his mouth. She drew her lips back and looked down. His free hand still held a to-go cup.

He noticed her gaze. "Coffee."

Nodding, she took the cup from him then placed it on the shelf behind her. "Now," she said, framing his face with her hands. "Let's do that again."

She was the one to kiss him this time. He didn't hesitate to get right back to where they'd left off. Their mouths were fused together as Cassie rubbed against him.

He moaned and she swallowed the sound. He tasted so damn wonderful. Like coffee and something banana with just a hint of a spice. She could lose herself in his flavor and wouldn't regret it at all.

He pulled at the hem of her T-shirt until he managed to get it hiked up. At the first touch of his rough palms on her stomach, she began whimpering.

"Oh, hell," he panted against her lips. "You feel so good."

"Yeah." She leaned harder into him.

The doorbell rang. They froze.

"Maybe they'll go away," she said hopefully. She didn't want to stop. Yes, they probably weren't ready to just fall in bed together, but the attraction between the two of them sizzled.

Max started to step away from her and she tried to hide her disappointment.

"It's probably for the best," he replied. "I need to check in with Alex about the additional cameras and look for weak spots."

She understood that he had a job to do. However, it didn't stop her from almost obsessing about having his hands on her.

Cassie tugged her shirt back down then smoothed the material just as she heard the front door open.

"Cassie?"

"In the studio," she called out. "That's James, my assistant. He has a key," she explained to Max.

He nodded. He turned to walk away but paused at the painting again. "That is truly beautiful."

"Thank you."

James knocked on the open door and stuck his head in. "Hey."

"Hi." She waved him forward. "James this is Max, who is here as security. Max, my assistant James."

"Security?" James looked between the two of them.

"After the break-in, Alex thought we needed to be more careful. Max is going to help get the house and studio better covered and is staying until the person is caught."

"Wow!" James stuck his hands in his pockets.

He was young, still attending college, and a very talented artist himself. They'd met at the gallery and she had been taken with his enthusiasm for art. "I didn't realize it was such a big deal."

Cassie frowned. "Of course it is. Someone broke into my home and the studio. Months of work was destroyed!"

James nodded. "Yeah, it's just no one was hurt and Canyon is usually such a safe place."

"I'm here to make sure it stays that way," Max said.

Cassie noticed he was watching James closely. She knew that he had to be suspicious of everyone who had access to the studio, but there was no way she would believe that James had been involved.

"I guess I was just hoping it was a mistake or something. It's scary."

"It'll be okay, hon," she assured him while wrapping an arm around his shoulders.

His bleached, spiked hair tickled her cheek when she embraced him.

"Wow!" James noticed the canvas of the black wolf and broke away. "This is so awesome!"

She met Max's gaze and smiled. She thought the man was pretty awesome himself.

"I'm going to get started," Max stated, "so don't leave the house without letting me know."

"No problem," she assured Max. "We're going to go through the inventory list from the gallery to see just how many more pieces I need. I don't want Alex to cancel the show if he doesn't have to."

Max glanced over his shoulder to where James was admiring the painting from different angles. Max's hand brushed against hers as he strolled from the room. The tingle that followed his touch gave Cassie something to look forward to.

Max turned the screw to secure the last additional camera Alex had purchased and sighed with relief. He'd been at it for hours. He was finally comfortable about the new security around the entire Wilson ranch.

"Hey, man."

Max looked over at Alex who had joined him on the porch. The man held out a beer and Max almost moaned in gratitude. It was damn hot out today and he was tired. He climbed down from the stool he was using for mounting the camera above the front door and accepted the cold bottle.

He rubbed it over his forehead before taking a long pull. "Thanks, I needed that."

Alex nodded. "Looks like you got the last one up."

"Yeah, I also put new locks on all the windows and installed a chain on the front door. Cassie seems to use the balcony doors a lot and I want to get some better locks for that."

"She likes to smell the fresh air," Alex said.

Max noted that Alex seemed a little uneasy. He took another long drink and lifted an eyebrow. "Everything okay?"

Alex shook his head. "Let's sit."

Max followed him to the wooden porch chairs then settled down with his beer. "What's up?"

"You've heard about the Church for Humanity?"

"Sure, they are the ones who are trying to get the government to make shifters register."

"They're also the reason that the wolf Council worked so hard in setting up the new shifter Coalition. The main guy was arrested in Nevada for kidnapping and all sorts of other crimes against the wolves."

"I remember reading about it right after I got home," Max told him.

"I received another letter today at the gallery that they want the showing canceled due to the *nature* of the show pieces."

"Cassie's work?" Max guessed.

Alex leaned forward and rubbed his hand over his face. "Yeah. I called and left a message for Alpha Shawn, but he hasn't called back yet. I'm worried. I know our Pack isn't public, but the church can cause us all kinds of trouble."

"Do you think they might be responsible for the break-in?"

Alex blew out a breath. "I don't know. I mean, how would they have known we weren't home?"

"Someone was watching."

"And if someone is watching, what else have they seen? We shift all the time. Almost everyone around these parts does."

Max could completely see why Alex was worried. The members of the church had been getting more and more vocal about how unnatural the shifters were. After their leader had been convicted, it had seemed to spread to being downright nasty between the church and shifter communities. "We need to call the Council."

"That's why I wanted to talk to Shawn. He'll be able to contact them and maybe even the Coalition."

"Fuck!" Max muttered. This just got worse every minute. If they did have to bring the Coalition in, there was no way they would be able to remain hidden. "What are we going to tell Cassie?"

"I don't know. I'm not sure we should tell her anything right now. She needs to concentrate on the upcoming show and I don't want her more worried than she already is."

"Then maybe you shouldn't discuss it on my front porch."

Max jerked his head to the side and saw Cassie standing in the doorway. Alex groaned and stood.

"I'm sorry, Cass, but I didn't want to scare you." Alex held out his hand.

Cassie moved to him and snuggled into his arms. "I'm a big girl, Alex. You can't protect me from everything." She looked over at Max. "Plus I've got a pretty good bodyguard."

Max grinned, although he fought not to blush. He really admired how calmly Cassie seemed to handle everything. Yes, she was struggling, but her natural instincts seemed to take over and she showed trust in the men around her.

Alex chuckled and patted her back. She stepped away then leaned against the rail while Alex retook his chair.

"You can't keep things from me, Alex. If there is more going on than just a break in, I need to know."

Alex nodded. "I know, you're right."

"We'll handle this," she told him. "But what about the boys? Are they safe here?"

"I sure hope so," Alex said just as his cell phone rang. He dug it out of his pocket. "That's Shawn. I need to take this."

Max waved him off and waited until he'd walked down the porch steps. He then turned his attention to Cassie. "You okay?"

"Yeah. No. I don't know," she said, sighing deeply. "I can't help but wonder if I caused all this with my paintings? Is the Pack in danger because of me?"

Max stood and encircled her in his arms. "No, I don't believe so. These people are so hell bent on causing trouble for us they could have found anything."

She laid her head against his chest. "I hate the idea of someone watching us. Planning ways to hurt us. I don't understand why they can't just let us be."

Max buried his hand in her hair and tightened his embrace. "Ever since the beginning of time, people have feared what they don't understand. This will pass. We have the Council and now the Coalition. It's going to be okay."

"I'm glad you're here. Everything is crazy and happening fast, but I feel safe with you. Like I can get back to my art and not worry about what is going on around me."

"I'm glad I can give you that kind of security," he replied. It was funny that from the moment he'd set eyes on Cassie, he had felt something settle deep inside him. Like even his wolf was at home with this woman. "And we'll figure out what to do about the church."

Her eyes sparkled as she gazed up at him. "Kiss me again?"

He cupped her cheek while he lowered his head. "Yes," he whispered against her lips, brushing his over hers.

She pushed into the kiss eagerly and responded so beautifully that he had to draw back so he didn't end up embarrassing them both. Her brother might return at any time.

"Be good," he warned playfully when she tried to chase his mouth.

She lifted a brow. "Oh, I can be so very good."

He snorted, stepping back. "Not with your brother close by," he teased, popping her on the ass with a light slap.

Her carefree laughter warmed his heart. They might have a lot of concern, but they would get through it. He would make damn sure.

Max spotted Alex heading back toward them and retook his seat. Cassie smirked at him and returned to lean against the rail.

"Shawn is calling the Council right now. He and Chase will come over to the house as soon as they can," Alex informed them as he stepped up to the porch.

"I'm going to call Jacob and make sure he can make it too. I thought we could have a barbeque. It's a nice evening and we need to return to some sort of routine."

"Sounds good," Cassie agreed. "I'll make a few side dishes. The least we can do is feed everyone if we're going to put them in danger."

"Hey!" Alex strode up the steps and to his sister. "This is not your fault."

"I know," she said softly. "Really, I do, but I can't help but... This sucks!"

Alex nodded as he chuckled. "It does. Just remember there are five artists in the showing, four of them are shifters, and we don't even know why this show is being targeted. We've had many over the years. Let us figure this out."

She nodded. "I'm going to go start on some food."

Max kept himself from reaching out to her as she passed. He wanted to comfort her, to take her back to the moment when she was laughing happily. As she stepped back inside, Alex growled. Max turned to him.

Alex stood, hands fisted at his side. "I want to kill whoever is doing this to her, to us all."

Since Max felt the same way, he couldn't really offer anything to say.

"I've got to call Jacob. Stay close to her?"

"I will," Max promised. He waited until Alex was stalking back to the main house, then Max turned and followed Cassie.

He found her at the kitchen sink scrubbing potatoes. "You okay?"

"Fine," she answered shortly.

He moved up behind her and placed his hands on her hips.

She sighed and leaned back into him. "I forgot for a minute outside. With you. How can I be happy and so scared at the same time?"

Max nuzzled her neck. "It's natural. You've got a lot thrown at you right now. It's okay to feel good while you're still worried. It's okay to feel pleasure."

She turned and faced him. "I just keep thinking if all of this wasn't happening, I wouldn't have met you again. You wouldn't be here with me."

Max leaned closer and rubbed his nose against hers. "I think we would have. Somehow we would have found each other. This, between us, is too good for us not to have found a way to each another. "

"Max," she whispered. "Kiss me."

Max did as she requested. He could spend forever kissing her.

Chapter Seven

Cassie felt better. She'd made potato salad, dips for chips and coleslaw for dinner, then she'd stepped into a quick, hot shower. Max hadn't even tried to join her and she was little disappointed. She kept telling herself that they'd have time together, but she was struggling with patience. She wanted the man.

While she'd cleaned up, Max had linked all of the new cameras from her place, the main house and Jacob's residence to his laptop. He'd taught her how to work the programs and she appreciated the fact that he was including her, showing her how he was keeping her safe.

He had the laptop on the deck table as they waited for everyone to arrive. Alex had started the grill before pulling beers out of the cooler and passing them around.

There was a nice cool breeze that Cassie welcomed as she sat next to Max, admiring him. With his head bent over the computer screen, she was able to watch him without him noticing. He was so damn attractive with his black hair and tanned, muscular body. She could still feel his hands on her from earlier in the kitchen and felt arousal shoot through her.

Max lifted his head and looked over at her. Upon catching her staring at him, he winked. "Later," he murmured quietly.

She ducked her chin, raising her gaze to Alex and flushed when she realized her brother had been watching her while her attention had been on Max. Alex was grinning at her, but luckily footsteps sounded and she turned her head to see Alpha Shawn and Chase arriving.

Max pushed the laptop away and stood. He greeted his brother with a quick hug then he shook hands with their Alpha. She liked the way his hazel eyes brightened around the other men. He stood next to Chase and Cassie could easily see how close the two brothers were.

That was important to her. It had just been her and her siblings for so long. Both Alex and Jacob made it a point to take care of her while she did her best to take care of them. She didn't like to leave the ranch, so they did her shopping and visited her a lot. While there was no getting out of gallery shows, one of them stayed with her the entire time.

Alex had even been the one who had hired James for her. He'd wanted the young artist to get more attention and had asked Cassie to help him. Since her and James had hit it off right away, she was happy to assist in his training.

James didn't have a lot of money, so the income that came from protecting Cassie provided him with some cash, while at the same time, the experience of working with another artist had really brought James' art to the front.

There would be half a dozen of James's work in the next showing which was one reason why she didn't want it to the postponed. This was really James' true first shot.

Since he was human, he wouldn't be at the barbeque, but she had spoken to him earlier about what was happening. She had assured James that the show would still proceed as planned. His art would be seen.

James had been relieved. Since he didn't know about the shifter aspect of the break-in, he had been more upset that someone was trying to hurt the gallery.

She wished she could be honest with him. Since her Pack wasn't in the open, she had to continue to be careful.

"What are you thinking about so hard?" Max asked as he slid to her side.

"The show. I told James it would still go on. It's his first art exhibition and I want to make sure that he has enough support."

"How long has he worked for you?"

"Almost a year now. He applied for the job over the Internet and moved up here. He doesn't have any family so he sort of became part of ours. Plus he's a big help. I don't have to worry about ordering supplies or anything else other than painting."

"He seems kind of young."

"Yeah, but he is talented. A few more years and he'll probably have a show of his own." She nudged his hip. "You're looking into him?"

"I am," Max admitted. "He has access to the ranch and knows all of you."

"There is no way he's involved."

"Then he has nothing to worry about. Let me do my job, Cassie. He won't even know I'm looking if he doesn't have anything to do with this."

She had to trust Max. If they were going to be able to explore the attraction between the two of them, she'd have to take Max at his word. "Just be careful. He's been through a lot."

"I will." He squeezed her shoulder before moving over to the grill.

"So I take it everything is working out between you and Max?" Alpha Shawn asked as he took Max's place at her side.

She grinned over at him. "Did you have any doubt?"

Shawn chuckled. "Nope." He swung his arm over her shoulder and led her away from the others. "I knew Max would be a big help here. And I was sure that you would be a good influence on him also."

Cassie checked over her shoulder to make sure no one else was within hearing range. "Tell me you're not playing match maker."

"No, actually, I'm not," he assured her. "But Max needs to do something that will make him feel good about himself again, make him feel needed. Plus your family is one of the best I've ever known. He needs time to heal and less time to think."

She tipped her head back to get a good look at him. "You're worried about him?"

"Yes," Shawn admitted. "I have plans for Max, but he needs to settle things in his mind before I can proceed."

"What kind of plans?"

"The kind I'm sure he'll fight me on. I want to name him as my successor if anything happens to me."

She couldn't hold in her gasp. "That's awesome! Why wouldn't he jump at the chance?"

Shawn looked over to where the other three men were laughing next to the grill. "Since he's a non-shifter, Max has never felt truly part of the Pack. Even though everyone respects him, Max doesn't see himself able to lead the others. I want to show him he's wrong."

"What can I do?" She wanted to help Max see that he could be a great leader.

"You already are. He seems comfortable here. Once we find out what is going on, I think Max will see on his own that he has even more to offer."

She didn't have time to respond. A loud commotion announced the arrival of her nephews, younger brother and her sister-in-law.

Her two nephews, Kyle and Korrie, raced up the wooden steps to where she and Shawn were standing.

"Alpha! Alpha!" Kyle, the youngest at four, cried out.

Shawn crouched down to catch the small boy. "Hey there, little man!"

"Me too!" Korrie called, jumping up and down.

Shawn easily picked him up in his other arm. It was a sight to see the two children in the arms of their powerful leader.

Cassie leaned over and kissed both boys on their cheeks. "Well, hello to you too."

Kyle laughed. "Hi, Aunt Cassie."

"Hi, honey," she said, hugging her sister-in-law. Peyton had been her best friend since grade school. When Peyton and Jacob had gotten married, Cassie had been so happy. Peyton had always been like a sister to her and now she truly was.

Cassie accepted a quick hug from her brother. Pulling away, he then joined the other men.

"Come on, you monkeys," Peyton said to her children. "Let Alpha Shawn breathe."

Their Alpha set the kids down, patting them one last time, then he hugged Peyton, then strolled toward the grill.

"Well, look at Max Lawson," Peyton murmured. "He sure is looking good."

Cassie grinned. "Uh-huh."

"Jacob tells me he's staying at your place?"

"Yes."

Peyton faced her. "And?"

Cassie laughed. She ran her gaze over the boys then back to Peyton.

"Oh, an adult conversation? Nice!" Peyton commented. "How would you boys like to play with the Legos?"

Kyle and Korrie hooted then raced over to where Alex had a small play area in the corner of the porch. The entire family enjoyed hanging out together, so Alex had made sure the boys had plenty with which to entertain themselves.

Peyton put her arm through Cassie's and pulled them even farther away from the crowd. "So?"

Cassie shook her head. "I don't really know what to say. You've seen him, he is sexy as all get out, and he seems to be a really great guy. We kissed last night and ever since then I can't seem to get him out of my mind. There is just something there, you know?"

"I do, but are you ready for that? You've been fighting Alex on finding a mate for a long time. "

"But that's because I never felt any sort of connection. Max is different. I don't know what will happen between the two of us, but I do know that I have to find out. I want him, but I'm worried about scaring him off too. He might not be ready. "

"Huh." Peyton frowned. "All I can say is that if you are truly interested in him then don't give up. Let him set the pace, yet let him know you're interested."

"I guess." Cassie turned so she could watch Max.

He was standing between his brother and Alpha Shawn, talking and gesturing. His tight T-shirt was stretched against his chest muscles and damn if that sight didn't make her mouth water.

Max glanced over at her and the heat in his eyes called to her. She licked her lips, watching as his gaze followed the motion.

Peyton bumped her arm. "Well, let's go join them."

As they made their way over, Alex declared the burgers were ready. The next several minutes consisted of everyone filling plates and grabbing new beers. The group settled at the wooden picnic table.

Cassie was filled with love. This was what family was all about. These people had come together to figure out how to protect one another and the entire Pack.

She sat between Max and Alex and felt one hundred percent safe. Of course, having a successful show would really prove that she had gotten her life back after the break-in. Let whoever was responsible know that they hadn't won.

She'd felt compelled to bring Max's wolf to life for him. There was no way that she would let that piece of art go into the show, though. The canvas of Max's wolf would be for Max alone.

Even if he wasn't able to shift into his animal, sometimes she could sense how close his wolf was to the surface. Even at a young age, she'd known that Max was different. It wasn't until the night before that she'd really started to understand, though. She'd always taken the ability to shift for granted.

Now she was seeing things differently.

There was so much more to Max than what she had first considered.

"So, I spoke with the Council and they are sending out two guards to aid us in the investigation. The leader of the Church for Humanity was arrested in Nevada, but the Council has been keeping an eye on the other locations. However, owing to a problem with one of the people, they've pulled out all the shifters they had under cover in the church," Alpha Shawn told them. "Now they have to watch from the outside."

"What about the Coalition?" Max asked.

Shawn shook his head. "They said we can wait. The Council has dealt with the church before and the two guys they are sending already brought one location down. Since we want to remain in secret, we won't bring in the Coalition until we have no other choice."

This was great. At least it wouldn't lead her Pack to having to reveal themselves. There were a few humans who lived around the canyon or in town, but not many. Luckily their community was mostly made up of Pack.

"With the security measures we've taken here and in town, I'm confident about what we'll be coming up against," Alpha Shawn assured everyone.

She felt Max's hand on her back and leaned into his touch. She hoped they caught whoever was causing the trouble quickly.

The others spoke more about who could be involved and why, but Cassie just listened. She finished her burger. She accepted her bottle after Alex stood and grabbed another round of beers.

They were connecting the church with the break-in to her studio, but Cassie couldn't really see the link.

Okay, so the church didn't like the art that featured animals since they were fighting against shifters, however there was no actual proof that her art had any association to shifters at all. It was a great chance someone from the church had to take.

No, the culprit had to be closer to home.

She didn't realize that she'd spoken out loud until everyone turned to her. She flushed while ducking her head. "Sorry."

"No," Max said. "We want to hear your ideas too."

She glanced over at their Alpha and saw him nod.

"I just don't see how the church could know enough about me to break in."

"They would have had to be watching."

"How?" She motioned, indicating the property. "Our land isn't easy to get to. And if strangers were wandering around, someone would have scented them."

Alex and Max shared a look and she stiffened. "You don't think it's a stranger either."

No one said anything. She glared at her older brother.

Alex sighed. "No, we don't. We think that whoever is involved with the break-in has a connection to the church."

"Who?"

"Your assistant," Max informed her.

"James? There is no way! I already told you that!"

"Think about it, Cass," Alex responded. "He has access to the house and studio. He knows if you're out. No one would think it was strange for him to be around, and since his scent is already familiar to us, we wouldn't notice it."

She shook her head as she stood. It wasn't possible that the sweet kid who she had spent so much time with would do something as horrible as destroy her work. No way.

"You're wrong. I'll prove that you're wrong," she told them and stalked away.

She heard someone start to follow her but didn't look back to see who it was. Her heart ached and she wasn't exactly sure why. It didn't seem right that her family, who knew James, would accuse him.

Cassie also wanted to silence the small part of her that wondered if they were right. Everything they said was true and she really needed time alone to think about it.

Chapter Eight

It had been three days since the barbeque, and Max was finding Cassie both intriguing and aggravating.

She refused to talk to him about James or the break-in. Alex had warned him that she would act this way, but Max just didn't get it. Cassie had no problem discussing what they were investigating and had met the two wolf shifters the Council had sent. However, she wouldn't hear of James being involved.

Since she spent most of her time in her studio, Max was glad to see she was back doing what she loved. They'd also made it a habit of sitting together on the porch late each night talking and sharing a few kisses. They were growing closer each day. He felt himself start to heal too. During the day, with Cassie working, he hung out with his Alpha, Alex and Chase. He was beginning to feel like the man he used to be. Even though he knew the camaraderie with the other three men was helping him, it was really Cassie to whom he attributed the change in him. He wanted to be the man she deserved.

He hated to leave her every time he ushered her inside and into her bedroom. He just wasn't sure they were ready to move their relationship to the next step. Oh, it wouldn't be long. He ached to have her against him. However she was busy, and he wanted to insure her safety above everything else.

Getting to know Cassie better by keeping their relationship at a slow pace had the added benefit of making Max feel like he really knew Cassie. Max found that Cassie was a talented, smart and warm woman. While she didn't like to be in a group of people in strange surroundings, she loved to be with family and enjoyed gatherings with them.

She spoke to her brothers and sister-in-law at least once a day. He liked that they were so important to her.

The more Max learned about her the more he liked her. He'd started to connect to her right away, and over the last couple of days, he knew that he'd started to fall for her. Their connection was more than just sex, especially since they hadn't had sex yet.

The nightmares that he'd been plagued with since he'd returned home had eased. In the last two nights, Max had dreamed of some good times with his team.

Cassie asked lots of questions about what he'd done in the Navy and his friends. Out of all the stories he'd shared, he hadn't been able to talk about losing Evan just yet. But he shared stories of his best friend, glad that she seemed to want to listen.

It was nice just relaxing on the patio with her.

His wolf did not fully agree. Every time Max was close enough to smell Cassie, his animal wanted to claim her. The human part of him understood that Cassie needed time to get to know him better, but the wolf wanted to mate.

As he locked up the house and checked the security, he heard Cassie's shower turn on farther back in the house. His cock, which had been half hard the entire time he'd sat talking with her, grew even more so. He palmed himself thinking about how she would look, naked and wet, under the hot spray.

He bit back a moan and yanked his hand away. He'd jacked off every single night since he'd started staying with her. Tonight would be no different. He needed to get to bed. It was already after midnight. Hopefully Cassie would be turning in soon too.

She'd gotten only a few hours' sleep before she'd risen to start painting again. It seemed to Max that she got very little rest, but she assured him it was normal for her. She painted when she could and, once she was done, she would be able to catch up on her sleep.

Max worried she wasn't taking proper care of herself, but he also didn't want to interfere.

He closed his bedroom door behind him and pulled his T-shirt off. Walking around the end of the bed, he folded the comforter back before dropping his shorts and boxers. He didn't have to sleep in the nude even though he was more comfortable that way. However, he'd found with Cassie close by, the need to jack off every night was strong and the only way to really calm himself enough to fall asleep.

He climbed in the big bed and lay on his back. The overhead fan turned silently while creating a soft breeze. Max ran his hands down his chest and played with his nipples. The pull made his cock even harder. Keeping his fingers of his left hand busy, he used his right to stroke himself.

It felt good, like it had the past several nights, but Max still wanted to experience what Cassie's talented fingers would do to him.

He sped up his movements as he thought about Cassie climbing in bed with him. What she would feel like under him. He thrust his hips up, imagining being buried deep inside her. He craved to hear the sounds she would make while he took her. He hoped she was vocal. He enjoyed a woman who didn't hide her pleasure.

Max pumped himself faster, already close to the edge.

Cassie had a small, compact body. She liked to wear soft cotton pants and tank tops while she painted. Even her cute painted toenails were a turn on for him.

And her mouth! God, she had a talented tongue. They'd kissed probably a dozen times a day and he couldn't get enough of her unique flavor.

He came, biting his lip to keep from crying out as he covered his hand with his seed. He fell back onto the sheets and panted. If just thinking about being with Cassie pushed him over so quickly, he had no idea how he would handle it when he finally got to have her in his bed.

He reached over and grabbed a handful of Kleenex to clean up the mess he'd made. He tossed them in the waste basket beside the bed then rolled over, burying his face in his pillow.

Sleep started to cover him and he didn't fight it as he looked forward to what the next day with Cassie would bring.

* * * *

Cassie dried off with a clean, fluffy towel then pulled on a pair of sleep pants and a black tank top. She ran a brush through her hair, thinking about the canvases that she needed to have picked up.

She'd told James that she would call him once she was ready for everything to be moved to the gallery, and was almost out of space. She'd avoided having her assistant out to her house since she knew that Max and Alex believed he was involved.

In the meantime, she couldn't figure out if James was actually involved or not, she decided to just avoid the entire thing. Max let her, to a point. He still told her everything that the two Council shifters were finding out about the church close by. Apparently they were watching the church to see if any members were showing too much attention. They had reported that while the church was fully prepared to stop the showing, or to picket it, none of the members had traveled near the ranch.

Cassie felt both better and worse about that.

If the church had not been involved in the break-in, then the only suspect was James. But she also didn't want to think about strangers being in her house.

She felt safe having Max with her while she completed the last of the new projects. Each time she was on a roll, he left her alone, just making sure that she had food or a snack close by. And if she needed a break, he would sit with her and talk with her for hours.

The stories that he told were amazing for her inspiration. She'd made sure that Max hadn't seen any of the paintings just yet. After the show, she wanted to present them to him. She'd managed to make a series of works detailing each member of Max's unit. She knew that they weren't shifters, but she could take what Max shared with her and bring them to life. She'd just completed the last one.

Evan. Who Max had said was his best friend. Each time he spoke about Evan, she could pick up on the tension and sadness inside Max. She hadn't asked, yet she was pretty sure that Evan had been killed.

If that was what had happened, it was no wonder Max had been so depressed when he'd arrived back in town.

She wanted the painting of Evan to be perfect. To reflect every feeling that Max had shared with her. The moment Max saw it, Cassie hoped that he would have a lasting, loving reflection of his friend.

Now, since she was done, she wouldn't be able to put off calling James any longer.

She set her hairbrush down then strolled out of the bathroom connecting with her bedroom. Her soft mattress called to her, but she continued past it.

She'd been so close to finishing the entire series that she couldn't relax until she was finally done. She really wanted to spend more time with Max, but she just couldn't *not* work on her art. That was the way it was with her. When her muse struck, she painted obsessively then just stopped.

If she were going to have a relationship with Max — and she was going to make sure she got the chance — it was better the man learned her quirks now. So far, he had been very understanding.

She took the cover off her last canvas and let her gaze wander over the scene she'd created. The color and shading were just what she'd wanted.

There was just one more addition. She knew what it needed. She picked up her brush and chewed on the wooden tip. In her mind, she didn't see Evan as a wolf. No, the way Max described him there would be a difference in his best friend.

Cassie had gone with a panther. A powerful, sleek, black panther.

She retrieved the paint palette and started mixing the colors. The panther crouched low in a field of brush. Its hind legs poised to jump, ready and willing to defend his friends.

Working furiously, she lost herself into her special world. She didn't have to think, just let the image in her mind out.

As her fingers started to cramp, she returned to awareness. The fog of concentration lifted, and she stepped back, drawing in a deep breath.

It was perfect.

Elation swamped her.

The intelligence that was shining from the panther's crystal-green eyes looked back at her. As Max had spoken about his best friend, it was this image that she'd seen. Now she could finally share her gift with Max. Let him see how she saw the world and the people in it.

Tears of pride and exhaustion prickled and she rubbed at her eyes with the heels of her hands.

She'd accomplished what she had set out to do. Turning in a circle, she took in each piece of work. The way that Max had described each man and the stories he'd shared had allowed her to see them in an animal form and turn them into their animal counterpart.

She smiled. She couldn't wait to show Max.

But a glance at the clock on the wall showed that she had been busy. It was just after three in the morning, so she would have to wait to share her gift with him.

Now, hopefully, she would be able to sleep.

She started toward the bathroom. She turned on the water before scrubbing the dry paint from her hands and under her nails.

Clean, she shut off the faucet and stared into the mirror. Now that she was finished with the series, she could take the time to decide how to proceed with Max.

There was no doubt that they wanted each another. And it was time to let him know that while she enjoyed getting to know him, she had to have him. She flicked off the bathroom light and headed toward her bed. Just as she reached it, she heard a faint noise from down the hall.

Cassie tiptoed to the door and pressed her ear against it. A soft moan, like from a wounded person, drifted to her. Quietly as possible, she pulled the bedroom door open and peeked into the corridor. All of the lights remained off and she couldn't sense anyone near. She paused and strained to pick up the sound again.

There! Coming from Max's bedroom.

She inched forward until she heard him cry out. Bolting to his bedroom, she grabbed the handle, relieved it was unlocked. After twisting it open, she rushed inside.

Max laid on his side, thrashing his head against the pillow. His long legs were tangled in the sheets as he kicked. He moaned again and Cassie couldn't stand to see him struggling in a nightmare.

"Max," she called as she crept closer.

"No!" he cried out, still asleep.

"Max, wake up! Max!" she tried again. Her knees hit the edge of the bed and she lightly shook his shoulder. "Max."

His hand grasped her wrist and he yanked her forward. Cassie fell on top of him but ended up trapped under his heavier bulk as he rolled. His hazel eyes popped open but were cloudy. She wasn't sure he even saw her.

With her free hand, she cupped his cheek. "It's okay, Max. It's Cassie. Wake up for me."

Although he had her pinned under his body and his hand was still wrapped around her wrist, he wasn't actually hurting her. In fact, under any other circumstances, she would have loved being in this position with him.

"Max, it's me," she repeated over and over.

He grunted, easing back. His gaze started to clear, and he blinked down at her. "Cassie?"

She smiled. "Hi."

He frowned. "What?" he asked looking around. "Oh, God! Are you okay? I didn't hurt you, did I?"

He released his hold and sat back on his haunches.

"No," she assured him. "You didn't hurt me."

Since his breathing was still a little too fast, she rubbed his chest. "You were having a nightmare."

"Shit!" He closed his eyes. "I'm sorry."

"Hey" — she lifted one hand to rub his jaw — "look at me."

She smiled as he complied. "It's okay. I finally ended up in bed with you."

Chapter Nine

Cassie's words startled a laugh from Max and he shook his head. He was so embarrassed that she had heard him having a nightmare, but thankful he hadn't hurt her.

Max slowly lowered his head so that Cassie could tell he planned on kissing her. If she didn't want him to, she could still pull away. Cassie didn't. Instead, she lifted her head and their lips brushed.

She gasped, giving him entrance, and he took no time thrusting his tongue inside. Her nails dug into his bare shoulders as she held him tightly and moved her mouth against his. He'd gone to bed naked and knew that if he didn't put a stop to their making out, it wouldn't be long before he was begging to take her.

He tried to pull away, really, he did, but when she chased his lips with hers, he groaned and slanted his mouth over hers again.

She smoothed his hands down her body and under her tank. She arched into him while wrapping her legs around his waist. His cock was already hard and leaking.

It took everything he had to finally yank his head back. "If we don't stop…"

"Don't want to stop," she told him, gripping his nape and trying to pull him down.

Her confession had him fighting once again for control. "We don't have to do this right now."

Cassie sat up and Max was enraptured by her soft expression. "You're right, we don't. But I want you and I know you feel the same way. We're adults."

Max shook his head. "I want you for more than just sex." He needed her to understand that she meant more to him. He wanted a real relationship.

She grinned. "I know."

He lifted an eyebrow. "And?"

"You're not going anywhere, Max. We are going to see this to the end. And I've finally got you just where I want you." She pushed at his chest and he followed her directions to lay back. She threw her leg over his waist and planted both hands on his chest. "And I am going to take care of you tonight."

"Yeah?" he replied, trying to tease, but it came out breathless.

"You bet." Cassie shimmied down his body until she was between his legs. She lifted his cock and he had to bite his lips as she pumped him. Already he was so close.

"I want to taste you," she said.

"Yes," he hissed out when she did just that.

She ran her tongue over the mushroom head while stroking the length. He gripped the sheet under him to keep from grabbing her head.

She looked up at him then she started to swallow him deeply. She was so damn sexy going down on him.

"Christ!" he growled.

Humming, she pulled back up. "I love your flavor."

He wasn't going to able to survive her seduction. It took every ounce of his control to not pump his hips as she went back to sucking him. He let out a long moan, as she started to cup and roll his balls with her left hand.

Cassie was expertly bringing him to the edge, so he stopped fighting it. He let go of all his tension and just closed his eyes, enjoying the pleasure she was giving him. He lifted his hips and Cassie adjusted easily to let him slide deep before backing off again.

She licked, sucked and hummed and it wasn't long until he felt the familiar tingle at the base of his spine.

"Cassie!" he called out a warning.

She only dropped down and suckled harder. Taking that as permission, he bucked and came.

She swallowed down his seed, then popped off his cock with a smile. "I knew you would taste good."

"Come up here," he demanded.

She stroked him one last time, causing him to hiss again, then she complied.

As soon as her body covered his, he rolled her under him before devouring her mouth. She pressed up into him, reveling in his power. Panting with need, she begged with her body. Max wasted no time taking off her clothes as she tried to get control of herself. His hands on her body, however, did not help at all. She was drowning with her need for him. Once he had her bare and stretched out for him, he began to slowly trace over her with his tongue.

Shivering and panting, she rewarded him with moans and pleading. He plunged a finger inside her wet pussy as he lowered his mouth to her clit. She screamed and convulsed, climaxing for him.

Max lifted his head and watched as Cassie gasped for breath.

He removed his fingers and slowly rose back over her. She blinked at him, grinning widely. "Wow."

He couldn't have agreed more. He kissed her once again, wrapping his arms around her and holding her tightly.

They came down from their sexual high while embracing each another. Max found that he could have stayed just like that forever. He rotated their positions, lying back with Cassie draped over his chest. He buried his hand in her short hair as she petted his chest.

"I'm glad you came in here," he said quietly.

She laughed. "I was going to wait until tomorrow, but then I heard you, and I had to make sure you were okay."

He nodded. "It was a bad one."

"Can you...? Do you want to talk about it?"

He wasn't sure. He'd shared stories about his team with her, leaving out the last day. He still felt unable to tell anyone about that day.

"You don't have to," she said softly. "I don't mind listening if you need to talk, though."

He took a deep breath. "On my last mission, Evan was killed."

She didn't show any surprise, just patted his chest.

"We'd gotten the hostages away and were almost to the rendezvous location when we ran into another group. We managed to hold them off long enough to hide in an old abandoned house. The bullets just kept coming through. I didn't know Evan had been hit until later."

He shuddered and choked on the words.

"It's okay," she soothed.

"I remember dropping to my knee to reload and looking around the room. My team had spread out to cover all the entrances and Evan was beside me with his body in front of the people we'd saved." He sniffed. "I was so proud that even injured he'd put his life before the lives of others. I thought he would be okay. He told me he would be. Sanchez was trying to reach someone on the radio and everyone else was just attempting to cover our asses. I went back to my window to hold off the incoming enemies as best as I could."

Tears filled his eyes. He ignored them, wanting to finish. "It was an RPG, rocket-propelled grenade, right through the wall. Evan and I used our bodies to shield them."

"Oh, honey." Cassie kissed his neck.

"He lived for another two hours, in pain and still trying to do his job." It had been awful. The worst thing Max had ever been through. He hadn't been able to help Evan. He'd held his best friend's hand until Evan took his last breath. "I lost it. Just completely went crazy. If I hadn't had the shifter's quick healing, I don't know that I would have survived the gunshot wounds. I just stood next to my team, firing until there was no one else left."

Cassie crawled over him before she gripped his chin, making his gaze meet hers. "I'm glad. Do you hear me? I'm so glad you survived and are here now."

He nodded. "Me too. For the first time since that night, I feel like I'm finally healing."

She kissed him thoroughly until his cock perked up again. He ran his hands down her body, but she pulled away. "I'd like to show you something."

"Oh, yeah?" he murmured, teasing his fingers lightly down her spine.

She laughed. "Not that. Okay, not just that."

Cassie surprised him by rolling away and landing beside the bed. She held out her hand. Confused, he took it. She pulled him up and he went willingly, wondering what she was up to.

He did enjoy the view of her naked body.

She glanced over her shoulder and winked at him. "Save that thought for later."

Gladly, he thought. One taste of her was not enough. He wasn't sure why she'd insisted they leave the bed, but he was game to find out. He wasn't surprised when she pushed open the studio door. She did spend most of her time in there.

"Listening to your stories, I felt like I knew your team," she started to explain. "But I always picture someone, whether they are a shifter or not, I picture their animal. I hope this is okay."

Max allowed her to grip his hand and pull him toward the canvas on the easel. His breath caught as he looked at the powerful panther. "Evan."

"Yes, this is how I saw him."

It was the most amazing sight he'd ever seen. It was like Cassie had read his mind and pulled out Max's own impression of his best friend. "Cassie, this is... I..." He turned to her and urged her forward. "Thank you!"

She beamed at him. "I have more."

Max didn't want to step away from the painting Cassie had done of Evan, but he was curious to see what else she'd been working on. He followed her to where more canvases leaned, covered, against the wall and watched as she removed the cloths.

"Oh, shit!" he said, astonished. His entire team came alive in front of him. He had no problem identifying each member of his unit. The talent she had to bring the subject out in her art staggered him. "Oh, baby."

Cassie held the covers while watching him. "So you like them, right?"

"I love them," he confirmed quietly. He stepped forward and ran his finger over the snow-white wolf that somehow he knew was Matt Wallace. "I can't believe you did this."

"For you," she told him. "After the show, I want to give them all to you."

He faced her and saw the emotion shining from her eyes. Deeply touched, he moved forward and embraced her. "Thank you." The words didn't feel like enough to express his amazement, but he would make sure she understood. Every day of their lives, if he was able.

Cassie lifted her face and their lips brushed. Max needed more, so he pressed her tighter and nibbled on her bottom lip until she opened for him. He plunged his tongue inside her mouth, his blood pumping and his heart racing as she moaned and gripped him harder.

Inside, his wolf was frantic to mate with the woman that both man and beast recognized as their own.

He ripped his mouth away. "I want you."

"Yes," she hissed while he ran his fingers down her back.

They were already naked with his erection brushing against her stomach. It would be so easy to drag her down to the floor and lose himself inside her, but he knew Cassie deserved to be worshiped and for him to take his time.

"Come on." He tried to lead her back to his bedroom.

She tugged on his hand. "Here, now."

He was helpless to resist. He didn't want to. His wolf clawed at him to make sure Cassie knew she belonged to them. Until now, he'd never felt this intense need to claim anyone.

Max brushed his thumbs over her nipples, smiling at her sharp intake of breath. He cupped her firm breasts, loving the fact that they fit perfectly in his hands. "On the floor," he commanded.

She dropped gracefully, kneeling in front of him. She rubbed his palms down his stomach while bending forward to lick the bead of pre-cum from his cock.

He gasped and bucked but didn't take advantage of her mouth like she obviously expected. Instead, he joined her on the floor and pushed her to lie back.

Starting at her neck, he ran his tongue down her body, stopping to pay close attention to every spot that made her whimper. He wanted to learn each and every place that he could use to drive her crazy. By the time he reached her glistening pussy, Cassie was begging him to fill her.

He tormented her by playing lightly with her clit and softly rubbing his fingers over her moist folds.

"Please!"

He took in her flush body and the heavy need in her features. "Turn over."

She quickly moved to obey and get to her hands and knees.

"I'm going to take you," he told her. "Claim you so you know who you belong to."

"Yes, yes!"

He grasped his cock and slid up against her. He massaged her opening with the head of his cock.

"Don't tease," she begged. "I need you."

Max thrust deeply, causing her to cry out in ecstasy. Her inner muscles clamped down around his cock and he moaned.

Cassie pushed back against him and Max felt the last strand of control snap. He pulled out slowly before driving back inside.

It was fast and furious and so fucking good that he couldn't think straight. All he knew was it felt so right being buried inside Cassie.

He snapped his hips over and over as he drove himself closer to completion. Cassie threw her head back and screamed just as she climaxed. Max plunged inside, his body tightening, and he joined her, crashing over the edge.

Sweat dripped down his forehead to land on the back of her neck. She sighed deeply, the sound full of contentment and pleasure.

Max rolled them to the side and cuddled her close. "Damn."

Giggling, Cassie nodded. "We need to do that again."

He couldn't have agreed more. "Yeah, but now I don't think I can walk."

He pulled out and pushed on her shoulder so she would turn onto her back. He poised over her. Cassie made a sight with her pink-tinged cheeks and hair tangled. "You are so beautiful."

She snorted. "I'm sure I look it right now."

"Always," he told her, cupping her face.

She lifted her head to kiss him softly. "Come on, shower then bed."

Bed. That sounded good to him. He rose, helping her along the way. He couldn't stop running his hands over her shoulders as they left the studio. He wasn't near finished with Cassie for the night.

Chapter Ten

Cassie wrapped the canvases up one more time so they could be taken to the gallery. The acrylic paint was already dry and ready to be picked up. She'd called James, asking him to come by this morning to set up a delivery time. He would be there any minute and she was hoping that he would be gone by the time Max returned.

Just thinking about Max brought a smile to her face.

After the night before, or early morning would be more accurate, she found herself longing to just see him. They'd spent most of the morning in bed and it wasn't until Alex had phoned asking Max to meet him at the stables that the two had managed to actually get up.

Max was a passionate lover and she could honestly say that she'd never been with anyone who was so intent on ravishing her. She was pleasantly sore as she moved around the studio.

Now that she was finished with the last of her series, she could enjoy a few days just to explore what was happening between her and Max. They planned to ride the horses into the canyon in the late afternoon so Cassie could share some of her favorite spots with him.

Since several of those places were very secluded, she looked forward to getting Max horny and naked.

Laughing at that thought, she squealed when someone touched her arm. She whirled around, heart beating frantically. "Shit!"

"Sorry!" James held up his hands. "You were lost in your own world."

She blushed. Wasn't that the truth? "It's okay, I was just thinking."

"Good thoughts, apparently, since you're blushing."

She nodded.

James grinned. "I can't believe you got so much done in just a few days." He took in the covered pieces around the room. "I figured it would take a month or longer for five new paintings."

"I did too," she confessed. "I wasn't even sure I was going to add any more to the show. I'd only lost two pieces and we have enough to go forward, but I just...got inspired."

James sighed. "It's unbelievable what you can do."

"Hey." She didn't like the sadness she heard in his tone. "You are just as talented. This is going to be a great first show for you."

"No, it's not."

Cassie frowned, walking toward him. "James?"

"Don't," he snapped and held up a hand to stop her. "You know, I thought this was going to be so easy."

Unease tingled down her spine. James was acting so out of character. "What?"

"All I was supposed to do was find out as much as I could about you and your family. I couldn't believe it when you saw my work and thought it was good.

And then Alex! He offered to show some of my pieces!"

"Of course," she replied cautiously. "Because you *are* talented. He wanted to give you a chance."

James shook his head as he reached behind his back. Cassie gasped, catching sight of the black gun.

"Wha… What are you doing?"

"I didn't actually think you'd do it. I'd like to see your paintings before we leave, but we just don't have time. I didn't come inside until your bodyguard left."

"James, you don't have to do this!"

"But I do. You see, the show is never going to take place. Right now a couple of my cousins are at the gallery, and in just a little while, there will be nothing left of the building. The fire should burn pretty damn hot with all the supplies we keep in the storage room."

Cassie started shaking. Everyone had been right about James. How could she have misjudged him?

"The fire here shouldn't be as bad. Maybe there will be something that can be saved. I don't figure your brother or bodyguard will be far."

He waved the gun toward the doors. "But we won't be here to find out."

"Where are we going?"

"There are some people who want to talk to you. They know you are familiar with some shifters. Hell, they even tried to convince me that you were one. I told them that was crazy, but I can't deny that there is something about your art that draws the monsters to you. I have cataloged where all of your paintings have been shipped. Several pieces have gone to known shifters."

Of course they had. Cassie knew where each and every piece had ended up. The fact that James did too was unsettling. "You're working with the Church for Humanity?"

James snorted. "I've been a member all my life. My uncle leads the division in Texas. Since Bruce Carter and the California chapter have been arrested, it is up to us to stop the madness of people actually accepting the shifters. I mean, can you even imagine someone being able to turn into a wolf or some other kind of animal?" He visibly shuddered. "Horrible."

Cassie was shocked that James felt that way. On one hand, it was probably in her best interest that he didn't believe she was a shifter, but she wanted to set him straight that they were not monsters.

"Anyway, we'll stop the show. There were going to be several shifters who have already RSVP'd and we don't want their kind in town. After you talk to my uncle and tell him what he needs to know, he'll let you come back as long as you promise to stop supporting the shifters. They shouldn't be able to buy your work. They're…they're just animals really. Your art is too good to be wasted on the shifters!"

Cassie knew damn well that if the church got a hold of her, she would not be coming back home.

"And you're going to burn my house and gallery down?"

James nodded. "It's the only way we can insure Alex doesn't go on with the show. I don't know how long you'll be gone." He shrugged. "But I'll make sure they know you're okay.

"Now, we really do have to go. My friends should be here anytime to set the fire, and we don't want to be anywhere near here when it goes up."

"You're talking about burning my house down!"

"Shh!" James stomped toward her. "I know and I'm sorry, but it's the only way! Now hurry up, we have to leave." He grabbed her shoulder and shoved her forward. "I wasn't kidding when I said it was time to go."

Cassie shuffled her feet as she was propelled toward the balcony door. She knew she had to figure out a way to get Alex or Max's attention, but her mind raced and she couldn't think straight.

James pressed the muzzle of the gun against her arm and she considered turning and trying to grab the weapon. Even if the gun went off, there was a good chance it wouldn't kill her. Plus if Max or Alex heard the shot they would come for her.

"Don't try anything," James whispered. "My brother is over at your nephews' house and we really don't want to hurt the kids."

Oh, God! Cassie didn't want to believe him, but what if they were prepared to get a hold of the boys? She nodded and unlatched the double doors.

"Head straight for my car."

Once she'd pushed open the doors, she saw that James had parked close by. There was not a lot of room to form a plan before she would be inside his vehicle.

She felt James nudge her with the gun again. "Walk."

Her bare feet didn't make a sound when she crossed over the small deck and down the couple of steps. She looked around hoping someone, anyone, would be close by. Instead, all she could see was the empty yard.

"James, this isn't going to work. Let me get Alex and we can talk this through."

"Talk?" James stated. "So you or your brother can try to sway me to the side of the shifters? I don't think so. After you talk to my uncle and hear what he has to say about them, you'll understand. I told him you didn't know any better. He'll help you."

She didn't know what James' uncle thought he knew, but it was obvious that James believed the man's preaching.

The grass was cool and moist under her feet. She stopped and turned to James. "He's wrong. Shifters are not monsters. They are not evil."

"I know you believe that."

"Listen to me!" she said desperately. "The church—"

"Stop!" James snapped. "Just get to the car."

Cassie dropped her hands and turned back around. She almost wept in relief as she saw Alex step into view.

"Shit," James muttered. "Just act natural. I'll take him with us if I have to, but my uncle will not be pleased."

The gun was jammed harder into her and she hissed.

"Hey, sis. Hey, James," Alex called out.

Cassie figured her brother couldn't see the weapon as he walked toward them. She knew as soon as he was close enough, he would pick up on her fear.

"Hey, Alex!" James waved with his free hand. "We're just going to run into town real quick."

Come closer, Cassie mentally begged her brother.

"Cool!" Alex hollered back. "Can you stop at the gallery and pick up a box I need?"

"Uh, sure," James replied.

"Good." Alex started to jog over.

She felt James stiffen.

Cassie braced herself for whatever would happen next. Alex wasn't giving any kind of message that he knew something was wrong. But he had to know. There was no way that her leaving with James, barefoot and in pants and a tank top, would be normal.

"Drop the gun."

Both Cassie and James jumped when Max's deep voice sounded behind them. Cassie whirled and saw Max had clamped his hand around James's wrist. She backed up from the two men and almost squealed when she ran into another solid form.

"It's okay." Alex wrapped his arm around her shoulders.

"Oh, God!" She whimpered and relaxed into his hold.

"I won't repeat myself again. Drop the gun."

James yelled and released his hold on the weapon, causing it to fall to the ground.

"You okay?" Max asked, his gaze raking her up and down.

She nodded.

"Now..." Max gave his attention back to James. "You and I are going to have a little talk."

"Let me go! I wasn't doing anything!"

Max gripped James' shoulder with his free hand. "We have your buddies from the gallery."

James paled, but Cassie didn't have any sympathy for him. There was no telling what would have happened to her if James had delivered her to the church. James might not believe she was a shifter, but if anyone else had suspected, she could have been in real trouble.

"I just wanted to help her. To help all of you! You don't know what kind of monsters you're dealing with!"

"Monsters?" Max growled.

"James thinks that the reason my art is so popular is because shifters keep buying my work. That is why the church wanted to stop the show. They don't want shifters in town," Cassie told him. She prayed that Max understood the unspoken part of that sentence. If James didn't think her family were shifters then hopefully they could get by without having to reveal themselves.

"I see," Max said. "I think holding an innocent woman at gun point makes someone a monster. Not if someone has the gift to turn into an animal."

"You're wrong! Let me take you to my uncle. He'll show you how evil they are."

"I would love to meet this uncle," Alex spoke up.

Cassie would be happy to stay away from the man. She was relieved to hear that the men from the Church who were at the gallery had been caught, but what exactly where they going to do with them?

"Damn!" she yelled. "There are more men coming! They were going to burn my house down."

"We've got them, plus the ones watching Jacob's place."

Cassie spun and saw Jacob, Chase and Shawn joining them with three other men. She placed her palm over her racing heart. "Please, no more surprises. I can't handle anything more."

Max frowned and motioned his brother closer. After he pushed James toward Chase, he marched up to her side. "Are you sure you're all right?"

She moved from Alex, and her brother stepped away to join the other men. "I'm okay. I just don't want anyone else sneaking up on me."

"Well, we have the two Council representatives bringing the men from the gallery over. We should probably go meet them at the main house so they don't have to look for us."

She bobbed her head in agreement. "Alcohol. There will be alcohol in the main house."

Max intertwined his fingers through hers and lifted her hand. He kissed her knuckles, smiling. "I'll get you whatever you want."

"Okay," she agreed. She sure could get behind that idea. "I can't believe I was wrong about James."

"I understand. And I really do think he believes he is helping you."

"He was going to burn down my place!"

Max stopped them and waved for the others to continue on. Once the group was far enough away to not overhear, Cassie found herself held tightly as Max dropped his mouth to hers.

She opened to him and grasped at the back of his T-shirt to keep him close. The scent and flavor of him calmed her wolf and even managed to make her forget about everything for a few minutes. He pulled away and she was surprised by the stress lines on his forehead.

"I was so scared. Kurt and Clint called and said that they'd caught a couple of guys trying to break into the gallery and knew for sure James was involved, I just about lost it. Thank God for your brother. He managed to calm me down enough so I didn't barge into the studio and wait until the two of you came out."

Cassie cupped his face. "I was trying to figure out what to do."

"I know. And I knew that you'd be upset that James had turned on you."

"I am," she admitted. "But I also know that he doesn't understand. He's been surrounded by hatred. I wish he could see how much being a shifter is a gift."

"Maybe someday he will. Let's head up to the house. Kurt and Clint will help clean up this mess. They'll deal with the church so we can go on remaining hidden."

"I'm glad we weren't exposed. But I have to wonder how long it will last."

Max sighed. "Me too. But we'll figure it out. Shawn won't let anything bad happen to the Pack. I bet he is already working on whatever needs to be done."

"I know Shawn will do what he can. What if it's not enough, though?" She didn't say anything about her talk with their Alpha. She believed that Max was going to make a great Alpha one day. If Shawn did get his way and Max accepted the role of next Alpha in line, he would have to deal with more instances like this. She honestly believed that Max would thrive as an Alpha. He was both smart and kind. Hopefully Max would take Shawn up on his offer once the Alpha spoke to Max about training him. "And I'm glad this is over."

Max hugged her. "Yeah."

They walked quietly to the main house, entering though the back door. The low sound of voices reached her as they strolled closer to the den. Cassie paused in the doorway and watched as Alpha Shawn spoke with James and several other men. The two strangers that she suspected were from the Council stood glaring at the other group. Apparently not everything was going well.

Alex spotted them and tilted his head forward. Max pulled her out of sight until Alex joined them in the hall.

"James and a couple of the others want us to talk to his uncle. They seem determined to make us see the light about accepting the shifters. The other group won't say a word. Kurt has a call in to the Council to see what exactly they want them to do next. Clint thinks they should go to the church."

"But they can't!" Cassie exclaimed.

Alex shook his head. "We're pretty sure that someone from the church would recognize them, so I agree. But they're right too. We need to know more about this chapter. From what James is saying, his uncle is good friends with the senator who is trying to pass a law to make all shifters register."

"I still don't get that," Max said from beside her. "How would that help?"

"I don't know, but I don't like it. No one actually thinks it'll pass. We worked with the government when all the shifters announced their presence, so we already have their support. Human and shifter leaders both agreed long ago that all shifters would be treated just like humans. I know the Shifter Coalition is involved in speaking with our government officials to make sure that nothing has changed, though."

Cassie groaned. "I wish they would all just leave us alone."

Alex patted her shoulder. "I don't think that will happen. There will always be someone who fears us because we're different."

"You're right. I'm just tired."

"Why don't you and Max head back to your place? I'm sure it will take a while to get things settled here."

Cassie glanced at Max. "If you don't mind I'd really like that."

Max massaged her shoulder. "No problem. I know how to relax you."

Cassie flushed since they were in front of her brother and Alex laughed. "I don't need to know."

She smacked Max's chest when he chuckled.

"What? I was talking about a massage," he protested.

Glaring, she turned on her heel. "Right."

He caught up with her and threw his arm around her shoulder. "I didn't mention what part of you I was going to rub down."

She almost stumbled as arousal spread all over her. "Hurry," she whispered.

They jogged down the steps and back to the yard. Max grabbed her around the waist, lifting her up and over a shoulder.

"Hey!"

A sharp painful slap to her ass surprised her. "Hush, you know you like it."

Well, that didn't mean she had to make it easy on him. "All the blood is rushing to my head."

He smacked her ass again. "Good, I don't want you thinking about anything other than me."

Like that was even possible with his ass flexing so nicely right in front of her face. "Hmm."

She received another smack.

"I'll show you hmm."

That was what she was hoping for.

Chapter Eleven

Max was still reeling after his conversation with Alpha Shawn. He couldn't believe that his Alpha wanted to start training him to lead the Pack. He'd never even considered the possibility of becoming Alpha since he was a non-shifter.

But Shawn was adamant that he wanted to pass the job on to Max when he retired or in the case of his death.

Max hadn't given him an answer, but he was seriously considering it. Just in the week since he'd confronted James and the other members of the Church for Humanity, Max knew that he was not going to let anything else hurt his Pack. He wasn't going to quit and would see to the safety of everyone he loved. He was a new man. His relationship with Cassie seemed to help, plus he had to admit that talking with Alex and Chase and sharing what he had been through had taken him a step forward.

He now felt needed and useful so Max was truly happy. He hadn't moved back in with Chase, either. He'd brought up the possibility to Cassie, but she had distracted him from the conversation and they'd spent the afternoon in bed. The second and third time it had happened, he'd finally got that Cassie did not want him to leave and that was her way of letting him know it.

She seemed to be dealing well with everything that had happened. They made sure to keep the house and studio locked up and the alarm set just in case there were further issues. Kurt and Clint from the wolf Council were still in town. They were now being helped out by the wolf division of the Shifter Coalition. So far the Pack had been kept away from what was happening. Shawn made sure they were kept in the loop.

One of Max's first jobs would be to work with the Council and Coalition to insure the safety of the Pack.

First he had a date to get to.

Cassie had texted him coordinates in the canyon for him to meet her at. He drove his Harley, taking in the beautiful surroundings. It was the first time he'd been to the deepest part of the canyon but could see himself going there more often.

He knew Cassie loved shifting and running in the area, so he was trying to keep an eye out for her. However, he kept getting distracted by the amazing sights.

The bike rumbled under him as he followed the trail that would lead him to where Cassie had instructed. It was only about half an hour or so until sunset, and excitement filled him just imagining what Cassie had planned. He slowed and made the final turn taking him farther from the more popular trails.

Another ten minutes of riding brought him to his destination.

He knew he was at the right place when he saw the plaid blanket and picnic basket. He turned off his Harley and let the bike still under him. He brushed the hair from his forehead and glanced around him. He didn't see Cassie anywhere.

After throwing his leg over the side of his bike and stretching, he whistled sharply. If Cassie was in her wolf form, she should be able to hear him.

He strolled over to the blanket and stood with his hands on his hips. He drew a deep breath and brought in the wild scents in the area. He could smell where Cassie had been and figured it was about an hour since she'd left. There were also other animal scents. Small critters and even a coyote.

The air was fresh, and with the slight breeze, it was a perfect spot.

Movement ahead of him drew his attention and he watched as a small tawny wolf slowly approached. He hadn't seen Cassie in her wolf form. She was breathtaking. Pride and satisfaction flooded him as he thought about the fact that she was all his.

Both the woman and the powerful creature were his to claim and protect.

She paused on the ledge right above him then lowered to the ground. Max closed the distance before dropping to his knees beside her. He buried his hands in her soft fur and tugged lightly.

Cassie rolled, exposing her belly to him and he got the hint to give her a rub down. It was amazing to be able to share this with his lover. He'd stayed away from the Pack for so long that he had forgotten that even if he couldn't transform like everyone else, he enjoyed being around them in their shifter form.

Cassie was sharing her wolf with him and he fell just a little more in love with her. His feelings were new and growing, but he had no doubt they'd be able to make things work between the two of them.

Cassie licked at his hand before turning back onto her stomach and getting to her paws. She shook her body and he backed up, laughing.

As she started her shift, Max made sure to keep his senses open to insure her safety. Once she completed her transformation, he grinned at her. "Nice run?"

"Yes," she answered. "I'm glad you got here before the sunset, though. I wanted to show you the view."

Max ran his gaze over her naked body. He could stare at her all day. Slight and compact, she was a little firecracker.

"Not me!" She smacked his chest.

"Sorry, but when you don't have any clothes on, I don't see anything else."

Her brown eyes sparkled in delight and she rewarded him with a kiss. "Well, I packed a picnic for us. And it includes a bottle of champagne. After the sun goes down, you can make love to me right here."

He caught her hand and pulled her closer. "What if I don't want to wait?"

She didn't get a chance to respond as he lowered his mouth and kissed her deeply. Her arms went around his neck and he lifted her off her feet.

"O-okay" she panted when their lips parted.

Max carried her to the blanket. "We'll stick to your plan for now."

Disappointment flashed in her eyes, but Max just grinned. "Now where is the champagne? Are we celebrating something?"

She flopped down then dug into the wicker basket. "Us. I know you asked if I wanted you to go back to Chase's, but I really don't. Although it happened fast, I like having you around. I want you to stay."

He joined her, wrapping his arms around her waist and pulling her into his lap. "I'm not going anywhere, baby. My place is next to you."

"Good, so see, we're celebrating us!"

"I'll drink to that."

Max filled the two glasses with the bubbly liquid and turned just as the bottom of the sun passed behind the canyon.

Colors exploded in the sky and it was so stunning that it actually took his breath away.

"It's amazing, isn't it?" Cassie whispered.

Max nodded. He didn't have the words to describe what he was seeing. He tightened his hold on her as they silently watched the sun lower. Drinking their champagne, Max was awed by the perfect moment. Once the sunset, he turned his face to hers. She was watching him intently.

"My fingers ache to paint the look on your face."

He set his glass down before taking hers and placing it next to his. "Later, first I want to show you how much I want you. Always need you. It doesn't matter if I haven't seen you for five minutes or five hours. I can't stop thinking about you."

"I feel the same way," she responded softly.

"You'll be mine forever, right? You and me, we're a team." He laid her back gently, nibbling her neck.

"Yes, Max. I'm yours. Show me."

"I'm yours too," he vowed.

Since she was already bare for him, he took his time kissing down her body. The air around them had started to cool, but he wasn't worried. He would keep her warm.

The taste and feel of her was already so familiar. He'd been telling her the truth when he'd said he always wanted her. Every part of his mind, body and soul belonged to Cassie. He needed the same from her. He would have the same as he showed her his love under the darkening night sky.

He skimmed his lips over her soft skin and Cassie shuddered in need.

"Max," she gasped his name as he slipped a finger through her wet folds then inside her. He added a second finger, opening her to prepare himself to bury deep in her body.

"It's just you and me out here. I'm going to claim you again, make you mine."

Cassie lifted her hips and rolled into each thrust of his fingers. "Yes!"

Max leaned back over her and lowered his mouth to hers. She gripped his shoulder tightly. Her pants and murmurs grew in volume. Before she flashed over the edge, he removed his fingers.

"In me, please, Max!"

Covering her body with his, he positioned his hard cock at her entrance. "Open your eyes and let me see you as I take what's mine."

Her soft brown eyes met his and he slowly pushed inside. He groaned as her inner muscles clamped down on him. On his knees, he lifted her hips and held her firmly. He withdrew gradually then snapped his body, slamming back into her.

Cassie cried out in pleasure.

He pumped deeply, connecting the two of them in the most intimate of ways. There was nothing like the power of the strong woman he was making love to calling out his name and giving in to the pleasure he gave her, the pleasure they gave each other.

The tingle at the base of his spine signaled his coming completion. He sped up his movements even more.

He lowered his head and took her mouth once again, climaxing together. They kissed through the powerful release until she had to pull away to catch her breath.

Cassie was absolutely breathtaking, looking thoroughly sated.

"Mine," he whispered against her mouth. "Mine."

PACK BETA

Dedication

A big thank you to my Facebook Fan Page members.
Your encouragement has helped make each Were
Chronicles book possible.

Chapter One

Kayla Webb raced past another alleyway without slowing down. She could hear her best friend Randy at her heels breathing heavily and fighting to stay with her.

She wasn't sure how they'd ended up running for their lives through the deserted streets of Lubbock, Texas. All she was certain of was that they had to get away.

Ahead she saw what she was looking for. Slowing only slightly, she motioned Randy to the right. Together they made the turn, bringing them to the opening of an old, abandoned building. Kayla slipped through the small gap first before reaching out to grab Randy's hand.

Her friend clutched her as they collapsed on the cold, dirty concrete floor.

"Do you think we lost them?" Randy managed, panting.

Kayla held up her right hand to have Randy quieten down as she strained to pick up any sound of their pursuers. Taking a chance, she peeked around the opening to look out into the night. "I think so," she whispered.

Wiping the sweat from her face as she leaned her head back, Kayla tried to calm her breathing. She wouldn't have thought she was so out of shape but a chase for over a dozen blocks had her feeling sick. Plus she wasn't sure she could stand if need be. Her legs shook and her muscles cramped.

"What the hell was that all about?" Randy asked as he twisted to try to look out into the alley.

"I don't know, but they sure know who we are," she said. "That wasn't a random mugging. Did you see how they immediately zeroed in on the two of us? How they expected us to run?"

Leaving a restaurant together, Kayla and Randy had been headed to her truck when three men had stepped out of the shadows and advanced on them.

Her wolf had sensed the threat, making it difficult to stop from shifting. She'd managed to hold her wolf back and grabbed Randy's arm, pulling him to a stop. They had been too far from her vehicle. She would have chanced a sprint across the parking lot until she had spotted movement in that direction too.

Three more men had blocked her and Randy from their escape. They'd had no choice but to run—and run fast.

There was no way that anyone, even six large men, should have been able to keep up with two shifters. It should have been an easy escape. Instead, Kayla had barely been able to lead Randy to safety.

If she could call an old building that was about to collapse safe. She'd attended a party—an illegal party—there almost ten years ago. The structure hadn't been stable then. It was in even worse shape now.

"We can't stay here long," she said.

"We can't go back to the restaurant."

Randy had a point.

"I have a friend who lives a couple blocks from here."

"We're in the middle of an industrial zone," Randy argued.

"He's a metal artist," she explained. "He converted one of these old warehouses into a studio with a loft. If we can get to him, we can at least think about our next move."

"Okay, let's do it."

Standing, she reached down to help Randy to his feet. "Is your leg okay?"

He shrugged. Damn, she hoped he could make it as far as Justin's place. She would carry him if she had to, but that would slow them way down.

"I'll make it," he said.

She wanted to hug him, promising that everything was going to be all right, but she couldn't. Also, just because Randy had an old injury and limped a little didn't mean he would put up with her coddling him.

"Stay close," Kayla warned.

Stepping through the opening, she paused long enough to insure no one was around. She picked up on the scents of trash, rotted food and vomit. Those were the only smells, though. No humans around.

As quietly as possible, she crept away from the building. Keeping to the shadows instead of using speed, she hoped their stealth would prevent them from being discovered.

Randy's presence at her back provided a solid reassurance as they carefully maneuvered in the dark. Justin's building was part of an area that the city had once tried to bring back to life. The plan had never really gotten off the ground but Justin had told her he was happy about it.

He enjoyed the privacy of the area. If he was up all night working with a welding machine or other tools, he had no neighbors to worry about disturbing. She didn't get it herself but she had no reason to judge him.

As the structures in the area started to become familiar, she found herself calming. If they could just get off the streets, she knew they could regroup as they tried to figure out what was going on.

Coming up on the backside of Justin's building, Kayla could have wept with relief. She pressed herself up against the wall, drawing in long, deep breaths. She motioned to Randy to do the same. While Justin didn't normally like surprise visits, she hoped he would make an exception this one time.

"Um, my friend can be a little weird sometimes," she told Randy.

He snorted. "Well, he *is* a friend of yours, so that's to be expected, right?"

It seemed so strange to smile at a time like this but she found herself grinning over at Randy anyway. "I guess so. I mean, I am friends with *you*," she teased.

"Exactly."

Shaking her head, she patted his arm. "We'll have to make a run for it, just in case the pursuers remained close by. The stairs lead up to the front but it's three flights. They're all outside and the door is sturdy metal, solid, so we can't break in to his place. Keep an eye out."

"You got it."

Breathing deeply, Kayla mentally counted to three then took off at a full run. She leaped over several steps and rushed up the staircase. Pounding on the door, she prayed that Justin was inside.

It was early enough that if he was in town, he should still be home.

Repeatedly beating on the door, she finally sagged in relief when she heard Justin's cursing coming from the inside.

He swung the door open, frowning. "What?"

Instead of answering, she pushed him back into the interior, allowing Randy to slip past her. She slammed the door closed, quickly turning both deadbolts.

"Kayla? What the fuck is going on?"

Leaning against the door, she took in Justin's appearance. He hadn't shaved, which gave his looks a dangerous edge. His mussed black hair fell around his face, framing the deep frown lines on his forehead. Dressed in only a pair of thin sweats, he looked irritated and suspicious.

"Hi." *Fuck. That was stupid thing to say.* Now that she stood in front of Justin, she was at a loss for words. After all, it wasn't everyday she raced away from attackers.

Amusement flittered briefly in his eyes as he pressed his lips together. When he crossed his arms, she sighed.

"I can explain."

"Come on in, then," Justin said as he turned on his heel.

Kayla followed, but only after she glanced over her shoulder at Randy, who still stood off to the side. Randy looked at Justin with a mixed expression of awe and a little bit of fear.

Well, Justin could be intimating but Randy wasn't normally frightened either.

The narrow hall led to a large, open kitchen. Kayla had been there enough times to be comfortable in Justin's home. The third floor consisted of the kitchen, bedroom, office and bathroom. Below, Justin used the other two levels for his art. Kayla had never been to those areas, even though she'd tried numerous times to talk Justin into giving her a peek.

Standing at the counter, Justin had his back to them as they reached the granite island. Kayla pulled out a bar stool and sat, nodding for Randy to do the same.

"Coffee?" Justin asked.

"Sure," she replied.

Justin played his long fingers along the pot as he prepped the machine. The strong muscles in his back rippled when he reached for mugs above the sink.

They'd first become friends when she'd moved into town. Justin had been taking a business course located right next to her math class.

Something about him had called to her, resulting in a quick friendship with the reserved man. Although, at the time, Kayla had been hoping for more.

After a few dates, they both realized that the chemistry between them just wasn't there. They'd known the relationship would never progress, so they'd remained good friends.

Once he'd got the coffee brewing, Justin turned to face them. "Who're you?" he asked, looking at Randy.

Shit, he must be in one of his moods. The hostile edge to his tone was not what they needed after running for their lives. Justin could get rude and defensive when anything unexpected happened but he usually showed more patience than jumping his guests like this.

Randy started to laugh, cutting off her response. "Randy O'Hare," he answered still grinning. "I'm a friend of Kayla's."

"The musician? Huh."

Glancing between the two men, Kayla tried to gauge how the meeting was going but she wasn't sure. Justin appeared just as grumpy as he normally was. However, Randy's amused manner threw her off on what was going on between them.

"Yep, you're the temperamental artist."

She started to stand when Justin shocked her by laughing—a full, loud, belly laugh.

"I like you," Justin said, as he pointed at Randy.

"My heart is all aflutter," Randy replied but he winked at Kayla.

Relaxing back onto the stool, she knew everything would be okay. Randy and Justin were two of her best friends. They were bound to meet eventually anyway.

As he turned back to the coffee pot, Justin lowered his voice as he grew serious. "So you want to tell me what you two were running from?"

"I guess we'd better," Kayla told Justin. While she spoke, she could see Justin listening carefully by the way his features changed, tightened with worry then relaxed with relief. It was a short story, although by the time she was done, her stomach had soured.

She sat blowing on her coffee as she waited for Justin to say something, anything.

"You both are all right?" he finally asked.

"Yeah, sure," she said, exchanging glances with Randy.

"Did you hear them say anything?" Justin inquired.

"No, they just went after us," she replied.

"Uh, I did." Randy waved his hand.

"When?" Kayla asked.

"What?" Justin looked at him intently.

Running his gaze from her to Justin, he sighed heavily. "Just as we exited the restaurant, I heard a voice say 'get the wolves'. I didn't see who said it, though. I didn't have time to really think about it."

"The only thing you heard them say was to get the wolves?" Justin pressed.

"Yes."

Kayla tried to go back in her mind but she couldn't recall hearing the men speak. But if Randy said he did, she believed him.

"Stay here. I have to make a phone call."

Stunned silence filled the kitchen as she watched Justin flee.

"He's kind of…"

"Intense?" she offered.

"Yeah."

Nodding she placed her hand over his on the counter. "I don't trust anyone for something like this other than you and Justin."

"I can't scent him."

In the time she'd known Justin, she had never been able to get a trace off him either. Normally when she was around a shifter, their unique fragrance was a connection to their animal. Humans tended to have a more chemical or fabricated odor. Justin had neither. There was no smell whatsoever.

At first it had bothered her but she eventually got used to it. For thousands of years nature had shown that there were always exceptions to the rule. Over time, Kayla had chalked up Justin's unusual non-scent to just being a part of him.

"I know. I never figured that out." She shrugged to show Randy it didn't bother her.

Randy hummed but didn't say anything more on the subject. She suspected he wouldn't let it go, but they had a bigger issue at the moment. Justin's low voice traveled through the building but even with her superior hearing, she couldn't make out the words.

Since she couldn't eavesdrop on his conversation and not wanting to dwell on what happened earlier, she thought about Randy's words. Justin was more than he appeared — she knew that for sure. Justin had known right away that she was a shifter. Kayla hadn't realized that she had given any signs to her true nature but obviously, she had. Justin had asked her before they were ever intimate. The way he'd asked had made it easy for her to be honest.

Luckily, he'd accepted her shifter half.

Justin reentered the kitchen, causing Kayla to snap out of her thoughts.

"I think it would best if both of you stayed here tonight."

"What? Why?" Kayla questioned. Sure, she had come to Justin for help but she hadn't planned to hide.

"There have been rumors for the last few months about a group targeting shifters. I've only heard bits and pieces but from what I've put together, if you're being stalked, there is a real danger."

"That's crazy!" Randy slid off his chair. "How would these guys even know what we are?"

"I don't know," Justin responded. "How *would* they?"

Shaking his head, Randy stood, trembling, revealing his upset. "I've got a family here, a younger brother. I need to go check on them."

"Give me their address. I'll send someone discreetly to watch over them. The first thing we need to do is figure out why you two were chosen."

"Who are you, *really*?" Randy asked, his voice dropping dangerously low.

Kayla stepped in front of Randy. "He's my friend." She waited until Randy met her gaze. Randy's eyes were already glowing, the wolf inside striving for release. "You need to calm down."

"Calm down!" Randy hollered. "Are you fucking kidding me?"

"Hey! I'm only trying to help," Justin interrupted.

"Really?" Randy swept his arm, grabbing a hold of Kayla and yanking her behind him. "I haven't heard anything about this group or other shifters being attacked. How is it you have?"

This was getting out of hand fast. Kayla knew the best course of action was to get both men under control but that require settling them down. "Stop, both of you!" she yelled drawing their attention. "This isn't helping."

"Randy, sit and drink your coffee. Justin, start explaining."

For several tense minutes, the two men stared at each another in challenge. Finally, Randy sighed before placing his hand on her shoulder. "I'll hear him out. But I make no promises."

"Fine," she conceded.

As Randy dropped back onto the bar stool, she faced Justin. "You're not just an artist, are you?"

If she was being honest, she *was* a little hurt. She'd been friends with Justin for over twelve years. The first person she could say she had connected with when she'd first arrived in town. If he was hiding something major from her...she just didn't know if she would ever be able to forgive him.

"Actually, I am."

Randy snorted.

Giving Randy a furious glare, Justin took a step toward him.

Holding up her hand, she caught Justin's attention again. "Don't."

A small growl escaped Justin as he spun around to begin pacing the length of the kitchen. Kayla relaxed her shoulders, rolling them and moving her neck from side to side. They didn't have time for Randy and Justin to keep going alpha on each other.

Kayla sat back down closely watching Justin's measured steps as he paced. Picking up her cooling coffee, she took a sip. The strong bold brew tasted like heaven.

She took a larger drink, enjoying the bitterness. *Damn, that was good.*

"Okay," Justin said, coming up to stop in front of her. He placed his hand on the island. "I'll tell you what I can but this isn't my story to share. There are people...family that could be hurt if any of this information gets out."

"Look man," Randy interrupted. "I'm sorry I lost my cool. It's been a hard night. All I can think about is what if those men had gone after my brother or mom. There is no way they'd be able to escape as we did. But we wouldn't put anyone else at risk. Whatever you tell us stays in this kitchen."

"Thanks. For hundreds of years and long before the shifters came out publicly, there was—and still is—a group that operates behind the scenes. They protect nonhumans. They've always worked in the shadows. Very few people know about them."

"You do," Kayla pointed out.

"There has been a member in my family involved with this organization going back as far as my great-great-great-grandfather."

"What do they do?" Kayla questioned. She really didn't like where this was going."

Justin looked up, steadily meeting her gaze. "Whatever they have to."

Chapter Two

"This latest arrest makes it appear to this reporter, that the Church for Humanity is now finished. With its leaders accused of kidnapping, attempted murder and terroristic threats, the doors have closed on the religious faction."

Grinning, Chase Lawson clicked the television off. The Wolf Council had come through, once again ridding the Packs of the latest danger to them.

He had to give the council credit. It had been a long investigation but finally, after a year, all five divisions of the Church for Humanity were now shut down.

Hearing a shout, he strolled to his office window to look out. Alpha Shawn stood hands on hips as Chase's brother, Max, remained beside him in deep concentration as he stared out over at the property.

Pride washed over Chase as he watched the scene play out in front of him. Max was in full Alpha training and Shawn was not going easy on him.

Although Max was one of the rare non-shifters, Shawn believed Max would make the best replacement as Alpha, should something happen to the leader.

Chase agreed. In the time that Max had been home, he'd changed. Instead of the lost and angry military man Chase had worried about, Max was open, more confident. A lot of his personal alteration had come from Max's mate, Cassandra Wilson.

He hadn't known when he'd asked Max to watch over her that the two would form such a tight bond.

Chase had always been close with the Wilson family, as Cassie's older brother Alex was Chase's best friend. So when Cassie had been in trouble he, of course, would have done anything in his power to help.

He'd never imagined that Cassie would be the one who would save Max and the rest of his family.

Slowly, they had been losing Max to his demons. It had been all Chase could do to hold on to his brother. Nothing he'd tried had worked to return Max to the man he once was.

The next day, Max met Cassie. Finally, he'd found a reason to let go of his past.

Chase was happy for his brother, although there was a small seed of jealousy inside him as well. Chase was so busy with his restaurant and Pack duties that he'd never regretted not finding a mate—until he saw how happy Max was with Cassie.

Neither held positions with the Pack structure, but both were instrumental in insuring the Pack's happiness and survival. If they could make it work, maybe it was time to concentrate on his own needs.

Then again, with the threats against them, in addition to the newly proposed legislation to require all shifters to register into a database, Chase knew he wouldn't actually change anything any time soon.

A lot had been changing in the last few months. Even though Chase's Pack wasn't public to the world, they still had had to be careful. Already the Church for Humanity had targeted them. The entire population of Canyon, Texas needed to be ready to defend their homes against any other danger.

Staying hidden hadn't actually worked out as he'd imagined.

When the shifters around the world united, deciding to come out to the public, it was left to every Alpha to decide if they would be open or remain hidden.

Chase's entire Pack still lived in secret.

The past several months had put that secrecy at jeopardy and it was why the representatives from the Wolf Council were in town. Chase's Pack couldn't aid in their endeavor without revealing themselves, so they'd only played a minor role.

Still, Chase was proud of everyone, especially his brother and Cassie. Pushing himself away from the window, Chase sat back at his desk again. He had a little more work to do before he could head to the town diner that he owned.

Luckily, he had a good staff that was covering the place well as he took care of his Pack duties. Sue Ellen had worked for him for years as the head server. He was going to have to reward her for really stepping up.

He'd been considering promoting her to manager and hiring another waitress to take her place. That way, he could insure that as Beta, he was available to the Pack.

As Beta, it was his responsibility to make sure that everything ran smoothly for his Alpha. When someone needed advice or help but the problem didn't actually require the Alpha, Chase was there.

That left Shawn the opportunity to take care of serious matters, as well as spending time with his people.

Unlike a Beta who was also an Enforcer, Chase didn't discipline any members, so he had a good relationship with all of them. Some even came to him for his counsel, not even wanting to see the Alpha.

It made Chase feel good. He enjoyed helping others. Just like at the diner when he fed them. It was part of a circle that he had created — to care about his fellow shifters in every way.

Opening his laptop and powering it up, Chase waited as it loaded. A knock on his office door surprised him. He hadn't heard anyone approaching his office. He stood, making his way to the entrance then pulling open the heavy wood door. Upon seeing the two representatives of the Wolf Council, he grinned.

"Hey guys!" he greeted. "Come on in."

Kurt Moore and Clint Price sauntered into his office. Both men carried themselves with a strong presence that screamed Alpha male. They'd arrived in town to handle the church's threats, working in the shadows the entire time.

The men were so talented at what they did that Chase hadn't even heard from the townsfolk about the strangers. They'd managed to hide their presence while accomplishing what they'd set out to do.

As Beta, Chase had been aware of their mission and had become friendly with them. He'd be sorry to see them leave. "Coffee?"

"Please," Clint nodded, grinning widely.

Kurt snorted. "His mate has turned him into an addict."

Chase had heard all about Clint's mate, Sara Webb, who owned a coffee shop in their small town. "Well I'm sure it's not as good as hers, but I do try."

"Are you kidding me? I love your coffee, man," Clint told him.

After their first meeting, Chase had noticed Clint savoring his brew. Chase had long ago cut back on the amount of caffeine that he consumed each day. So, instead of filling up on tons of coffee, he went for an expensive blend that he could enjoy a few cups of daily.

As he walked to a small cabinet, it saddened him to know his friends would probably be leaving soon. He busied himself making up two mugs instead of thinking of the loss. He remembered how both men took their drinks, so it didn't take long to brew it and serve them.

"Looks like Max is doing well in his training," Kurt said from his position in front of the window where Chase had been watched from earlier.

"Yeah, he's taken to it quickly. He's a born leader," Chase said with pride as he passed Kurt his cup.

"You have a good Pack here," Clint commented, accepting his own mug. "A strong Alpha with a tight inner circle. You're going to need that in the upcoming months."

"So it's not over?" Chase questioned with concern. "I thought with the closing of the Church for Humanity we would be safe. "

"You are," Kurt assured him. "From them, anyway. But there is more going on here than we first thought. There are still unexplained circumstances that have me concerned, starting with the fact that we weren't the ones who brought down the church."

"Wait! What? I thought...the news stated..."

"The Church for Humanity is finished. The arrests will stick. But our team and the officials we were working with weren't responsible. Someone got there before us."

"Who?" Chase questioned, confused. There was no pack in Lubbock where the church had opened. The college town was considered open territory. As the closest shifter collection to the large city, Alpha Shawn had made it his business to insure any shifters in that area had someone looking out for them.

"We don't know. That's what bothers me. We can assume that they are on our side, since they did take down the enemy, but I don't like not knowing what is going on." Clint rose from the couch then started to pace. "I didn't catch another scent anywhere near us. There is no way that someone could get that close and leave no trace of being there."

"So what do we do now?" Chase asked.

"That's why we're here," Kurt informed him. "Your entire Pack needs to keep its eyes open. If you have anyone in Lubbock, that's even better. But we need to talk to your Alpha and Max. We've been called away."

"You're leaving?" Chase jumped to his feet. "Why?"

"The Council is sending us to Missouri, where there have been three disappearances of shifters. We leave today."

Dread trailed up Chase's spine. Not only was there an unknown person or group but they wouldn't even have the Council representatives to turn to.

"Hey," Clint stepped up next to him, gripping his shoulder. "We're still just a phone call away, plus you have resources here as well—one of them being your brother. Max's military record is strong and the man knows how to take care of his family."

"I know." He *did* know that. But that didn't help the fear now gripping him.

"Also, your Alpha has mentioned some of the other Pack members who have settled in the area. Ex-military, government, police — you are a strong group. We wouldn't leave if we didn't think you all would be okay," Kurt added.

"We've always been peaceful here. I'm just worried. You're right about our members but as you said, they *are* retired. They came to us to get away from things like this."

Kurt placed his cup on the side table before he stood. "Unfortunately, I don't think the Packs have that luxury any longer. Whether or not you came out publicly, you're going to have to deal with this."

Chase couldn't respond, as he heard heavy footsteps headed in their direction. A quick sniff informed him that Shawn and Max were almost to his open door.

Nodding, he walked back over to his coffee machine to get each of the new arrivals a cup. They had a lot to talk about ahead of Kurt's and Clint's departure.

* * * *

Marcus Webb's house was located low into the Canyon. It took almost an hour to reach the isolated dwelling. Chase made the trek at least once a week to check on the older man.

Even though he'd dropped by only two days previously, at the encouragement of Alpha Shawn, he was headed to discuss the new information they'd received with Marcus.

It had been fifteen years since the man had moved into the Canyon to join the Pack. He'd brought along his teenage daughter after retiring from some branch of the government. Alpha Shawn might know, but

Chase had never actually been told what Marcus had done prior to coming to town.

His daughter, from what Chase could remember, had been wickedly smart and very pretty. Chase didn't know her well, owing to the Webbs staying to themselves so much. He thought maybe Marcus' daughter had become friends with Cassie but he would have to ask his brother.

Pulling in front of the Webb house, Chase noticed the older man standing on the porch.

He was a picture to see. If Chase didn't know that Marcus liked him, he would be a little nervous. Even though Marcus was in his late fifties, he was still one of the most intimating men Chase had ever seen. He was even bigger than their Alpha.

He always pulled his graying hair back in a long ponytail that trailed down his back. Marcus wore camo pants with a black tank top. His muscles bulged as he stood with his arms crossed and eyes narrowed at Chase.

Smiling, Chase turned off the ignition before pushing open his door. "Hey, Marcus."

The other man nodded, still watching him closely.

Chase slowly strolled around the front of his SUV and up the sidewalk. He stopped halfway through climbing the steps.

"I *would* say that I'm surprised to see you so soon, but I can feel something is going on. What's wrong?" Marcus questioned.

It had taken years to earn Marcus' trust and to get used to the strange way the man spoke. Chase would call Marcus paranoid if he wasn't certain the guy wouldn't kick his ass.

"I need to talk to you. You know the raid that closed down the Church for Humanity?"

"I've watched the news," Marcus replied.

"Well, it turns out that the guys who we thought were responsible for the capture weren't the ones after all. Someone beat them to it."

Marcus twitched his lip in the start of a smile. "Really?"

Chase got the distinct impression that Marcus wasn't surprised by the news. Stuffing his hands in the pockets of his slacks, he eyed Marcus. "Alpha Shawn sent me over here to see if you know anything about this new group."

"Why would I know anything?" Marcus questioned.

Chase had gotten to know him pretty well. He was certain that Marcus did indeed have information.

"Why don't you tell me?" Chase stated, rocking back on his heels. He could play this game all day but he needed answers and Marcus was going to provide them to him. Sure that more was going on than he knew, Chase was tired of being kept in the dark. His patience snapped. "Just tell me what the hell you know!"

Marcus' gravely chuckle had Chase holding in his own. The rare sound had Chase lifting his eyebrows in question. "So your Alpha finally decided to let you in on all the secrets? I've been telling him you can handle them."

Not sure what Marcus was talking about, Chase shrugged.

"Well, come on in. I'll grab a couple of beers. We have a lot to discuss."

A loud crack came from behind him and it took several seconds for Chase to realize what was happening. Marcus grunted and fell forward as blood spread along his shoulders.

"Fuck!" Chase dropped to the ground. "Marcus?"

The man groaned.

Scrambling up the steps, Chase cursed under his breath. Once he reached his friend, Chase ran his hands over Marcus' chest, making sure he didn't touch the wound.

"Get down, you damn fool," Marcus griped at him.

"What?"

Several more pops followed. Chase jumped as pieces of the wooden steps flew at his face.

"Shooter in the canyon. Call the Alpha." Marcus' voice cracked.

Damn! Shit! Fuck! He pushed his hand into his pants then yanked out his cell. He glanced over his shoulder to see if he could pinpoint the location the shots stemmed from.

"And stay low. We need to get to cover."

Marcus could sure be demanding, even when he was bleeding out. Chase fumbled with the phone almost dropping it. He couldn't believe what was happening.

Beside him, Marcus groaned again. Chase needed to get his shit together. Tucking his phone between his cheek and shoulder, he kneeled over Marcus. "Hang on," he told him.

A pained grunt was his only reply.

Alpha Shawn's line rang in his ear as Chase struggled to get his free arm under Marcus. Luckily, with his shifter strength, he was able to gently lift Marcus and crawl behind the porch's low solid walls for protection. He didn't know if the assailant was still out there but he didn't want to take the chance. There was no clear route to the front door without putting themselves in the open.

"Hello?"

"Alpha! We need help. Marcus has been shot."

"Where are you?"

"In front of his house. Taking cover on the porch."

"Stay there. We're on our way."

The call ended and Chase cursed. It would take too much time for his Alpha to reach them. Marcus was bleeding heavily and Chase needed to get him help.

Crouching, he peeked over the rail.

"Don't," Marcus whispered.

"I have to get you out of here."

"Wait for the Alpha," Marcus insisted.

Chase peered down at the other man, who was too pale.

"It'll be okay," he promised.

"Stubborn ass," Marcus wheezed.

Grinning at his friend, Chase shrugged. If he could make it back to his vehicle, there was a good chance he could pull close enough that the SUV would block him getting Marcus inside.

It was a risk, but one that he had to take.

He grasped Marcus' hand in his. "Don't you dare die on me, old man."

"I'm too damn mean to die," Marcus replied softly.

Chase sure the hell hoped so. Putting his plan into action, he leaped over the rail, landing back in the yard.

Immediately ducking, shots rang out as he began running and he barely managed to keep from being hit. That answered his question of whether the shooter was still there. He made a break for the passenger side, yanking the door open when he reached it.

More cracks, sounding too close for comfort, hit the opposite side of the vehicle. When they got out of this, he was going to have a serious talk with his Alpha.

Chase liked to think of himself as more of a lover than a fighter. This kind of shit should be left to his brother. Max would have probably already shifted and tracked down whoever was after him.

He stayed low, thrusting the key into the ignition before climbing into the driver seat. Relief flooded him as the engine caught and the car came to life. He grabbed the gear shift, throwing the vehicle into reverse and slammed his foot on the gas. Whipping the wheel around, he drove over bushes so he was directly in front of the stairway.

Three more bullets hit his SUV.

Chase wasn't sure how much more damage his ride could take. Pushing the door open, he then dropped to the ground, scrambled up and back to Marcus' side.

"Hurry, he'll be headed toward us soon. If you're going to get us out of here, do it quickly," Marcus advised.

"Here we go," Chase said as he hefted the other man to his knees.

Gritting his teeth, Marcus cursed through them. "When I get my hands on this fucker..."

"Easy," Chase said with a smile. If anyone could lighten the situation, it was Marcus. "Calm down, killer. We can worry about that later."

Glaring at him, Marcus huffed.

"Ready?"

He waited until Marcus nodded.

"Let's go!" Chase half-dragged Marcus down the steps to the vehicle. Pushing the older man in through the open driver door, he followed closely, climbing over him and into the driver's seat to avoid exposing himself to the sniper.

Since no shots struck them, Chase could only guess that Marcus was right and the assailant was coming after them. Not wasting any time, he stomped on the gas and took off.

Lying on the passenger floorboard, Marcus groaned, holding his shoulder.

"You are both incredibly brave *and* stupid."

Chase nodded. "Yeah."

Flying down the dirt road, Chase tried to spot any trouble ahead. There were too many places an attack could come from. While living deep in the canyon kept Marcus isolated and protected, it meant once someone found Marcus' location, he or she could keep well hidden until it was time to attack.

"What the hell is going on?" Chase demanded.

"Alpha may have waited too long to fill you in," Marcus replied.

"So why don't you?" Chase snapped. Now that the adrenaline had started to ease, Chase had problems processing the events that led him to driving his buddy to the hospital. Even with him gripping the steering wheel, his hands still trembled and his stomach remained in knots.

The low groan that came from Marcus had him glancing over. *Shit!* Marcus' head had dropped and there was no color in his face at all. Chase shifted to reach his cell.

Trying to get a hold of either his Alpha or brother, he got both of their voicemails. Hopefully Shawn and Max were close to Marcus' house and could catch whoever was responsible for the attack.

Leaving a message telling them he was taking Marcus to the hospital, he prayed that he would get there in time.

"Hang on, Marcus," he demanded.

There was no response. Chase glanced over to see that Marcus had passed out. If it wasn't for the fact he could still hear Marcus's heart beating, Chase might have driven off the road in panic.

Chapter Three

Kayla rolled over in the bed and buried her face in the soft pillow. Muffled sounds came to her from under the closed bedroom door but she really just wanted to go back to sleep.

It hadn't been easy settling down for the night. Since Justin didn't have a guest bedroom, she'd ended by sleeping with him while Randy had taken the couch. Justin's large body beside her was a comfort.

Resting next to him was no big deal to either of them. Her love for Justin had evolved into seeing him as only a brother.

Since Justin was no longer in bed, he was probably in the kitchen. Randy was no doubt awake also. The two of them alone? That was cause for concern.

Which meant she had better get her ass in gear. Slowly climbing from the soft mattress, she padded over to the door and opened it silently. A soft chuckle came from the direction of the kitchen. Okay, her boys were getting along.

In her borrowed sweatpants and T-shirt, she sauntered into the bathroom to the sink. Washing her face then using her finger as a toothbrush, Kayla went about freshening up as much as she could.

Justin had promised to throw hers and Randy's clothes into the wash. She needed to get dressed and find out what last night was all about.

She didn't want to worry her dad but he needed to know what had happened. And if there were a group targeting shifters in the city, she would have her father alert their Alpha.

Canyon, Texas was only a little over an hour's drive. Since Canyon was a shifter town still living in secret, any threat in Lubbock could spill over to her friends and family.

Strolling into the kitchen, she spotted Randy sitting at the island. Justin busied himself at the stove.

"Morning," Randy greeted her.

"Hey, did you sleep okay?" she asked as she passed him. She'd left her phone charging on the counter and she grabbed it.

"Fine. How about you?"

Glancing at him, she saw his lifted eyebrow and nod toward Justin. "Justin is a perfect gentleman."

From his position behind her, the *gentleman* snorted. "Please don't try to help my reputation."

He turned, smiling at her. It didn't look like he'd slept at all by the dark circles under his eyes. She remembered him getting into bed with her but she had passed out right away, the excitement of the evening too much for her.

"Did you rest at all?" she asked him.

"Some. I sent some friends to Randy's parents' place and to both your apartments. There is no sign of anyone having been around any of your homes."

"Thank God." A weight lifted from her shoulders and helped to loosen some of the tension inside her.

"I also talked to my father and sister. Angel should be here shortly. She wants to talk to you."

Kayla definitely wanted to hear what Angelica Salvatore had to say. Justin had been so vague about the group his sister was supposedly a part of that Kayla had always been highly suspicious.

While she knew that Justin was a good guy, that didn't automatically mean his family wasn't involved in something questionable.

No one wanted to believe that their loved ones were involved in evil plots. So she would have to talk with Justin's sister herself. As much as she would have loved to trust them, she couldn't. Something weird was occurring.

"I need to call my dad," she told him.

Justin held up his hand. "I know you want to talk to him. Can you just wait?"

Stepping back, she eyed Justin. He appeared earnest as his gaze met hers. Still unsure, she strolled over to the coffee pot. Taking the time to pour the brown liquid into a mug and add sugar and creamer, she thought about his request.

"I'll wait to call him," she relented.

"Thanks," Justin said, turning back to the stove. He pulled the skillet off the burner. "And I made breakfast."

"Taking her cup back across the kitchen, Kayla sat beside Randy. He rubbed his hand down her arm before linking his fingers with hers.

"We'll get to the bottom of this," he whispered.

"I know." She nodded. Of course, that wasn't completely true. She didn't really know anything.

Everything had happened so fast. She and Randy always tried to meet at least once a week for dinner. But it was never on the same day of the week. There was no way for anyone to have advanced knowledge that they met last night.

Since it was a Friday, they could have had dates or other plans. It just so happened that they'd both been free.

Either someone had followed her or Randy — or that person had just stumbled on to him and her leaving the restaurant. She didn't believe the latter was the case.

And if anyone were targeting Randy, why would he or she leave his family alone?

The sick feeling in her belly made her think that she had been the objective.

Her dad had always told her to trust her gut. Now was the time to have confidence in herself.

She smiled up at Justin as he placed a plate of ham and eggs in front of her. "Thanks."

"You're welcome," he replied softly.

They ate in silence. She and Randy sat at the large tiled countertop and Justin leaned back against one of the counters with his own breakfast.

Glancing at the clock on the stove, she saw it was almost ten-thirty in the morning. She was usually an early riser and couldn't believe that the morning was almost gone. She hoped that Angel would arrive soon. There was no way she could wait around all day.

Between the strong coffee and the wonderfully prepared food, she started to feel more secure in what she needed to do. After she heard whatever it was Angel had to tell her she would call her dad then start looking for whoever had been after them last night.

Her dad had taught her how to handle a weapon and she was licensed to carry concealed.

She wouldn't be caught off guard again.

Beside her plate, her phone rang. She picked up the small device, not recognizing the number. Glancing at Justin, she pressed the answer sensor.

"Hello?" She met Justin's gaze as he stepped closer at the same time Randy stood and leaned against her side.

"Kayla Webb?"

Not able to place the man's voice she tensed. "Yes?"

"I'm Chase Lawson. From Canyon. I know your dad."

Kayla vaguely remembered who Chase was. He was the Beta for her Pack, so of course she knew. "I know who you are, Mr. Lawson."

"Call me Chase, please. Anyway, the reason I'm calling is that…um, I think it would be best if you came home this weekend. You're in Lubbock, right? I can even send someone to pick you up."

In all the time she'd lived in Lubbock, she had never received a call like this. Wary from the events, Kayla wasn't sure she could trust the phone call. "Why isn't my dad or Shawn calling me?"

"I'm sorry. Uh, I was with your dad at the house when…when he was shot."

"Shot?" she yelled.

"He's okay! Or he will be. He's out of surgery and they were able to remove the bullet. He hasn't woken up yet and I got your number from his phone."

"Where is Alp…Shawn?"

"He and my brother Max are looking for the culprit. I can have him call you as soon as he gets back. I just wanted to make sure you knew what's going on."

The guy sounded so upset and solemn.

"How do I know you are who you say you are?"

"What? What do you mean?" he asked sharply. "Are you okay? Why would I make this up?"

Since she didn't know whether the call was for real, she had to consider that it could be a trap. A way to lure her out. But what if it wasn't?

She locked gazes with Justin silently asking what to do. He shrugged, looking as upset as she felt.

"How did you know to call me?"

"What?" His voice rose. "You're his daughter."

She waited.

"You want me to prove who I am?"

"Yes," she confirmed.

"How?"

She wished she knew. Randy tapped her arm and grabbed the phone and putting it on speaker.

"What kind of cell do you have?"

"Who's this?"

That doesn't matter. Answer the question."

"An iPhone 5."

Randy covered the mouthpiece. "Do you know what this guy looks like?"

Nodding, she thought she was catching on to his idea.

"Kayla will call you right back at this number on video conference."

"Hold on…"

Randy disconnected the call.

"If he is who he says he is then this shouldn't be an issue. Plus we'll be able to see in the background," Randy explained.

"It's a good idea," Justin confirmed.

Kayla took the phone back and hit redial with video call. The line only rang once before she saw Chase Lawson. "Can you see me?" Chase asked.

"Yes," Kayla answered. "What happened to my dad?"

Chase ran a hand roughly over his face. "Honestly? I still don't know. I went over to his place this morning to talk to him. We were headed inside, when out of nowhere, a bullet caught his shoulder. I didn't see anyone, but the sniper kept firing. I called our Alpha and got Marcus to the hospital and that's really all I can tell you."

"Where is Shawn?" She noticed Chase had slipped and said Alpha but she wasn't going to point it out. When in public, they weren't supposed to use the Pack ranks but Chase was obviously distressed.

"He's still searching the canyon. As soon as we knew Marcus was okay, Shawn and Max left to try to find the guy."

"I'm on my way. I should be there in about an hour."

"Wait!"

She stopped from disconnecting.

"Are you okay? What's going on that you didn't believe me?"

"We'll get into that when I arrive. I'll meet you at the hospital."

This time she didn't give Chase a chance to reply. She leaped from the stool. "I've got to go."

"Hold on!" Justin grabbed her arm as she tried to pass. "We need to think about this. You were almost attacked last night too. They could be waiting for you to head back into town."

"My dad's been shot!"

"I know. I do. But we have to be careful."

"I'm going, Justin," she told him.

"I'll go with her," Randy said.

Justin gripped his hair and yanked. "Fuck," he yelled, frustration evident.

"I have to go."

"We're all going. I'll call Angel and have her meet us in Canyon. I'm not going to let you two go off by yourselves."

She grabbed his face and kissed him. "Let's go!"

"You have to get dressed first," he hollered at her.

After hanging up with Kayla Webb, Chase's anxiety rose to an all-time high. There had been something majorly wrong that she hadn't shared with him. Now that she was on her way, he wouldn't be able to relax until she had actually reached the hospital.

Pacing the ICU's waiting room—helpless once again to do anything—Chase grimaced as aggravation boiled up in his gut. A member of his Pack had been shot right in front of him and he hadn't been able to do anything about it.

At times like this, he wished he were more like Max.

Max had shown up at the hospital with their Alpha. Both men had shifted then ran the whole way to the Webb residence. By the time they'd arrived, the shooter was nowhere to be found.

Two of the Pack's other members had driven to Marcus' with the Alpha and Max's clothes and phones. After they'd heard Chase's message, they'd high-tailed it to the hospital.

Max had sat with Chase while Shawn had demanded updates from the staff. While his brother had tried to make him feel better by stating that Chase had done his part getting Marcus help, Chase didn't feel like he had done enough.

Plus he really wanted answers.

"Hey."

Chase jumped when someone's hand came down on his shoulder.

"You okay?" his best friend, Alex Wilson, asked.

Chase took a deep breath and tried to smile. "Yeah, sorry. I guess I'm a little…"

"Freaked out?"

"Yeah," Chase admitted.

"It's all right, man. Here. I brought you coffee from the bakery."

Gratefully, Chase accepted the Styrofoam cup from Alex. "Thanks."

"You're welcome." With a hand on the back of his neck, Alex led him to the row of hard plastic seats. "Now tell me what's going on. Max called and asked that I come sit here with you but didn't give me much detail. He said he had to take off for a little bit and didn't want you here alone."

Slowly sinking into the chair, Chase flipped up the top of the drink and inhaled. Had it only been earlier in the morning he'd had coffee with Kurt and Clint in his office?

It seemed like days had passed since their meeting. Who knew that conversation would lead him into witnessing an attempted murder and he'd wind up in the hospital waiting for something more to happen?

How had the good news of the Church for Humanity being closed down come to all of this?

The Pack should be celebrating. They were safe once again. Sure, they still had to watch out for one another, as the world wasn't as accepting of the shifters as they first thought others would be, but his family was supposed to be okay.

"Chase?"

He jerked at the sharpness in Alex's tone.

"Are you okay? You didn't get hit, did you?"

Pulling himself from his thoughts, he peered over at the other man. "Nah, I'm fine. It's just a lot to take in."

"I bet. Now tell me what happened."

He started from the beginning. First, what Kurt and Clint had told him up to the point he'd driven up into the emergency lot.

"How's Marcus now?" Alex asked when Chase had finished.

"Okay. The doctor said he would recover fine. I called Marcus' daughter and she's on her way up. I haven't heard from Max yet."

"He's still looking. They did find where the gunman had been when he'd shot at you guys. So they have his scent. That's good news."

"I just don't understand what this is all about. Why Marcus? What is going on?"

"I don't know. But we will find out. We'll protect our people."

Chase wanted to believe him. "I felt so helpless," he admitted. "I didn't know what to do. I should have shifted or something. Gone after the guy myself?"

"And get yourself killed?"

Shrugging, Chase lifted his head. "At least I wouldn't have run away."

The shame of his actions was still eating at him. If it hadn't been for Marcus, he might have been shot himself since he'd frozen. It had taken too long for him to realize what was happening.

"You didn't run. You rescued Marcus and got him the medical attention he needed."

"If Max had been there, we probably wouldn't still be searching for this man. Max would have ripped him apart before he saved Marcus."

"Hey." Alex lowered his voice and leaned close. "Where is this coming from? You did the right thing."

Closing his eyes, Chase didn't want the reassurances Alex was offering. He knew he'd fucked up.

For his entire life, all he'd wanted to do was take care of the Pack. He'd pushed to better himself so that when Shawn took over as Alpha, he could apply for the Beta position.

As one of the youngest Beta's in any Pack, Chase was proud of what he'd accomplished. But now he wasn't sure what he'd done was really best for the Pack.

So many Packs now had their Beta and their head Enforcer also. Since Chase had never been too keen on the discipline of the job duty of Enforcer, he'd never trained for that station. That might have been a major mistake.

"Listen, I don't know what is going on in that head of yours, although from the look on your face, it isn't good. I want you to hear me now, though," Alex said gruffly as he slid off his seat and kneeled in front of Chase. "If it wasn't for you, Marcus might not have made it. We'll catch whoever is responsible for this. You're job now is make sure that Marcus' daughter gets here and he stays safe."

"I will," he promised. He might have failed earlier, but he would insure that Marcus was kept under guard and no one hurt him again. Also, since he still wasn't one hundred percent certain Kayla Webb wasn't in danger too, he would have to work something out for her.

"Good."

"Gentlemen." The doctor cleared his throat as he entered. "We've moved Marcus from ICU and have placed him in a private room. I can take you up to him if you'd like."

Chase rose and smiled at the older man. "We would appreciate it."

As they followed behind the physician, Chase tried to remember whom the man was mated with. Since the doctor wasn't a shifter himself, Chase didn't know him as well as others in his Pack. Most of the residents in Canyon who were not shifters were either mated with or related in some way to one another. A few were aware of their kind and stayed, knowing they would always be protected.

Having a doctor as part of the family was a real benefit to everyone. In fact, just having an entire hospital of their own was rare and a true treasure. Their injured and sick didn't have to be treated off site. The Pack could go into the privately funded hospital.

Of course, it was the Pack that funded the medical facility — Mindy Bright! That is whom the doctor had mated.

"How is Mindy doing? I haven't seen her in a few months," Chase asked, as the three of them stepped into the elevator.

The man's smile lit up his entire face. "She's wonderful. Really enjoying retirement, although she does miss the little ones."

"I bet. The kids always loved it whenever they had her class," Chase replied truthfully.

They made small talk as the elevator took them to the sixth level. Once the ding sounded and they'd exited, Chase looked around the quiet floor, trying to work out what needed to be done.

"I'll be assigning a guard until Marcus is out of here. Also, his daughter should be arriving shortly," Chase informed the doctor.

"Anything you need. You just let me know. The head nurse is Barbra Knight. You know her well, I believe."

Chase chuckled. "Yes, I am familiar with her. The woman has been my mom's best friend for my entire life."

"She'll page me if Marcus needs anything, but I really believe he'll be okay. He's over here."

There weren't many people around but the two women who Chase passed waved at him. Knowing family was caring for Marcus helped relax Chase.

He would still demand that there be security, but he knew Marcus was going to be safe.

The door to the room stood open. Chase knocked on the heavy wood as he entered.

"He still hasn't woken but it should be soon," Barbra told him, as she looked up from a clipboard in her hand.

Nodding, Chase moved to her side. "Glad to hear it."

Running his gaze over the older man in the bed, Chase's heart contracted painfully, as he viewed his friend.

Marcus had always been intimating. Pale and bruised under the harsh lights, he looked years older than his actual age. Tears burned behind Chase's eyes but he wouldn't let them fall. He had to be strong.

"He's going to be okay," Barbra said quietly.

"Yeah," he replied but didn't look away from his friend. "He's going to be just fine. I'm going to make sure of it."

Chapter Four

Kayla didn't remember the entire drive from Lubbock to Canyon. All she knew was it took much too long. When Justin finally did pull up to the small building that served at the Canyon Medical Center, she jumped out of the vehicle.

"Kayla, wait!" Justin called after her.

Ignoring him, she rushed through the automatic doors, bypassing other people, and running straight to the nurses' station. "I'm looking for my father, Marcus Webb. He was shot."

The young woman looked up startled then smiled kindly. "Yes ma'am, we've been expecting you. If you'll take the elevator to the sixth floor, we'll call up for Chase to meet you."

"Sixth floor?"

"Yes, Ms. Webb. Your father has been moved to a private room. You'll be taken directly to him."

Sagging against the counter, Kayla wiped at her eyes. She hadn't realized she'd been crying. "So...he's okay?"

"I am *so* sorry!" the young lady stood as she reached over and grasped her hand. "I thought you had been in contact with the Beta—uh, Chase. Your dad came through surgery fine and is resting comfortably. He woke about half an hour ago."

"Thank you," Kayla managed. She sensed a presence behind her and turned to see Justin and Randy hovering close by. "He's okay," she told them.

"Of course," Randy replied as he embraced her. "Let's get up there and see him now."

Twisting back around to the nurse, Kayla held out her hand. "Thank you."

"You're very welcome. I'll call up to his floor now so they will be expecting you."

Randy kept his arm around Kayla's shoulders, for which she was grateful. Still a little bit shaky, she needed the support.

They didn't speak again until the elevator doors opened.

"Here we go," Randy said gently.

Stepping out, she immediately recognized Chase Lawson. The Beta of the Pack was leaning against the wall with his hands clasped together. Kayla had met the man a couple of times but it had been a while.

Since she'd left home right after she graduated at eighteen, the few times she'd been in Chase's presence she'd been underage and more worried about small teenager needs than the Pack.

During her visits home, she'd stayed around the house with her dad. A loner and a bit of a recluse, her father didn't like to leave their place. She knew Chase visited him often and the two men had become close friends.

Now that she was face-to-face with the high-positioned shifter, Kayla wished she'd paid closer attention to what her father had said about him.

Maybe then she wouldn't have been so shocked by the man's good looks.

Tall, dark, nicely built, and mouth-wateringly handsome, Chase Lawson appeared to be in his early thirties

A few strands of gray at the sides of his black, short hair gave him a distinguished edge. His deep chocolate eyes met hers as he smiled with perfect white teeth.

In other circumstances, she wouldn't have thought twice about seducing him.

Chase pushed off the wall, standing tall, then moved his slim, sleek body closer.

Kayla had to curl her hands into fists to keep from reaching for him. His gaze, full of compassion and caring, met hers. Randy tightened his arm around her shoulders, yanking her attention away from the hot shifter and back to the present.

What in the hell am I thinking? Checking out the Pack Beta while her dad lay in a hospital bed? She needed to get a hold of herself.

"Ms. Webb, I'm relieved to see you made it safely," Chase said as he held out a hand.

Stepping away from Randy, she placed her palm against Chase's. The jolt that flowed between them almost had her jumping. Instead, she smiled. "Call me Kayla, please. Thanks for meeting us."

"Of course." He dropped her hand and looked at her two friends.

"This is Randy O'Hare and Justin Salvatore, friends of mine."

Chase shook hands with both men. When he faced her again, any signs of the attraction that had sparked between them had vanished. "I'm sure you'd like to see Marcus. He woke a little while ago but, because of the pain meds, he almost instantly went back to sleep. The nurse did say that his reaction is normal and he will be in and out for a while."

"Makes sense," she murmured, trying to figure out why he'd change in his demeanor. In seconds, he'd gone from kind to businesslike.

"He's just over here." Chase waved for them to follow.

In front of the door stood a well-muscled man. Taking a discreet sniff, she recognized him as a shifter. As they approached, she tensed at his stance and cold gaze.

"Since we still don't know who is responsible, I have assigned a guard to Marcus until further notice."

"Thank you." Having her father protected was a huge relief — one less worry. She stayed close to Chase as they entered the small room. "Oh, Dad." Rushing to his bedside, she peered down at her father.

He looked both better and worse than she expected. With the sheet folded down, revealing a white bandage on his shoulder, Kayla got her first look at his injury. Placing her hand on his upper body, she thanked God that his chest moved under her palm.

While his face remained drawn and thin, he still seemed as strong as ever.

"I'll inform the doctor that you're here. He will want to speak with you," Chase said behind her.

She watched as he hurriedly left.

"Interesting," Justin murmured, stepping up beside her.

"Hmm?" she asked, distracted. The man's ass was just as fine as the rest of him.

"Earth to Kayla!"

Jerking her head back, she smacked Justin's hand away from in front of her face. "Stop it."

Chuckling, he elbowed her. "Nice guy."

Knowing she had been obvious in her interest and not really caring about being teased, she ignored him.

"Kind of hot," Randy added. "I wonder if he's single."

Kayla was *so not* going there. Instead, she returned her attention to her dad.

He'd never been hurt in all the time she could remember. Traveling so much when she was young, Kayla had lived half the year with her grandparents until her dad would come home. While her childhood might not have been normal, it had been happy.

She'd loved her grandma and papa. After they'd been killed in a car accident when she was only ten, her father had retired from his government work and they'd moved to Canyon to settle down.

Still uncomfortable around other people, her father hadn't been involved deeply with the Pack. Kayla had gotten to know the members better since she did attend school and made friends.

In all those memories, she could never remember her dad even coming down sick.

Now that he's been injured, she needed to stay home with him. He'd bitch and complain but she was certain remaining home with him would be for the best.

While he never pressured her to come back to Canyon, he did love it when she came to visit. Kayla could never see herself living in a small town for the rest of her life.

Or away from other people, like her dad.

Kayla loved being around others. As an administrative assistant, she made schedules and phone calls all day. Organizing her boss's business meetings and keeping up with notes made her feel important.

Although it wouldn't be easy, she knew her boss would be able to deal without her if she took a couple of weeks off. She'd have to call and tell him her father had an accident and she was needed at home. He'd want to know why her father had been shot and Kayla hated to lie to her boss but it wasn't as if she could tell him the truth. She didn't have those answers. There shouldn't be a problem with the request. Rarely did she use all of her vacation time anyway.

Aware that Justin and Randy had moved into a corner to speak quietly, Kayla sat on the side of the bed, still keeping her hand on her dad's chest.

She'd get him healthy again. Make sure their Alpha found out who was responsible, instead of worrying about what had happened the previous night.

Being in Canyon would keep her away from whoever had been hunting her.

Returning home might just be the best plan.

Justin's cell rang. Glancing up at him, she saw him wince.

"It's my sister," he told them.

Justin had left a message for Angel about what had happened. She'd send Randy back with Justin and let the two men work on what was really going on in Lubbock.

Once she knew everything was okay here with her father, maybe she could talk to Chase about her own mystery.

First and most importantly, she had to get her dad out of the hospital and on his path to healing.

* * * *

Chase cursed himself as he stalked down the hall looking for the doctor. *Talk about unprofessional.*

He'd practically been drooling over Kayla Webb.

As Beta and the man who was with her father when he'd been shot, the last thing the girl needed was him staring at her like a piece of Grade A beef.

The minute he had seen her, Chase's mouth had gone dry as his heartbeat increased and desire roared straight to his cock.

If Chase had written a list for his perfect mate's traits, Kayla would have been the woman.

Her shiny brown hair was pulled back away from her face, revealing her soft dark eyes and pert nose. She wasn't short, so for a man just at six feet tall, he could easily look into her eyes.

There was more muscle and sculpture to her body than he was used to from the women around Canyon. The spark that had sizzled through him at the very first touch had instantly hardened his cock.

He hadn't even seen the two men accompanying her until the man with his arm around her moved. That had quickly drawn his attention and highlighted how he was supposed to behave.

"Hey, Barbra, can you tell the doctor that Marcus' daughter has arrived?" he asked upon reaching the nurse's station.

"Sure thing, Chase." Barbra picked up the phone.

He strolled away.

Now that Kayla was there and the guards had been arranged, there really was no reason for him to continue to hang around. Marcus might not even want to see him now.

Kayla probably wouldn't want to set eyes on him, either, once her father informed her how Chase had frozen when the incident had happened.

Yeah, it would be a lot better for everyone if Chase just took off. So why wasn't he? Finding himself a couple of doors down from Marcus' room, Chase stopped.

He could hang around Barbra or go back to the waiting room. That way, he would still be close if something happened but he wouldn't be in the way.

Staying close and discreetly hidden was even better.

Mind made up, Chase started for the other end of the floor when the elevator opened and his Alpha and brother stepped out.

"Hey, bro." Max strode over and gripped his shoulder. "You hanging in there okay?"

Rolling his shoulder to dislodge his brother's hand, he nodded. "Of course."

"Why aren't you with Marcus?" Shawn questioned, glancing between him and the room.

"His daughter and friends arrived. I just had Barbra page the doctor so he could speak with her."

"Great, I have a few questions of my own," Shawn said, strolling forward.

Hanging back, Chase waited for the other men to enter.

"What are you doing?" Max asked, after realizing Chase was with him.

"They don't need me in there. I should take off." He waved his hand in the opposite direction.

Frowning, his brother changed course and marched back to him. "What's wrong?"

"Nothing," he assured Max. Of course, he was lying but his brother was the last person he wanted to have this conversation with. Chase just needed time to get his head on straight.

"Then why are you leaving?"

Sighing, Chase wasn't sure what to say to get Max to back off. As close as the two of them were, this was Chase's problem and he didn't want Max involved.

Besides how embarrassing it would be to let his brother know what a big failure he really was.

"Talk to me, man."

Raking his gaze over his brother, Chase recognized the stubborn set of his jaw and concern in his eyes. "I just need to get away for a bit. That's all. With Marcus' family here and now you and the Alpha, I'm not needed."

"Okay, if that's what you want. I'll tell the others you'll be by later."

"Yeah, sure." Spinning around, he hurried back to the elevator.

Stopping his escape, Shawn called him. "Chase! Marcus is awake and asking for you."

"Fuck!" he murmured. No choice in the matter. Chase spun on his heel.

Max was still standing in the same spot. Avoiding his gaze, Chase rushed to Shawn's side. He could get through this then he was going home and losing himself in a bottle of tequila.

"You're awake," he said with fake happiness.

Marcus sat up with his daughter at his side. "I told you I was too mean to die," Marcus replied with his usual gruffness.

"Yeah, you did, old man," he agreed. The room seemed a lot smaller filled with so many people.

Kayla's two friends stood in the corner by the window. Both men openly stared at him. Paying them no mind and turning his back on Shawn and Max, Chase made the effort to look only at Marcus.

"Come here, son," Marcus commanded.

Leaning forward, the strength with which Marcus grabbed the back of his neck surprised Chase.

"Thank you."

Staring into Marcus' face, Chase had to swallow hard to clear his throat. The emotions in the man's features were unexpected. Unable to say anything, he simply nodded.

"Mr. Webb."

At the doctor's arrival, Chase took his chance to distance himself from the others in the room. Putting his back to the wall, he observed as the doctor spoke with Marcus and Kayla.

Shawn shouldered his way into the conversation. Chase thought everyone should leave and was about to suggest it when Marcus started to raise his voice.

"While I appreciate you patching me back together, I am going home!"

Oh, hell. Chase should have predicted this argument.

"Now, Marcus, you need to recover," Shawn advised.

"Mr. Webb, you were in surgery only a few hours ago," the doctor tried.

"Dad, listen to your doctor," Kayla added.

From his position, Chase could see Marcus was about to lose his shit.

"How about a compromise?" he suggested, joining the small group.

All eyes turned to him.

"At least stay overnight. If you are still feeling well enough to go home tomorrow instead of a few days, we can revisit the subject. One night, Marcus."

The silence in the room seemed to turn to tension as no one moved.

"One night," Marcus finally grumbled.

Like a balloon popping, the atmosphere immediately eased.

"I'll let you visit for a few more minutes but after that, I'm afraid I'll have to ask most of you to leave. If my patient insists on checking himself out early, I will make sure he is well rested when he does go."

A chorus of affirmatives followed the doctor out.

"I really wish you would reconsider," Shawn told Marcus. "He's just looking out for your wellbeing."

"I can take care of myself," Marcus argued. "All I want to know is if you found the son of a bitch who shot me."

Chase should have hightailed it out with the doctor. Sliding his feet back, he retook his stance against the wall.

"No," Shawn said roughly. "Bastard got away. But we got his scent. We'll keep a guard at your door here and watch the house."

"I don't need any damn protection. I can take care of myself."

Opening his mouth to argue, Chase quickly thought better of it. Shawn could strong-arm Marcus if he had to. It would be better if the Alpha handled this.

"You'll keep the guards," Shawn told him. "Right now we have a gunman lose, who could go after all of us. The Pack is on high alert. My family will be kept safe."

Marcus didn't say anything but his gaze left their Alpha until it landed on Chase. Chase didn't look away until Marcus did.

"You think they found me?" Marcus finally asked Shawn.

"I don't know. It's a possibility."

"What are you talking about dad?"

"Maybe I can help answer that."

The room came alive with activity as a new voice joined them.

Chase jumped at the woman's voice as Max and Shawn practically pounced on her.

"Hey!" The tall man who had arrived with Kayla jumped forward. "Get your hands off my sister."

"Where's the guard?" Chase demanded angrily.

The noise level rose until Chase couldn't hear anything in particular. Whistling sharply, he gained everyone's attention.

The woman held by Max and Shawn smiled as she glanced over at him.

"Thank you, Mr. Lawson." She then turned to Marcus. "How are you, Marcus?"

"Fine. You can let her go," he told the two protectors. "She's not here to hurt me."

Shawn and Max released the woman, who nodded to them. "Gentlemen."

The young man with matching features to the woman moved forward quickly. "Angel, are you okay?"

She waved away his concern, instead hugging him. "Yes, of course."

"Sorry, Alpha," the guard said from the doorway. "She showed a badge and said she was authorized to enter."

"It's okay, Jeffrey. She just took us by surprise," Shawn assured the young guard.

"I apologize for interrupting. I tried to call Justin but my call went unanswered so I just came up here. Angelica Salvatore."

As introductions were made, Chase took in the newcomer. She had the same black hair and crystal clear, blue eyes as her brother. About the same height as Kayla, she was probably around five seven or so. Intelligence gleamed from her gaze as she locked it on him.

"What are you doing here?" Marcus asked the question Chase was dying to voice.

"After the incident with Kayla and Randy last night, Justin called. When word about your shooting came in — and since they were already on the way — I detoured here instead of heading onto Lubbock."

"What incident?" Marcus and Chase asked simultaneously.

Chapter Five

With the addition of Justin's sister to the mix, all of the information floating around had given Kayla a headache.

She should have prepared her father better for hearing the news that someone had been after her and Randy the previous night, but she hadn't had the chance.

As he glared at her, she shifted nervously from foot to foot.

"That settles it," Marcus said trying to sit up farther. "I'm not staying here while my daughter is in danger."

Three sets of hands—hers, Shawn's and Chase's—all landed on him to keep Marcus in bed.

"Dad, I'm fine," she soothed.

"Marcus," Shawn growled in warning.

With a thunderous expression, her dad settled back against the pillows.

"There is too big of a coincidence to ignore," Angel stated, as she sat in one of the chairs by the window.

She'd never met Justin's sister and now she was kind of glad she hadn't. Angel was pretty intimidating, even surrounded by shifters.

It wasn't her appearance exactly, but Angel just had a certain presence about her that screamed 'I'm in charge'.

"This is a major concern for the organization. We think they've found you and your daughter," Angel spoke directly to her father. "There are more of us on the way."

The heavy sigh was full of so many emotions Kayla couldn't have guessed what was going through her dad's mind as he lay there.

"I've brought danger to the Pack," Marcus said to Shawn.

"You've spent your life protecting us and are part of my family. We'll handle this," Shawn replied easily.

"What *exactly* is going on?" Chase asked from across the room.

Peering over at him, Kayla took in his crossed arms and frown. The man was not happy with the information that was unfolding.

"We'll discuss it, but not here." Shawn turned to Max. "We need a safe place for everyone to stay. I don't want Marcus alone at his house when he's released — at least not right now."

"The main house has enough space. Between Alex, me, Chase and Jacob, we'll cover security. Also, we'll assign a few more guards close to the Canyon opening," Max offered.

"I agree. That will be the best place for everyone right now."

It only took a matter of seconds and a few sentences for the two men to organize everything. Stunned, Kayla sat as they spoke softly to each other.

The others in the room seemed to take in the two with varied degrees of amusement. Angel sat back smiling. Randy bobbed his head from one to the other. Justin kept rocking back on his heels just listening, and Chase simply smirked.

"Uh, if I can ask a question," Kayla raised her hand as if she was still in school.

The Alpha paused and looked over at her.

Now that she had his attention, Kayla didn't know what to say. Finally, thinking of what brought her to town, she questioned. "What about the man who shot my dad?"

"That is being investigated," Angel informed her. "We should know more once we get settled."

"You're responsible for the closing of the church?" Chase spoke up, aiming a fierce expression in Angel's direction.

"You could say that," Angel quipped.

With a shake of his head, Chase pushed away from the wall. "I figured. I have to go. I'll meet up with you all a little later."

"Where are you going?" Max blocked Chase's exit.

"To my diner. I need to check on things."

Max started to back away.

"Not alone," Marcus practically shouted.

"What?" Chase asked, frowning at him.

"He saw you. They'll know who you are by now, if they didn't prior to this afternoon."

"Look, I don't know what all this is about but I have a business to run. By the time everyone gets to the Wilson ranch, I won't be far behind. Nothing is going to happen in town anyway."

"I disagree," Shawn replied. "You are also the Beta of the Pack. Not only does that put you in danger, but you witnessed what happened at Marcus', so we need to make sure you are guarded too."

"I can take care of myself!"

Kayla sympathized with Chase. It was obvious he had been through a lot that day and needed some time away from the matter and everyone now involved. She wanted to offer to go with him but that wasn't possible. She had her own priorities.

Instead, she watched as Max gripped the back of Chase's neck and whispered in his ear.

The emotions that crossed Chase's face told her a lot. She wasn't certain why she felt the strong instant attraction to him.

All she knew was that she wasn't going to fight it.

Chase Lawson meant something to her and her wolf. She would find out what that was later.

"Fine," Chase said, throwing his hands up before stalking away from everyone. "I need to make a phone call."

Chase stomped out of the room and Kayla had to bite back a smile. The man needed some stress relief. Kayla had a few suggestions to help.

Max caught her gaze and grinned. There was no way that he could know what she was thinking but as a future Alpha, it wouldn't be hard to pick up on the attraction between her and his brother.

He nodded to her then quickly spun around, following in Chase's wake.

"You should get out of here," her dad said, drawing her attention.

"You do what the doctor says and stay in bed," Kayla demanded. She bent over and kissed his forehead.

"I will...for now," he replied.

Motioning for Justin and Randy to accompany her out the door, she led the way to the exit, leaving Shawn and Angel.

Why had her dad kept secrets from her? And they were some big ones too. Hurt by that knowledge, it would take some time for her to heal. In the end, she would forgive her father. She always did.

Knowing he was a good man was a comfort to her and whatever she learned—no matter how bad—would not change the way she looked at her dad.

Chase and Max stood next to the elevator with their heads bent toward each other.

"Any idea what's going on?" Randy asked from behind her.

Tearing her gaze away from the Lawson brothers, she turned toward her friend. "Not really."

They both glanced at Justin.

Tucking his hands into his pockets, Justin stared intently at the ground. "I told you what I could."

Kayla snorted. Justin obviously knew more about his sister's role in whatever was happening but was leaving it to the others to fill them in. Why she was more pissed about him hiding things than her dad, Kayla wasn't sure. However, the revelations were going to change her relationship with everyone who had lied to her—even if they thought they were protecting her. She was certain Justin wouldn't let her get hurt and it must have been hard to have his loyalty torn. Having to choose between her and his family wasn't something she could ask him to do. Eventually, hopefully, they would be better friends after all this was over.

Although she was pissed, she still loved him.

Shawn and Angel passed the guard, stopping to say a few words to the man before joining Kayla and her group.

"I spoke to Alex. Everything is ready for us."

"Let's head out," Shawn ordered.

* * * *

The large, comfortable living room in the Wilson's main house filled quickly with the group. One person handed out hot, fresh mugs of coffee to everyone as they each settled into his or her seats.

Chase sat in a recliner across from his Alpha. Seated on the sectional couch, Kayla, Justin, Randy and Angel spoke quietly, while Cassie and Max cuddled close on the love seat. Alex stood as he played host but Chase could see the tension in his friend's shoulders. They were all feeling the stress from the day.

While Alex was always helpful in Pack matters, Chase knew having a bunch of strangers in his home was still hard for him.

The only person missing was Jacob. The youngest Wilson sibling and park ranger was setting up the added security around the ranch. Now that everyone had arrived, it was time to get started. Alex would have to fill in his brother about what they discussed later.

Clearing his throat, Shawn drew all attention to him. "What you are going to learn today must be kept between the occupants of this room at all times."

He waited until every person had nodded.

"Also, by having this knowledge, you are putting yourself in danger. No one will think less of you if you decide to walk away right now."

Again, everyone gave an affirmative.

"Angel?"

The young woman glanced around after sighing deeply. She stood directly in front of them, which put her next to Alex.

His friend moved away, looking uncomfortable. Chase would have to dig into his friend's reaction later.

"For longer than we really know, there has been a group of people who were in charge of protecting those who were not human. This organization was started in secret and has always worked that way. Even when the shifters decided to go public, this group has remained dedicated to its mission," Angel explained.

"You're a part of them?" Chase asked.

"Yes. You can call it tradition. As the eldest child, I was raised knowing what my duty would be."

"What does this have to do with us?" Kayla questioned.

"A lot, actually," Angel replied. "Most agents don't retire. The ones who do have to live carefully so that they are never discovered."

"My dad?"

"Yes. After your grandparents died, he was given permission to leave and take care of you. He moved up here to live quietly and out of sight."

"When Marcus requested to join our Pack, I was advised of the whole story. I was also sworn to secrecy," Shawn informed them.

Chase wasn't surprised but he didn't like that his Alpha had being hiding this information. "And if something had happened to you?"

"Marcus would have shared with my successor, who would have to agree to the same as I did," Shawn replied, staring Chase down.

Sitting back in the chair, he nodded to his boss. There wasn't much Chase could do about the past. He'd just have to accept that even as Beta, he didn't know everything about his Pack.

"So why are they coming after Marcus now?" Max asked.

"And who are *they*?" Kayla added.

"Just like we've always fought to protect, there have been those who have known about the non-humans and are hell-bent on destroying us. We call them the Hunters. And we've been battling them a long time," Angel told them.

"This group that you're part of," Alex spoke for the first time. "What do you call yourselves?"

Angel turned to him and smiled. "We're the Guardians, of course."

Alex shook his head and muttered something under his breath. Chase couldn't make out what he'd said but by the rise of Angel's eyebrows, she'd obviously heard Alex.

"And these Hunters are after my dad?" Kayla asked quietly.

"So it seems. That's why I think you and Randy were followed the other night. That was right before the attack on your dad. If they'd gotten you then they would have used you to bring your father out in the open."

Now that they had the connection to Marcus and Kayla's attack, they could start planning a resolution.

Of course, that sounded a lot simpler than it really was. But there had to be a way to end this quietly and without disturbing the Pack. "What does this all mean for the Pack?" he asked, looking at his Alpha. It was his job to make sure none of what was happening affected their families.

"That's the long-term problem," Angel answered.

From the corner of his eye, he saw Max stiffen.

"What do you mean?" his brother asked with a growl.

"The Hunters know where Marcus is. Even though you all haven't made your status public, there is a good chance they know you're shifters. Their entire purpose is to eliminate your kind."

"They'll come after the Pack?" Chase pressed. He wanted her to say the words.

"Yes, I believe so."

The loud rumble that came from Max was full of anger. His brother jumped to his feet and started to pace. Cassie looked scared, with her knees pulled up to her chest.

Staying hidden was all the Pack had going for them. Their numbers weren't large and they didn't have enough guards for everyone. Running his hand roughly over his face, Chase knew he had to think of something, some way to defend the people he loved.

"Does the Council know about you and the Hunters?" he questioned. If Kurt and Clint had prior knowledge, maybe he could call them back.

"They are aware of our existence, although they do not work closely with us. They prefer to handle their own affairs," Angela said.

That was interesting, Chase mused. The Wolf Council was all about insuring the survival of the wolf shifters. They even collaborated with the Shifter Coalition.

"Not all of our organization is made up of shifters." She waved a hand at herself.

Since Chase was certain there was something off about Angel and her brother, her statement opened the door for him. "You are not one hundred percent human," he guessed. "Just what exactly are you?"

Angel faced him. The change in her demeanor was immediate and obvious. The fierceness in her gaze might have worried him if Max and Alex hadn't stepped closer to him. "I don't believe that is any of your business."

"You are staying in my home. I think we have a right to know," Alex argued.

Possibilities ran through his head but he couldn't settle on how Angel and her brother were different. Every shifter, wolf or other species had a unique scent to them. Chase might not always know from the aroma what animal they were but the shifter connection was always there.

Angel and Justin had no scents. He had never come across that ability before in his entire life. Humans picked up traces of their environment giving each a unique odor. So he was just as eager for answers.

"Why won't you just tell us?" Alex argued with Angel.

"Maybe I don't think you need to know, big guy," she taunted back.

Justin jumped up from his seat as Alex advanced on Angel. "Hey! Come on guys. We have bigger problems than this. We're on your side."

"How do we know we can trust them?" Alex asked Chase.

"Marcus does," Chase answered his friend. "That's good enough for me."

Besides, there might be a reasonable explanation. If Angel and her family were deep into the Guardian organization, maybe blocking their scent helped. Since the group has already proven to be secretive, Angel wouldn't be able to share that information.

"Justin's right," he said to the group. "We need to find these Hunters and concentrate on the Pack's safety."

Shawn had risen to stand close to Angel. "We need a plan."

As they settled down again, Chase noticed Angel eyeing Alex. Since Chase was surprised by Alex's aggressiveness toward the woman, he wondered briefly, what Angel thought about Alex.

"Here's how we'll start," Shawn stated, leaning forward in his chair.

Chapter Six

Chase strolled across the guest bedroom to the balcony doors. Pushing them open, he gazed out onto the expansive property.

The Wilson ranch was a second home to him. He'd ended up in this same bed many times over the years, too drunk or too tired to make the short drive to his own place.

After Max returned to Canyon, Chase had enjoyed having a reason to go home at night. With Max and Cassie's recent mating, though, he was once again alone.

Cassie's residence was the guesthouse only a few feet from where Chase now stood. From his bedroom, he could see the front door of Cassie and Max's place.

Knowing his brother was safe and close by made Chase feel a little better. Still, the danger the Pack was currently in made it difficult for him to sleep.

First part of the plan was to find the Hunter responsible for shooting Marcus. After that, they would have to work with Angel's people to see how much the group knew about the Pack.

He'd dismissed the idea of calling Kurt or Clint. The two Council members would no doubt be willing to help but by adding additional shifters into the mix, they would be giving the Hunters new targets too.

Information was power and Chase felt lacking in Intel. Angel had only been willing to say a little about the organization she worked for. As soon as Marcus was released from the hospital and rejoined them, Chase planned to get every detail from his old friend.

The Pack deserved honesty. Angel might not be family, but Marcus was. Chase was going to get answers.

But what was driving him crazy was that he couldn't do anything right now.

The Hunters could be setting traps in his town as he stood on the second-story balcony in the moonlight.

Restless, he paced the small area when he heard his bedroom door open.

Expecting Alex, it shocked him to see Kayla step into the room instead and close the door behind her.

Curious, he stayed in the shadows and watched while she took in the open space. The sway of her hips had his cock hardening as she headed in his direction.

Leaning against the rail, he crossed his arms over his chest when she strolled onto the terrace to him.

"I saw the light on," she explained, continuing toward him until she was almost touching him. "I figured you were too wound up to sleep too."

He had to swallow hard to keep himself under control. Having Kayla within arm's reach had a major effect on his body and on his wolf.

Inside, his wolf clawed to get out to the female. Rarely did Chase feel such an attraction so early after meeting someone. Oh, who was he kidding? He'd never experienced as strong of a pull as the one he did for Kayla right now.

"What's wrong? Cat got your tongue?" she teased.

Realizing she'd spoken to him several times and he hadn't responded, Chase shook his head. He needed to call on all his restraint to keep from backing away, since Kayla was now brushing up against him.

"Can I help you with something?" *Thank God my voice didn't shake.*

She chuckled softly. "Now that's a loaded question."

With more calmness than he felt, he raised an eyebrow in question, waiting for her to clarify her remark.

"I know you feel this spark between us."

He could lie, deny her claim, but what was the point? "Yes."

"I also think that you won't make the first move."

"And you will?" he taunted. Even knowing he was playing with fire, he couldn't help himself.

"I don't believe in wasting time," she answered.

With his heart pounding furiously and palms sweating, Chase went over his options. He could demand she leave or he could embrace the attraction between them. Uncrossing his arms, he placed his hands on her elbows and pulled her close. "What if I don't like a woman to make the first move?" he whispered, his lips just inches from hers.

"Then you don't know what you're missing."

A woman who knew what she wanted and wasn't afraid of going after it, actually did turn Chase on. With a low growl, he spun her around, backing her to the rail.

While Kayla's breathing grew more rapid, Chase slid his hands up her arms to her neck. With one palm behind her head, he used his fingers of the other to grip her chin.

"What is it you want from me, Kayla?"

"You already know." She shivered.

Yes, he did. Lowering his head slowly, he gave her the chance to change her mind. Once he laid claim to her mouth, he wasn't stopping unless she told him no more.

He didn't think she would deny him, since she's been the one to approach him.

Instead, Kayla grinned as she closed the distance.

The first brush of her tongue against his had Chase tightening his hold as a shudder ran down his spine.

Kayla intoxicated him. The combination of her scent and taste plus the way her body rubbed against his, made his head spin. He couldn't seem to pull his mouth away from Kayla's, even though he wanted to move them along.

Luckily, Kayla took pity on him by reaching down to rub his erection. Chase bucked into her touch, plundering her mouth with his.

The sensations were enough to have him almost coming in his jeans.

Instead, he tore his lips away from hers so he could gulp in long, ragged breaths.

"I knew we would be hot together," she said with a sexy rumble. As she spoke, she pushed down harder on his cock.

He gasped, grabbing her wrist.

So far, she had him hanging on the edge. *Time to turn the tides.* Grinning down at her, he released her arm to grip her hips and lifted her off her feet.

She squeaked as she clutched at his shoulders. Laughing, he strolled back into the bedroom, not bothering to close the balcony doors, before tossing her on the bed.

Bouncing, Kayla smiled as she settled on her back. Chase towered over the bed, peering down at her. He kept his gaze on hers as he lifted the hem of his T-shirt. He peeled the fabric slowly over his head then dropped the garment on the floor.

Her eyes widened and started glowing as her arousal spiked. Her reaction pleased Chase.

Keeping his movements unhurried, he started on his belt.

Kayla scrambled to her knees, placing a hand over his. "Let me."

Chase had no argument to that.

He allowed her to help him peel the rest of his clothes off then gently pushed her back down on the mattress. He took his time undressing her. Every new piece of soft skin that he placed a wet kiss on, every new piece of soft skin he revealed thrilled and excited him further.

Kayla panted with need by the time he was done. Chase knew he had her right where he wanted.

"You're killing me," she murmured, when he finally covered her body with his.

"Just warming you up," he whispered. Lavishing one pert nipple with only the tip of his tongue had her squirming.

She arched, dragging her nails down his back. "I'm warm! I'm warm!"

Chase was a firm believer that the best part of sex was the journey to penetration. He could spend hours worshiping a woman before he buried himself inside her.

But he was too strung out and his need clawed at him. Later, he would take his time, make Kayla beg and plead. Right then he needed to feel her wrapped around him tightly.

Bringing his lips back to her mouth, he kissed her deeply as he used his fingers to make sure she was ready to receive him. Sliding his digits between her wet folds, he found the opening of her sweet pussy and thrust inside.

"Yes," she hissed in pleasure.

Finding her ready, Chase withdrew his fingers so he could grasp the base of his cock. Positioning at her opening, he pushed inside, loving the feel of her inner muscles clamping down on him.

With her back bowed, breasts swaying with each of his leisurely thrusts, he wanted to watch her forever. Chase closed his eyes, losing himself in the intimate act of claiming Kayla.

The electricity that he'd felt at the first touch magnified each time he rocked into her. A light sheen of sweat covered both their bodies as he pushed them further toward the edge.

Leaning back on his knees, he cupped and lifted her hips to plunge deeper and harder.

Kayla's moans rose in cadence as he snapped his own body faster.

"Chase, Chase," she started panting his name.

He growled. The low sound escaping even as he tried to control it. Thrusting quicker, he just barely waited until she screamed, climaxing, before he joined her in his own orgasm.

Collapsing on top of her, he tried to clear his mind and regulate his breathing.

It took a few minutes but finally he could lift his head.

The soft, pleased look in Kayla's eyes pulled at Chase's heartstrings. He bent kissing her softly. "Stay?"

Nodding, she cupped his face. "Yes."

* * * *

Kayla wasn't certain how long it had been since she'd woken up in someone's arms but having Chase spooned from head to toe against her had her smiling.

She'd taken a chance by going to Chase last night but the results pleased her. Although she hadn't expected that they would end up in bed so quickly, she didn't regret it.

Already she'd learned a lot about the Pack Beta. Chase was smart and sexy, making Kayla want to spend all the time she could with him.

After they'd learned what they could from Angel, the entire group had sat together and planned their action.

He'd impressed her when he'd listened and accepted advise and help from her, Justin and Randy. At no time had he dismissed their opinions. She respected Chase a hell of a lot for that.

The attraction she'd felt immediately upon seeing him again had only bloomed further during that meeting.

Then she'd seen him out on the terrace with the moon at his back and had known she would have to nudge him. Secure in the knowledge that he felt the same strong pull toward her by the way he watched her approach, she couldn't resist him—didn't want to resist him.

If she hadn't made the first move, there was no telling when Chase would have. Kayla hadn't lied when she'd said she didn't like to waste time.

But the truth of the matter was that she felt something new and exciting for him. She wanted to get to know him better and privately. And wow, she sure had.

Having her share of lovers in the past, Kayla was far from a virgin. Nevertheless, she had never been with anyone who had dominated and demanded the reactions Chase had.

Chase had laid claim to a part of her no one had ever been able to touch. Instead of just giving him her body, Kayla had found she wanted to surrender her mind and soul too.

The new experience had her feeling a little off balance, though. So much was happening around her that she hadn't known about. A group of guardians protecting her for years without her knowledge with her father in their core was difficult to wrap her mind around.

She couldn't help the small hurt that flared whenever she thought about her dad keeping the truth from her. Oh sure, he had never outright lied to her, but he'd been keeping some pretty big secrets.

Not wanting to wake Chase, she slowly started to slide out from under him. Hating to leave the heat of his body, she needed to prepare for the day.

He tightened his arm as she felt his lips brush over her neck. "Where are you going?"

The sleepy, gravely sound of his voice washed over her, affecting her in a uniquely sexual way. "To shower," she responded quietly.

"Hmm," he murmured, caressing her shoulder with his fingers. The stubble from his beard scratched gently, causing a shudder to wrack her body.

Damn, how could one man make her need so much?

"You...wet...in a shower," he said slowly. "I like that idea."

Kayla gripped his thigh, pulling it more firmly against her. The change had Chase's early morning erection grazing against her rear.

"Yeah," she said, although she had completely forgotten what they were talking about. Pushing back into his body, she enjoyed his cock teasing her entrance.

Chase chuckled low right at her ear. She jumped when he caught her flesh between his teeth. "Shower."

Kayla squeaked before realizing that Chase had easily rolled back with her still in her hold and stood. As he started to carry her to the other side of the room, she laughed.

"I can walk," she argued, even as she wrapped her arms and legs around him.

"I'm not so sure about that," he teased. "You were getting distracted."

"True, but that was your fault."

They'd reached the bathroom and he set her down.

Grinning widely. "Uh huh," Chase agreed.

She went to smack him but he quickly avoided her hand. Instead, he twisted the knobs to adjust the shower. After testing the temperature, he motioned her closer.

The pure wicked expression on his face gave her an idea of the fun they were going to have. She could work with that. Running her fingers over her stomach, Kayla made sure she brushed seductively against him as she entered the tiled enclosure.

The sharp intake of breath from him delighted her.

"Little minx," he said then followed her inside.

He closed the door, the steam and hot water surrounding them. Sighing deeply, she let her head fall back as the cascade of water flowed over her. She hadn't felt the small aches until now.

"Feel good?" Chase asked her softly.

"Oh, yeah."

"How about this?" He gripped her shoulders and started rubbing.

That...that feels wonderful. His hands were slick as he massaged. Kayla didn't ever want to move again. Chase had very talented fingers.

Kayla closed her eyes, letting Chase have his way as he caressed her back.

Turning when he urged her to, Kayla blinked her eyes open, peering up at Chase. The edges of his lips lifted in a small smile as he concentrated on her front.

Having never been pampered like this, she wasn't sure how to show her appreciation. Going on instinct, she lifted to tiptoes to place her lips over his.

Chase stopped all other movement as their mouths connected.

He swallowed her moan. Kayla gripped his hips, bumping their bodies together.

Pulling away, Chase breathed hard as he looked at her.

She tightened her hold on him, letting him know she wanted more.

Flashing her a brilliant white smile, he quickly pushed her back against the wall.

He didn't torment her by making her wait. As soon as she stood braced against the tile, he entered her, thrusting inside deeply.

She cried out in pleasure, trying to hold onto his shoulders. Her hands slipped off so she wrapped her arms more securely around his neck.

Chase pulled out before plunging back inside, not giving Kayla time to catch her breath. Unlike the previous night, when he'd taken his time, this morning Chase needed to claim and own her body.

She was almost there. *Just needed a little extra. Faster...*

Snapping his hips, Chase drove into her over and over, spearing her with his cock, taking her higher. With his mouth on her neck, lips lingering as he clamped his teeth down on her flesh, it finally pushed her to where she needed to be.

She screamed, lost in her orgasm, uncaring if someone heard them. Her vision blurred and she went limp.

Two more thrusts and Chase joined in falling over the edge of completion.

It took several minutes for her to shake her head and gain control of her mind.

The water had begun to cool while Chase had pressed her to the wall, his weight heavy against her as he stood with his head bowed.

Kissing the side of his neck gained his attention, though. He stepped back, carefully lowering her legs, but kept a hand around her waist.

Their gazes locked.

He smiled sheepishly. "Are you okay?"

Nodding, she had to laugh. "More than okay. That was...incredible."

Relief flashed over his features, concerning her. She palmed the side of his face then kissed his softly. "Wonderful," she murmured.

"I don't usually lose control like that. Are you sure I didn't hurt you?"

Rolling her shoulders, she could tell she would have a few more aches due to their lovemaking however, she welcomed this sort of discomfort. "I'm positive."

"Let's rinse off and get out before the water turns frigid," he suggested.

As they washed off the sweat, soap and cum, Kayla could not stop smiling. She was proud that she'd made the normally careful Beta lose some of his restraint.

After she shut the water off, Kayla dried herself with a soft towel, keeping her attention on Chase. He kept running his gaze over her as well.

When he started to get hard again, she ran her fingers over his cock.

He hissed and thrust against her.

The loud pounding on the bathroom door startled them apart.

"Shit," he cursed, as he wrapped the towel around his waist.

Kayla covered up as well. Chase flung the door open with a growl.

"Sorry to interrupt but you don't have time to go at it again," Alex told them from the doorway.

Chase blocked Alex's view of her. Regardless, she flushed, knowing her face would be bright red. If Alex had been in the bedroom while their *shower* had been taking place, there was no way he hadn't heard them.

"What's going on?" Chase asked, not responding to Alex's earlier comment.

"Jacob found something. We need to go look," Alex informed him.

Chase stiffened his shoulders. "Give us ten minutes."

"Sure."

Chapter Seven

Chase kneeled, examining the tracks from the canyon that led up to the edge of the Wilson ranch. "The guards didn't see anyone?" he asked Jacob.

"No, we had two stationed close by and they never caught the scent of anyone."

The way Jacob worded his reply had Chase's stomach knotting. Chase stood slowly, his gaze finding Angel in the small group that had assembled.

Angel and her brother were the only two people that Chase had not been able to smell. They had no scent whatsoever. If their target had the same ability, there had to be a connection.

Since neither Salvatore would give them more information about why they were unique, he was suspicious of what they were really getting into.

Stepping away from the footprints, Chase tilted his head toward his brother. They met a little distance away from the others. With the superior hearing of the others, Chase still couldn't say what he wanted but he needed Max to know his concerns.

"I know," Max said as he pressed his shoulder against Chase's.

Nodding his understanding, Chase would have to leave the investigation into the Salvatore's background to his brother. "What do you think about this?"

"Strange, they left no tracks at Marcus' house. Pretty sloppy to do so now."

"It's a trap," Chase agreed.

"I think so. Alpha Shawn had already left to pick up Marcus. We can wait for him."

He shook his head. "I think I should take a small group and see what we can discover. We don't have to confront them but if we can get a better idea where they are, we'll be able to plan better."

"And if they are waiting for you?"

Chase eyed his brother. "We can take them."

"You sound sure of that. We don't even know who or what they are."

"Only one way to find out," he replied seriously.

"Why am I being the voice of reason?" Max asked grumpily. "Usually it's you who tries to talk me out of dangerous situations."

Since his brother had a point, Chase really had to think about his answer. Waiting for the Alpha made the most sense, however, since they didn't know when Shawn would return, that could put off the search for hours.

He wasn't willing to wait that long. He had been shot at, his friend injured and Kayla stalked. He wanted to know the hell was going on and he wanted to know now.

"We should go or they'll get too far away," he told Max.

Waiting for several tense minutes, relief flooded him when Max nodded. "You take a group of shifters. I'll go with Angel and follow behind. We'll leave Alex, Cassie and Justin here to wait for Shawn and Marcus."

"Okay, the tracks seem to follow Goldman's trail. We'll spread out from there if you two stay on it," Chase suggested.

"Keep your ears open," Max warned.

He slapped his brother on the back before rejoining the others.

"Are we doing this?" Jacob questioned when he reached them.

"Yeah."

The younger Wilson grinned. "It's been a while since I've hunted."

Shaking his head, he tried to hide the amusement at the younger man. Jacob was one of the best trackers the Pack had. His job at the Canyon as a park ranger also gave them an advantage. "Let's shift and do this."

They broke off into smaller sets. Chase stayed close to Kayla as she pulled her shirt over her head.

"Stay close to me," he whispered. "If they get their hands on you, they win."

Her eyes widened and she glanced around nervously.

"You don't have to come."

"Yes, I do," she corrected. "I *need* to."

"Okay."

Since it was normal for Pack members to run together as a unit, most shifters didn't have a problem with nudity. But Chase found himself wanting to shield Kayla's body from the others' view. He knew it was ridiculous but he couldn't help it.

His wolf wasn't interested in logic and, when it came to Kayla, his wolf made its presence known.

Chase had always seen the animal inside him as a separate but full part of him. Sort of like the other half. When he was in his other form, he felt complete.

It bothered him that his brother would never know the feeling.

Max had lived his entire life without the ability to transform. Although Max could still feel his animal, not being able to shift was hard to deal with.

Chase had spent the last ten years trying to find out why Max was different. When the Alpha in West Texas mated with a woman who was also a non-shifter he thought he had a good opportunity to get answers.

So far, the Texas Pack was able to change the old feelings that non-shifters weren't as important to the Pack. Sadly, Chase hadn't been able to put together all the pieces yet.

He was still working on answers, though.

Glancing over at his brother, he saw Max kissing his mate, Cassie, deeply. Chase grinned as he dropped to his knees. Kayla fell in front of him.

He nodded silently, telling her to go ahead.

Kayla's shifted quick and flawless. Waiting until she had changed into a beautiful tan-coated wolf, Chase was glad he'd gotten to watch. To be able to see her with his human vision, he could appreciate her that much more.

He wanted to run his hands over her soft fur and make her rumble in pleasure. Since he didn't have time for that now, he already planned on how he would get her in wolf form again.

Not wanting to be aroused in his other form, he took several calming breaths before he started to transform.

Changing into his wolf was a quick process. A tingle started in his body as he pictured the animal coming forward. He closed his eyes and just let the power that rose within him surround him.

Finished, he panted, standing on all four furry paws.

His vision altered too. A sharpness he didn't have before now helped him see further into the Canyon.

Stretching his neck out, he shook himself hard, Chase let himself feel as one with his wolf before nudging Kayla and starting off down the trail.

He took the west side, leaving Jacob and Randy the right. As they trooped off the path, he heard Max behind him. The wolves would be able to cover more ground while his brother and Angel actually followed the tracks left on the path.

If whoever they were after were trying to set a trap, it would look like Max and Angel were there for the taking. Chase would insure their safety, though.

Lifting his head, he tried to scent around him but could only pick up the smells that were common to the area. There were no unknown or troubling aromas to point him in another direction. While he wasn't surprised, it frustrated him.

Kayla stayed at his flank the entire time they traveled. To his left, he couldn't see or hear Jacob or Randy but that was to be expected. Just knowing they were there was enough to push him on.

Not having any sense of time, Kayla found it difficult to calculate just how long their journey was taking.

It had to have been hours later, leaving her only a little tired. The adrenaline that had spiked when she'd set out on the mission had bled out but she was still determined to find something.

The most aggravating part of the search was not being able to pick up the scent of anyone else.

Someone had been at the ranch watching them. They knew that much. While the evidence pointed to the group of Hunters, she still didn't understand how they could have gotten away.

Her mind whirled with thoughts that the missing clue linked to Justin and Angel's own absent trace.

She should have pushed Justin for answers long before now.

Movement to her right had her pausing in mid-step. She wasn't surprised when Chase stopped with her. They'd had been in perfect sync the entire time.

Crouching, she strained to see what had caught her eye. Chase crawled up to her as she caught another shift in the shadows.

Chase growled low, making the hair on her back stand up.

He saw it too.

Taking her gaze from the area for the first time, she looked over at Chase. He lay on his stomach with his tongue hanging out. The fur around her muzzle wrinkled as he snarled.

The sound was so soft that she was certain no one but she would hear it. When Chase turned his head and their gazes met, she could see his intent to move ahead.

She couldn't let that happen. She was aware that Chase didn't have nearly the same battle experience as his brother or the other members of the Pack.

Whining quietly, she brushed against him.

The hardness in his eyes eased as he blinked. Reassured that he wasn't going to go off half-cocked, she went back to staring to the right.

If the others didn't hear them continuing their trek soon, they would double back to her and Chase.

She wasn't sure how long it would take.

Wiggling to get more comfortable, Kayla kept her eyes steady as she waited for something to happen.

A man stepped away from a tree where Kayla had first sensed him. He didn't appear to be anything special. Maybe five foot ten or so, long black hair pulled back into a braid that hung down his back.

Although thin and pale, he'd obviously not been camping out long.

Wearing a black shirt, black pants, and black utility boots, there was no doubt he planned to stay hidden during the day. While his outfit worked for the night stakeout, he would have stood out under the bright Texas sun.

She wasn't surprised when he squeezed his way back into one of the caves.

They now knew where he was. If Jacob, Randy, Max and Angel caught up to them, maybe they could take the man. As deep in the canyon as they'd gone, no one else should be around. Only anyone with questionable intentions would travel into the secluded and off-limits areas.

Not dressing as a hiker had him standing out even more. If he'd tried to blend in. she would have wondered if this was the man they were searching for.

Although her instincts screamed he was the one. Soon, though, they would know for sure.

The questions and the danger could be over soon.

God, she wanted to attack, trapping the man who had shot her father and get her revenge. Keep Chase and his family from being hurt. Protect the Pack.

Chase repositioned next to her, drawing her thoughts away from where they were headed. She huffed, glad that he had been able to pull her from doing something stupid.

Unknowingly, she had begun to crouch, so she could launch herself toward the threat. A very faint sound reached her and she tensed. Beside her, Chase started forward. Two wolves headed in their direction.

Staying close to her partner, she followed Chase past Jacob and Randy until they were out of view from the cave.

Kayla stayed in her wolf form as Chase started to shift. Randy padded over to her. As always, it made her happy that she had her good friend.

It seemed like so long ago that they'd had dinner, teasing one another about when they'd finally find someone to call their own.

In truth, it had only been a couple of days — not even a full weekend. *How is it possible that so much has changed in mere hours?* She'd gone from not having a care in the world to being a target for a kidnapping, or worse.

Jacob had also changed back to a human to talk with Chase.

"Max and Angel are about twenty minutes down the trail," Jacob informed them.

"We have his location," Chase shared.

Jacob's mouth dropped open. "Fuck, yeah."

"He's hiding in one of the caves. I'll need you to take a look and see if you know if there is another way out."

"I know every cave in this area."

"Good, Kayla can show you. We'll wait here for Max. We don't have time to go back to the ranch. I think we need to take him now."

"Is he alone?"

"We have no way of knowing," Chase replied, shaking his head.

Jacob turned to her. "Ready?"

Kayla made sure to rub against Chase as she passed. He chuckled lightly as his fingers trailed over her back.

She felt the touch throughout her entire body.

Having to walk away from him wasn't easy. Not that she didn't trust Jacob. She just didn't like leaving Chase without her there to protect him. Even knowing that he would be only yards away and safe with Randy didn't seem to matter. She had to force herself forward.

"He'll be okay," Jacob said softly.

She jerked her head up.

"I'm good at reading people. You don't want to leave him. But Chase can take care of himself. Plus he has Randy, and Max will be here soon."

Since she couldn't reply, she led him away.

The closer they got to the area where they'd spotted the target, the more she slowed down, insuring she made no noise.

Jacob remained behind her, his footsteps silent, breathing barely audible. He made a terrific tracker. She could see why the Pack depended on him so much.

In position, she hunkered low to give Jacob plenty of time to study the area and the cave.

The hot sun beat down on her thick fur. A large boulder that reflected the heat right back at her also hid them. Trying to control her panting, she really couldn't wait for all of this to be over.

They stayed, keeping an eye at the entrance for at least fifteen minutes before Jacob patted her shoulder and they made their way back to the others.

Navigating back down took time but it was important that they didn't make too much noise, unsure if the target had the same superior hearing as the shifters.

Meeting with the rest of the group, Kayla noted right away that they'd moved into a heavily shadowed area. Randy had transformed and both he and Chase were dressed.

Luckily, Max and Angel had carried extra clothing and supplies for all the shifters.

Max pulled water bottles and granola bars out of a backpack.

Thirstier than she could ever remember being, she started her own change to become human.

Back on two feet, she glanced up at Chase, who had moved to her side. He handed her clothes, which she pulled on quickly, then accepted some water.

The refreshing liquid soothed her throat. She finished half the bottle quickly.

Chase remained close to her. She ran her gaze over him, taking in his strong shoulders and serious face.

He spoke quietly to Max as they discussed the merit of going after the guy.

Since both men sounded like they wanted to move forward instead of returning to the ranch, she was relieved. It would take hours to get reinforcements.

Something could happen, even leaving a few of them there to keep watch.

"Everyone agree with making our move now?" Max questioned.

After an affirmative given by each of them, Max nodded.

"Here's what we'll do," he said.

Chapter Eight

It was late afternoon by the time the plan was decided and they broke up into groups of two once again.

Max and Angel took the high ground, Jacob and Randy took the east, while Chase and Kayla would be the bait coming in from the west.

Everyone had agreed that entering the cave would be too risky. While there was no other exit, the interior was large. There were too much of a chance that anyone already in the cave could hide and orchestrate their own attack.

Hopefully Chase and Kayla's noise would draw out whoever was inside.

They waited for the others to take position, giving them about twenty minutes. After transforming back into their wolves, Chase ran his muzzle across Kayla's.

He knew he was putting her at risk by involving her in drawing out their target but she'd wanted to help. Giving her a quick lick then nipping her snout, he told her he was ready.

She took off at a full sprint. He chased her.

They broke out of hiding, racing into the area right in front of the cave. Making sure they were loud and that it looked like two wolves just playing around, they made as much commotion as possible.

It worked.

Just as Chase leaped over Kayla, their suspect peered out at them.

Perfect.

Kayla rose and tackled him so they rolled closer to the cave entrance — and their target.

After playing right in front of him for about five minutes, the man finally stepped outside.

Chase knocked Kayla down and snarled as the stranger lifted a handgun. Instead of shooting, the man stepped forward.

Chase howled, letting the others know to make the move.

Lifting the weapon, the man laughed evilly. "You picked the wrong place to play."

Since he wasn't certain whether the guy was just talking or if he knew Chase was a shifter, Chase just snapped at him again.

"All you fucking shifters think you're so smart. Maybe I'll cut off your head and send it to your fucking Alpha."

Okay, so the stranger knows I'm a shifter.

"How about we cut yours off instead?" Max said from above the guy.

The stranger jerked back, but it was too late. Max leaped down, knocking the guy to the ground and the gun from his hand. The weapon flew several feet to land at the trunk of a weathered tree.

Chase moved in to help with the killer.

Instead, the man jumped to his feet and leaped away.

Never had Chase seen anyone, shifter or not, move like that. Chase and Max sprang at him again but for the second time, the man moved too quickly for them to get to him.

Jacob bounded full speed into them but also missed the stranger.

They weren't even coming close to the man.

"Emilio?" Angel yelled, coming out from behind a tree.

"You know this guy?" Max demanded.

Everyone had stopped, giving the man time to dive back for his gun. Chase growled and lunged for the weapon also.

"What the hell?" Max yelled, going back after their opponent.

"I don't know," Angel confessed.

Chase managed to kick the firearm away with his back paw, receiving a vicious punch in his side for his trouble. The blow knocked the breath out of him. He'd never been hit so hard.

Max growled before kicking out just catching the guy's shoulder.

Angel leaped into the fray, finally getting the first direct hit on their enemy. He grunted, attacking in return.

The entire group surrounded Angel and her adversary but none of the shifters moved in.

Unbelievably, Angel moved just as fast as the stranger. In almost a blur, the two exchanged blow after blow.

Chase started barking and lunging for the man. Soon the others circled around and copied his moves. Their actions brought the enemy closer to Angel so she could spin and land a devastating kick to her opponent's head.

He crumpled, landing hard on the canyon ground.

Exhausted and in pain, Chase had to take a minute to catch his breath. Max moved quickly around him, grabbing a hold of the guy's arms and yanking them behind him back while rolling him onto his stomach.

"I need the rope out of the backpack," Max called.

Since everyone but Angel was still in wolf form Chase looked over at her.

She stood staring down at the stranger with a look of shock on her face. "I don't understand."

"Angel! Get me the rope," Max yelled again.

As she hurried to comply, Chase flopped down. Kayla brushed against his side. He nuzzled her neck, letting her know he was okay.

She butted her head back at him then started to transform.

Jacob and Randy began their change also.

"What the hell happened?" Jacob shouted once he was human again. "How did he move so fast?"

Max narrowed his eyes at Angel. "I would like to know that too. But first, you know him." It wasn't a question.

"Yes," she whispered.

"Who is he?" Kayla demanded on her knees beside Chase.

She lifted Chase's head, placing it in her lap then he closed his eyes to get control of the pain so he could shift. Keeping his ears open, he could still hear the conversation around him.

"He's...he's one of us?"

"What do you mean?" Jacob asked.

Chase didn't jump when Jacob placed a hand on his side but he did whimper at the pressure.

"He's part of our organization," Angel explained.

Kayla stopped petting him as Jacob stopped moving his hand against Chase's ribs.

"What?" Max asked, his shock evident.

"He's part of the Guardians. I've worked with him." Angel sounded upset.

The man groaned, obviously waking up. Chase opened his eyes. With the moves the stranger had shown earlier, Chase didn't want to leave his loved ones unprotected.

With great effort, he hauled himself off Kayla and stalked toward his prey.

The guy kept his gaze on him as Chase crept forward. "Filthy animals."

Growling, Chase crouched low.

"Emilio!" Angel stepped next to Chase. "What is the meaning of this?"

He laughed. "I guess I should have expected you to show up. You always did have a soft spot for these creatures."

"You're supposed to protect them," Angel argued. "You've worked your entire life to defend others and now you turn on them?"

Emilio struggled to roll over. Chase snapped at him, only to get a glare from the man

Max yanked the guy up to face them.

He tried to pull away from Max but the ropes were too tight.

"Emilio! Why?" Angel practically shouted at him.

He snorted. "In case you haven't noticed, darling, these animals that you are so fond of are going to get us all killed. Going public? That is the most absurd thing I've ever heard. They deserve to die, but we don't."

"So we just turn on one another?"

Chase jerked his head to the side, surprised by Marcus' presence.

Kayla stood as her father passed by. Chase let his Alpha take his place in front of their prisoner as Shawn and Marcus joined them.

The stranger stiffened at the sight of the two newcomers.

"Last time I saw you, Emilio, I was dragging your ass out of a four-on-one firefight," Marcus kneeled in front of Emilio.

"Last time I saw you, was through my rifle sight," Emilio responded.

Chase wanted to rip Emilio's throat out. It shocked him when Marcus laughed loudly.

"I should have known you were the sniper when I didn't die. You were always more of a planner and had trouble with the follow-through."

"Untie me and I'll follow through," Emilio threatened.

"You come onto my land and try to take out one of my people?" Shawn thundered.

The Alpha's voice boomed around the canyon.

Emilio couldn't hide his shudder of fear. Pride filled Chase as his Alpha's power traveled over them like a physical force. Knowing that the situation was under control, he stepped behind Kayla to shift. Once he'd gained to his feet, she held out his clothes.

"Are you working with the Hunters?" Angel questioned Emilio.

"Yeah, right. Like I'd ever get into league with those monsters. I'm part of a new organization—one that doesn't want to share-watch with an animal. And I'm not the only one of us who has defected. We've grown tired of protecting these *things*."

"I need to call my boss," Angel said to Shawn.

Their Alpha nodded while keeping his eyes on Emilio. "Why Marcus?"

"Are you kidding? How better to announce our purpose than to take a stab at the shifters and Guardians at the same time?"

Shawn growled but didn't attack Emilio. Instead, he grabbed a hold of the man and yanked him up and over his shoulder. "Let's head back."

Chase waited until the others passed by before grasping Kayla's hand in his. "You okay?" he asked her quietly.

"He's crazy," she whispered back. "Just look in his eyes."

"I know," he agreed.

"Are you okay?" She faced him.

"I'll be sore but I'll heal soon enough."

"When I saw him punch you and you went down, I was so scared," she admitted.

"Hey." Cupping her chin, he brought his lips down on hers. "I'm okay. When we get back to the house, I'll even let you help me clean up. A shower would feel wonderful."

She laughed just as he'd intended.

"You've got a deal."

* * * *

The hot water sluiced down her shoulders as Kayla ran the soap over Chase's back. He'd already washed the dirt and grime from her body.

The bruises on his ribs were already starting to fade, which had her feeling much better.

She gripped his shoulders, turning him to face her, then dropped on her knees, his cock already hard and ready for the taking.

She gently grasped his erection, placing a small kiss on the tip.

He groaned as he slapped his hands out onto tiles beside him.

Kayla lapped more at the salty pre-cum escaping from his cock and slowly wrapped her lips around his shaft.

"Yes," he hissed.

As she pulled back, his unique taste exploded on her tongue and she immediately wanted more. Keeping her teeth tucked, she started to suck him deeper and faster.

The feel of his hands buried in her wet hair encouraged her. Licking, sucking and swallowing, she quickly had Chase begging and pleading with her.

Using her hand to pump his cock as she tongued the slit in the tip, she grinned around his shaft as his knees started shaking.

Sliding both hands around to grip Chase's ass firmly, she encouraged his thrusts.

It only took about half a dozen deep plunges to have him tightening his grip in her hair and coming.

Pulling back enough not to choke, she took what she could until she popped off his cock finishing him up with quick hand pumps.

"Jeez," he panted out, almost collapsing against the wall.

Worried, she climbed to her feet, wrapping her arms around his waist. "Are you okay?"

He shook his head. "I think you just sucked my brain out of my cock."

She stared at him in confusion.

He lifted his gaze and she saw amusement shining in it. Sucked his brain...oh. "Ass!" she smacked his chest. "I thought I'd hurt you."

He chuckled, the smooth sound echoing in the small space. "Let's get out of here and I'll make it up to you."

Pretending to pout, she crossed her arms over her chest. "I don't know if you can."

Shifting enough to twist the knobs and cut off the water, he moved so quickly that she didn't expect him to grab her around the waist and lift her off her feet.

"Chase!"

"Hush, my turn to take care of you," he said as he carried her out of the shower.

As he placed her on the soft rug in the middle of the bathroom, he used a fluffy towel to dry her off. This man knew how to pamper. She'd noticed it before but he went even further by making sure she was warm and comfortable.

He only gave himself a light wipe down. She returned in his arms immediately.

"What is it with you carrying me?" she asked with a laugh.

"I like to have my hands on you," he answered.

She really couldn't argue with that. "Okay."

They reached the bed. "I'm glad you agree," he said as he dropped her onto the mattress.

She bounced and had to grip the sheets. Rolling over, she lifted an eyebrow.

Chase only grinned. He pounced on her but made sure that his knees landed at her sides.

Not having seen this playful side of him, she couldn't stop smiling. Easily, she pushed him back and flipped their positions. Straddling his legs this time, she leaned over him.

"Are you going to ride me, baby?" he questioned huskily.

Now that is one of the best suggestions I've heard in a very long time.

"Maybe," she teased as she lowered her mouth to his collarbone.

Peppering soft kisses on his flesh, she once again savored his wonderfully unique flavor — all musk and man.

She continued down, paying special attention to his pecks, before moving to the trail of hair down his stomach.

Chase tensed when she bypassed his cock and nipped his thigh instead, his cock hardening again. She could see in the way his body responded that his need matched hers. Cupping his sac with her left hand, she carefully grasped his cock with her right. Pumping a few times, making him lift to help, she couldn't wait any longer. In one smooth slide, she positioned herself over his erection then slowly lowered herself on it.

Chase gripped her hips once he'd fully penetrated her. With her hands on his chest, she began riding him, just as he'd wanted.

The seduction in the shower already had her ready and wet for him. It didn't take long before she wildly lifted and slid down, forcing him to take her faster.

She crested the edge, dragging her nails down his chest and leaving red marks.

He yelled out her name, filling her with his warm seed.

Chapter Nine

Chase stretched his legs out, making sure he didn't disturb Kayla too much. For the second morning in a row, he'd woken wrapped around an amazing woman and he hoped there would be many more mornings that he would be able to do so.

With her not living in Canyon, he wasn't sure how they would manage it but he was determined to find a way.

She was a beautiful woman anytime but there was something about her in sleep that made her seem even younger and more innocent. Her tangled brown hair lay fanned out against the white pillowcase. Chase didn't even try to resist the urge to run his fingers through the silky strands.

Kayla smiled with her eyes still closed but he could tell by the increase rate in her breathing that she was awake. Keeping his right hand buried in her hair, he trailed his left down her breasts and lower.

Fingering her damp folds, he started to open her sweet pussy with one then two fingers.

She lifted her hips, riding his hand just as he lowered his mouth to hers. They kissed deeply as he pumped his fingers deeper. Already his cock stood full and he was dying to bury himself inside her.

Once he had her wet and moaning, he pulled his hands away to roll her over onto her stomach.

Chase scooted closer to her and she rose to her hands and knees. The long expanse of her back was right there for his lips to caress. Grabbing the base of his cock, he pushed into her in one thrust.

There would never come a time when he didn't relish that first intimate contact with her. Withdrawing slowly, he didn't pull out completely then pushed back in deeply.

She gasped, moving her hips against him.

He wanted to take his time — to show her how much he craved being with her again — but he couldn't control the pace.

With her begging for more, he found himself complying, snapping his hips and riding her harder.

Her inner muscles clamped tightly around his cock, drawing out each amazing plunge until he came, crying out her name.

Shoving into her one last, powerful time, he then heard her low, long moan and she followed him over the edge.

Holding hands, she let Chase tow her toward the kitchen where he promised there would be coffee.

She needed the caffeine before they tackled what had happened the previous day.

"When Max called this morning, he told me that some of Angel's coworkers would be here a little later to pick up Emilio. They have him locked in one of the rooms with guards on him," Chase explained.

"I need to talk to my dad. I can't believe I never knew about any of this."

"Don't be too hard on him. He was trying to protect you."

Kayla snorted. "Didn't work too well, did it? And don't tell me that you're not just as upset. Both my dad and Alpha Shawn kept this from you too."

"I know, but after meeting Angel and seeing how she is, I kind of understand why they didn't tell me about the Guardians. They seem to like their secrets."

Chuckling, she squeezed his hand. *That's an understatement.*

"We'll work with Angel to insure that it was only Emilio and his small faction who know about us. She's already starting a search for anyone else involved."

"The men that came for me and Randy?" she guessed.

"Yeah, Angel wanted to ask you both some more questions. She should be in the kitchen."

Even though the immediate threat was over, that left her with another problem. Since she lived and worked in Lubbock and Chase's entire life was in Canyon, she wasn't certain about their future."

"Hey," Chase paused in the hall, turning to face her. "We'll figure it out."

"What?"

"Us."

Relief flooded through her that Chase's thoughts were so in line with hers. "Are you sure?"

"I just found you, Kayla. I'm not letting you go without a fight."

"No fight—not from me, anyway."

"Good." He kissed her until she grasped at his shirt ready to drag him back into the bedroom.

"Now let's fuel up so we can go back to bed."

"Good idea."

They started back down the hall when she heard voices coming from behind the closed door.

"What the...?" Chase muttered as he pushed open the entrance.

Taking in the scene in front of her, Kayla wasn't sure what to do. Alex Wilson had Angel pinned up against one of the walls with a hand around her neck.

Angel didn't seem to be in fear or even angry as she grinned back at Alex.

"Alex?" Chase said quietly.

The other man didn't even turn around. "No, I want answers from her and I want them now."

"We'll get them but not this way. Let her go," Chase replied.

When Alex didn't move, Chase sent Kayla a look of concern. Unsure if she should go get help or what to do, Kayla shook her head.

Chase started forward but Angel held up a hand. "Don't worry about it, Chase. If I wanted loose, I could do so myself. I'm quite enjoying this reaction from your friend."

That had Alex responding. He snarled, releasing Angel and stomping away.

Alex stalked to the other side of the kitchen before whirling back on Angel. "You have put my entire family—everyone I care about—in danger. I will not accept that you can't tell me what is going on. I want to know!" He ended his rant by slamming his hand against the marble countertop.

Angel nodded. Straightening her clothes, she stared at Alex.

The bright, intense look in her eyes worried Kayla. She had a feeling they were going to find out more than they expected—maybe more than they really wanted to know.

"Please have a seat." Angel waved her hand at the table.

Frowning, Alex opened his mouth but instead of responding, he strolled to a chair and yanked it out. He dropped to the seat, never looking away from Angel.

"I'll get the coffee," Chase said, as he placed a hand on Kayla's lower back, moving her past Alex.

Nodding, Kayla noted the explosive atmosphere. She didn't want to add to it by saying the wrong thing.

Angel took the seat directly across from Alex, leaving Kayla to scramble around toward the wall. For some reason, she could see the other woman flying across and taking Alex down. Kayla did not want to be in the middle of that battle.

No one spoke as Chase quietly moved around the kitchen until he placed four mugs on the table. He poured coffee from a stainless steel carafe then sat next to Kayla.

"Are you sure you're ready to hear this, Alex? Once I tell you, there is no turning back."

Alex snorted. "You mean you'll actually answer our questions this time?"

"I'll tell you anything *you* want to know."

The emphasis on you had Kayla and Chase exchanging a puzzled glance.

"Fine," Alex said to Angel. "Answer me this... Are you human?"

Talk about going straight for the jugular. Not that Kayla wasn't dying to ask the same question, but she expected Alex to ease into the conversation. Going off how pissed the man was, she shouldn't have been surprised.

Angel's expression didn't change. She still gazed at Alex with an open look. "No."

Alex didn't appear surprised and Kayla wasn't either. She and Justin were going to have a serious talk soon.

"Is that why you and your brother have no scent?"

"It is."

Kayla could see the short answers were starting to irritate Alex. "This organization that you work for...is everything you told us the truth?"

"Yes, the Guardians are a good group. We've always thrived in protecting others. That is our sole purpose."

"If it's such good work that you do, why the secrecy?"

"Unlike the Wolf Council or other shifter leaders, our agency does not discriminate against other paranormal types. Anyone who has the same beliefs is welcome to join."

"Beliefs?"

Angel's smiled grew. "The idea that no matter what—or who—you are, we are all equal. Everyone, including humans, should have someone looking out for them."

"What are you?"

Angel shook her head.

"You said you would answer!" Alex raised his voice.

"You're not ready!" Angel fired back.

"Damn it, tell me," Alex shouted, jumping to his feet.

"Alex," Chase called to his friend.

Alex turned on him. "No, there is something going on. I know she is doing something to me."

Kayla couldn't control her gasp of surprise. No one seemed to notice it, though. Chase had frozen beside her.

"I have to understand," Alex said more calmly. "What are you doing to me?"

"I'm sorry," Angel said sincerely as she walked closer to Alex.

Kayla wanted to tell her to back off and be careful, that Alex might hurt her, but Kayla didn't get a chance to say anything when Angel cupped Alex's face.

"Just…please…"

"They call my kind Day Walkers," Angel admitted in a whisper.

"I don't…what does that mean?" Alex questioned just as softly.

"It's what mythology would compare to a vampire—although our current culture has almost everything wrong about us."

"V…am…pire?" Alex managed to stutter out. "But…"

"And you, Alex Wilson, are my mate."

A silence fell so quickly that Kayla actually had to look at the three other people to see if they'd heard the same thing she had. Surely, she was mistaken and Angel hadn't just confessed to being a vampire. Vampires didn't exist.

Chase was the first one who seemed to snap out of the shock. "I didn't expect that. Alex?"

Just noticing how pale Alex was, Kayla found herself taking a step toward him.

Chase's strong hand on her arm stopped her movement. He shook his head. "Alex?" Chase called to his friend again.

They watched as Alex raised a shaking hand to Angel. As Alex laid his palm softly against Angel's cheek, Kayla found herself pressing against Chase's back and gripping his shirt.

"Amazing," Alex murmured.

Angel's eyes widened but a smile ghosted across her lips. "That's what I thought the first time I saw you."

Shocked and confused, Kayla stared at the scene in front of her. Chase drew her attention as he pulled on her arm to lead her away from Alex and Angel. She dragged her feet, not wanting to leave the kitchen. *Vampires? Real vampires? Wow, what else am I going to find out?*

When Chase actually lifted her off her feet and carried her from the kitchen, she peered down at him.

"Let's give them some privacy," Chase said.

"Okay," she relented.

They traveled through the swinging door before Chase set her on her feet. Leaning against the wall, he swept one hand roughly over his face. "Did you know?"

"What? How would I?" She was still reeling from the new information. After everything that the shifters had been through in the past year with going public, there had been no sign, no talk of vampires.

Just another secret that had been kept from her, because there was no way her father had worked next to vampires and not know about them. She had half a mind to track her dad down and demand that he tell her everything he knew. However, the look of doubt on Chase's face kept her rooted to the spot.

"Chase? What's going on?"

"Just trying to put everything together. The events from the last couple of days," he explained. "We went up against something that I have no idea how to handle. And even though no one was injured, they could have been, because we didn't know what we are up against. Now these are your friends—people you knew before me—so I'm asking if you knew about…what they are?"

The coldness in Chase's voice surprised her. For some reason, he truly believed she was hiding something.

"I don't know any more than you do," she said, stepping up against him.

He sighed, dropping his head back. Relief flooded her as he grasped her waist and pulled her into his chest.

"I'm sorry. I'm being an ass. I just… I don't know what to do."

His admission, spoken in a hushed tone, pulled at her heartstrings. She could see by the lines of stress on Chase's face just how hard he was taking this new information.

"I want to help you," Kayla said. "I just don't how."

"I have an idea where to start," he replied, turning his head.

Following his gaze, she saw Justin hovering in the hall. It hit her why Chase thought she had more information—her best friend.

She pushed away from Chase and whirled on the other man. "You have some explaining to do." Kayla pointed her finger at Justin.

"I couldn't tell you," Justin replied with a shake of his head. "It's against all the rules."

"You're going to tell us now," Chase said from behind her.

Justin visibly tensed but after a moment, nodded. "We wouldn't have let anyone get hurt. We were doing our best to protect you all."

"What we need now is to know what you do. If I'm going to protect my Pack, you have to tell me everything," Chase said firmly.

"Okay, but just so you know that once this is over, you can't let anyone know you are aware of us. Our life will be forfeited if our people knew we'd told."

Kayla glanced back at the bathroom door. Somehow, she didn't think the Pack keeping a secret was going to be a big deal. They'd been keeping plenty, and if Alex and Angel were mated — that made them Pack *and* part of the family.

Kayla glanced over her shoulder at Chase. They were all family. She wouldn't go anywhere until she knew they were safe. And yes, she was sure she was falling in love with Chase.

"There you are." Her dad turned the corner and stopped close to Justin. "I just got off the phone with my old employer and it seems they've caught all but three of the Guardians who left the company."

Alex brought his hand down on Angel's shoulder. "The three who went after Kayla and Randy?"

"We think so. But with the Guardians after them, they won't get away. I'm about to call the Alpha but I think we're safe enough for now."

Kayla turned to face Chase. He looked doubtful, mirroring how she felt. It wasn't over yet. She could feel it in her bones.

"It's going to be okay," her dad said to her.

Slipping her hand up to cover Chase's, she nodded. "I know."

The kitchen door opened as Alex and Angel stepped to join them. It was getting crowded in the narrow hallway.

"Maybe we should all go into the den?" Kayla suggested.

"Good idea," Justin agreed. "Angel and I will tell you what we can."

Twining her fingers with Chase's, she tugged him to follow the others. After they learned what they could, she would drag Chase back to bed. If there were no immediate danger to the Pack, she would enjoy her man while she could.

PACK SECRETS

Dedication

To my husband as we celebrate another year together.
I love you with all my heart and know I couldn't do
this without your support.

Chapter One

The strong fresh aroma of high-dollar coffee filled the kitchen as Alex Wilson went about brewing a pot. The last few days of having a house full of guests worrying over his best friend and other Pack mates had started taking a toll on him.

When his Alpha had first asked him to house their out-of-town company, Alex had figured it wouldn't be too bad. Since his sister had recently mated with Max Lawson, the two spent most of their time in the guest house, leaving Alex alone. Even his younger brother was already married and had two boys.

Alex was alone.

Although he wasn't opposed to the solitary existence, he'd found himself looking forward to socializing with others outside his immediate family.

He should have been more careful in what he wished for.

Not only were complete strangers staying in his spare bedrooms, but they'd also had to add guards to the property after Marcus Webb had been shot.

It was just the night before that the Alpha and others had found the man responsible for the attempted murder. They'd also found out that Emilio, the man accountable, worked for the same organization as Angelica Salvatore. Emilio was being held by the Guardians in one of his rooms, but his Alpha had assured Alex that Emilio posed no threat to his family.

Thinking about Angel reminded Alex why he needed to brew the coffee extra strong.

Ever since Angel had shown up on his doorstep with her brother and his closest friends, Alex hadn't been able to stop thinking about her. He shouldn't have been so damn hung up on some woman he didn't know, who was obviously keeping many secrets.

Alex didn't like drama and Angel appeared to be full of complications. She was also gorgeous, funny and mysterious. Fuck, he wanted to grab a handful of her black silky hair to yank her head back and plunder her mouth.

Cock more than half hard, Alex needed to calm down quickly before someone walked in.

Finally the beep indicating his morning beverage was ready sounded from the machine. Knowing everyone else would soon be up, he transferred the contents into a stainless-steel carafe before beginning another pot to brew.

As he picked up his favorite mug, the kitchen door swung open with a soft wisp of air. Alex didn't even need to turn around to know who had joined him.

"Coffee?" he asked, already reaching for another cup.

"Please."

Angel's voice sent a shudder through his body. Fighting against the temptation for doing all the things he'd been dreaming about, Alex went about making her drink. "One sugar and a dash of creamer, right?"

"You noticed."

Damn, damn, damn. He shrugged his shoulders. "I try to pay attention to my guests' preferences," he responded.

Her soft laughter came from right behind him. No longer was he only half hard. His erection now pushed against the zipper of his jeans.

Finishing stirring in the condiments, he turned to offer her the cup.

Angel was indeed close. She had Alex trapped against the counter, leaving him no way of moving without brushing against her.

"What are you doing?" he asked with suspicion.

"Accepting my coffee?"

He didn't miss the sparkle in her eyes. Breathing in deep, he tried his best not to let her know how she affected him. Since he couldn't get a handle on his emotions he really didn't feel up to battling wits with her right then. "Excuse me." He waved for her to back up.

"Anytime we're in a room alone together you have an excuse to leave. When are we going to talk about what this is between us?" she questioned as she raised a beautiful eyebrow.

"I don't play games," he told her. "If you need something just tell me."

Sighing, she shook her head before reaching down to place her mug back on the counter next to his. "I'm not trying to play games. I've been trying to get you to talk to me."

That sounded like a really bad idea to him. He didn't even know the woman in front of him yet was more entranced by her presence than he had ever felt about anyone else. It made him uneasy not knowing exactly what Angel was. He relied on his shifter senses so much that it was strange Angel was different from anyone he'd ever met.

"I should probably get breakfast started," he said, ignoring her words.

"You're doing it again," she accused.

"What?" He glanced over her shoulder, praying someone would walk in.

"Look at me, Alex," she demanded.

He was powerless not to follow that order. She had the prettiest crystal-blue eyes. They should have looked out of place with her long, dark, black hair, but instead the blue just seemed to stand out even more.

"Is there anything you want to ask me?" she questioned, pretty much throwing his words back at him.

He had too many questions on his mind that he wanted to ask but he didn't know even how to begin. What really held him back though were the questions he wasn't sure he was ready for.

There was something unusual about her. As a wolf shifter, he knew all about people who were different. Growing up in Canyon, Texas, Alex had been around shifters his entire life.

Angel and her brother Justin had no scent.

For a shifter who used his sense of smell to determine danger, the fact that he couldn't pick up anything from the Salvatore siblings messed with him.

"Why can't I scent you?" he asked cautiously.

Angel grinned up at him. At his six-foot height he peered down at the smaller five-foot-seven woman. "I knew that would be one of your first questions."

Alex nodded, although he wasn't certain why. She hadn't asked him anything. When she laid her hand on his chest he jolted in surprise.

"Wouldn't you rather discuss this attraction between us?"

It didn't escape Alex's notice that she hadn't answered his question. Placing his hand over hers, he gripped her. "Why don't you answer?"

"Because I don't want you to freak out. This is the first time you've really opened up and you're not ready."

"You're talking in riddles!" he exclaimed. "You say you want to talk, but you only want to dangle tidbits in front of me." He pushed her hand off before stalking away.

"Alex…" she called his name softly.

He spun around and saw — "Holy shit!"

Backing into the wall, he didn't know what to do. It wasn't until he felt the flat surface not giving him room to escape that he realized he was in deep trouble.

Angel's eyes actually glowed. Not yellow or red or anything like in the movies. Her normally calm blue eyes turned purple. He held up his palms to keep her from advancing.

She ignored them and walked right up against his body. "I told you that you weren't ready. But don't reject me."

"Back off," he growled. He might have been raised never to fight against a female, but he wasn't completely powerless. He let his wolf come to the surface in warning. Just enough that his own eyes would start to change and the animal inside could break loose if need be.

"You going to fight me?" she asked, grabbing a hold of his arms.

Fuck! She was strong.

"Go ahead," she taunted.

He had no other choice. He pushed his entire body against hers. As they banged against the wall, their breaths mixed as they panted with their faces so close together.

Even though fear spiked through him, he was sure to be careful with his strength. He didn't want to hurt Angel. That was the last thing he wanted, but he was so very much out of his element here.

"Is this what you want? Me pinned so you can ravish me?"

Why did her words have to be exactly the same as what he was feeling? As close as they were, she had to feel his erection, sure, but he got the distinct impression she always knew what he was thinking.

"Stop." Instead of the order he intended, the word came out as a plea.

"I won't stop you," Angel told him while she ran her hands up his arms. "In fact I want you to."

Alex was going to lose his mind. He didn't know which way was up or down. Biting his lip, he knew he should let her go. He tried to make himself. Really he did.

Then Angel strained up and covered his mouth with hers. Their lips touched once, then again, after that he was lost.

Opening up to her questing tongue, he let Angel control the kiss. Alex did the one thing he'd been dying to do. He buried his hands in her soft hair, using his body to keep her in place.

Bending at the knees, he pushed his hard cock against her.

She moaned, which he happily swallowed. He closed his eyes to block out everything else in the room.

A sudden barrage of pictures of the two of them popped up in his mind. Images of him and Angel on the kitchen floor, tearing at clothes and biting exposed flesh.

She gasped, jerking back.

The vision had been like a movie playing behind his closed eyes. *What in the hell?* Angel frowned with her eyes wide. She reached for him again but he shook his head, taking another step back.

"What are you?" he asked desperately. Angel had to be the one responsible for the clear images in his head. He'd never had an experience like his brain being taken over by such erotic and real-life pictures. Not knowing exactly what Angel was could be the only explanation.

"No," she said, her voice shaking a little. "I can't tell you."

"Tell me!" he demanded, gripping her shoulders.

"I..."

Touching her had been a mistake. Now that he had his hands back on her, all he could think about were the pictures of taking her once again. Had he ever felt so turned on before? He couldn't remember a time he'd been so out of his mind in need. Slowly he skimmed one hand from her shoulder to cup her chin before caressing lower.

He wrapped his hand around her neck without any pressure to harm her. He didn't squeeze, just held her still while he gazed at her. "Answer me, please."

The door opened behind them. Alex did not move.

"What the...?" Chase muttered from the entry.

Taking the time to explain to his best friend would have been smart. Instead, he was annoyed at being interrupted. He could scent Chase and Kayla as they entered the kitchen.

"Alex?" Chase said quietly.

"No, I want answers from her and I want them now," Alex snapped at his best friend.

"We'll get them, but not this way. Let her go," Chase replied.

He realized what it must look like. Instead of the intimate embrace they'd been sharing it may have appeared Alex held Angel in a hostile manner.

Chase started forward, but Angel held up a hand. "Don't worry about it, Chase. If I wanted loose, I could do so myself. I'm quite enjoying this reaction from your friend."

That had Alex responding. He snarled, releasing Angel and stomping away. *Why does she have to be so infuriating?*

He stalked to the other side of the kitchen before whirling back on Angel. "You have put my entire family—everyone I care about—in danger. I will not accept that you can't tell me what is going on. I want to know!" He ended his rant by slamming his hand against the marble countertop.

Angel nodded. Straightening her clothes, she stared at Alex.

The acceptance shocked Alex, but if he were going to get answers he would be happy.

"Please have a seat." Angel waved her hand at the table.

Never looking away from Angel, he strolled over to one of the chairs and dropped down.

"I'll get the coffee," Chase offered.

Nodding, Alex didn't speak, instead he breathed deeply, hoping to gain back some of his control.

Angel took the seat directly across from him. Having to push away the disappointment of not having her near him confused Alex. He'd only just met Angel and already he felt obsessed with running his hands over her body. What he needed was answers, not being distracted by his hormones.

No one spoke as Chase quietly moved around the kitchen until he placed four mugs on the table. Kayla helped Chase pass around the drinks before sitting back quietly while Angel remained staring at Alex.

"Are you sure you're ready to hear this, Alex? Once I tell you, there is no turning back," Angel stated.

"You mean you'll actually answer our questions this time?" he challenged.

"I'll tell you anything *you* want to know. But you don't get to just walk away when I'm through. You have to listen to all of it."

"Fine," Alex said to Angel. "Answer me this... Are you human?"

Angel's expression didn't change — she still gazed at Alex with an open look. "No."

Alex wasn't even surprised. "Is that why you and your brother have no scent?"

"It is."

Well at least he was getting some answers. "This organization that you work for...is everything you told us the truth?"

"Yes, the Guardians are a good group. We've always thrived in protecting others. That is our sole purpose."

"If it's good work that you do, why the secrecy?"

"Unlike the Wolf Council or other shifter leaders, our agency does not discriminate against other paranormal types. Anyone who has the same beliefs is welcome to join."

"Beliefs?"

Angel's smile grew. "The idea that no matter what — or who — you are, we are all equal. Everyone, including humans, should have someone looking out for them."

"What are you?"

Angel shook her head.

"You said you would answer!" Alex raised his voice, determined.

"You're not ready!" Angel fired back.

"Damn it, tell me," Alex shouted, jumping to his feet.

"Alex," Chase called to his friend.

Alex turned on him. Chase could sit at the table with Kayla at his side and have the ability to remain calm. Alex felt like everything was coming apart around him. "No, there is something going on. I know she is doing something to me." He didn't have another explanation. The images of them making love on the kitchen floor were still in his head. From the second he'd met her, Alex had been going out of his mind with need. "I have to understand," Alex said as calm as possible. "What are you doing to me?"

She stood slowly. "I'm sorry," Angel said as she walked closer to Alex.

"Just...please..." he begged.

"They call my kind Day Walkers," Angel admitted in a whisper.

"I don't... What does that mean?" Alex questioned just as softly.

"It's what mythology would compare to a vampire — although the culture we live in has almost everything wrong about us."

"V...am...pire?" Alex managed to stutter. "But..." How could that be? Vampires didn't exist. Surely someone would have spoiled that secret.

"And you, Alex Wilson, are my mate."

He blinked at her. He hadn't heard that right, had he? No, he really had to be losing his mind. But maybe... After all, he could shift into a wolf, and before they'd gone public no one had thought that was possible.

"I didn't expect that. Alex?" Chase spoke.

Alex heard him but it seemed so far away. He couldn't catch his breath and his hands were shaking. Angel was a vampire? She was truly remarkable.

"Alex?" Chase called again.

He softly laid his palm against Angel's cheek. He'd just kissed her. Been having dreams about her the last two nights and had never expected something like this. "Amazing," he murmured.

Angel's eyes widened but a smile ghosted across her lips. "That's what I thought the first time I saw you."

"Let's give them some privacy," Chase said.

"Okay," Kayla agreed.

Alex and Angel didn't move away from each other as Chase and Kayla left the kitchen.

"What does this mean?" Alex asked quietly, still in awe.

"There's a lot I have to share with you. I know you don't understand, but you have to trust me," she replied.

Trust, it seemed like such an easy thing to ask for. Could he give her that? What about the whole mate thing? "You called me your mate."

"Isn't that what the shifters call the persons they claim as their own?"

"Yes," he agreed.

"That is what you are to me. As soon as I saw you, I got a premonition that you were the person I was meant to be with."

"Oh," he responded, since he wasn't sure what to say.

She looked disappointed as she took a step back. Alex didn't want to her to move away.

"You don't feel it? I could have sworn you did."

Going with instinct, he grabbed her hand before she could get too far. "What?"

"I thought shifters recognized their mates. That's why you acted so weird around me."

Unsure how to explain things, Alex drew Angel back toward the table. This time he made sure she was right next to him. "Angel, shifters choose their mates. Yes, I've heard of two, maybe three, people who are believed to be fated mates. Only one of those recently. For the most part, it's the two people who find one another and perform a ritual that connects their spirit."

"I see," she said softly.

"We believe that the mate we choose is our match. The person that completes us. I've also heard there is an instant attraction and the relationship evolves from there."

"So you do feel a connection to me?"

He grinned. "Of course. I don't understand it, and not being able to scent you really messed with me, but I've wanted you from the first minute."

She rose, only to slide into his lap and straddle him. "So what are we going to do about it?" she asked, pressing her chest against his while gliding her hand down his stomach.

Alex sucked in a breath. "I..."

"Sadly, we can't do anything now," she told him. "I can hear everyone in the hall and I believe they are about to demand answers."

Now that she'd pointed it out, Alex could pick up on the voices getting loud outside his kitchen. "We do need to know if there is more of a threat out there to the Pack."

"I know. I tried to tell you as much as I could but I do have rules I have to follow. Although I can confess more to you than anyone else."

"Me?" he asked confused. It took a minute of her just staring at him before he understood. She'd claimed them mates. "Oh."

"What I can't tell the others I will share with you. You can repeat that information to your Alpha and we can go from there."

That sounded like a deal to Alex. "Okay."

Angel stood, however Alex didn't let her go far. He wrapped his hands around her waist. "Wait."

"Yes?" She peered down at him.

He didn't know how to ask for what he wanted. Instead he pushed out of the chair to take her mouth.

There was no hesitation in her response. When they broke apart he grinned. "I had to taste you one more time."

"There will be a lot more than just one," she declared, slipping her hand into his while pulling him toward the door.

Alex opened the door when they reached it, amused to see half the house standing there talking.

"Maybe we should all go into the den?" Kayla suggested.

"Good idea. Alpha Shawn is waiting for us," Justin, Angel's brother, agreed. "Angel and I will tell you what we can."

Turning to glance at Angel for confirmation, who nodded at him, he led the way. He guessed they were going to do this now.

Angel hadn't released the hold on his hand.

A few of his friends cast surprised looks their way but no one asked any questions. Chase smiled brightly at him before throwing him a wink.

Alex would have to talk to his best friend about everything. Chase now knew Angel's secret and, if it was so important that it not be revealed, Alex would do his best to keep her safe.

Justin sat in one of the large overstuffed chairs and was glaring at their linked hands. *Guess I'll have to deal with her brother too.*

His sister was also going to have to be one of the first he spoke with. Cassie nudged her mate, Max, nodding in his direction. Max only shrugged in response, getting a glare from Cassie. They hadn't been together long but Alex was still a little jealous about the ease in which they'd settled into their relationship.

He could only hope that if things worked out with Angel, he'd be as lucky.

"Angel?" Justin called.

Beside him, she took a deep breath. "Here's what I can tell you."

Chapter Two

Angel was more nervous than she'd ever been in her life. After all she'd revealed to Alex in the kitchen, she should be calm while explaining everything to the people in the room. They'd all helped her capture Emilio, proving they were good people. Plus, they were shifters, so being different themselves, they should understand the need for secrecy.

The fact that they were Alex's family and closest friends was what actually scared her. If they had issues with what she was they could stand between her and her mate.

She'd spent her entire adult life fighting for the people in the room. Shifters, humans and Day Walkers all needed someone out there making certain that they were safe. Like every group of people, the paranormals had the good and bad. Angel's job was to stop any bad from hurting people. It was something she'd been trained for from the moment she could walk.

As the oldest Salvatore child, her future had been decided when she was born. While her brother had received a good education and been able to concentrate on his art, Angel had always had responsibilities to the organization.

She wasn't jealous of her brother's freedom, well not much anyway—she liked what she did, even though she was lonely.

Glancing at the man next to her, she had to wonder what the future would hold for the two of them. Hopefully Alex could accept her as his mate and they'd somehow be able to manage around her job.

It was easier to look at Alex as she spoke. His was the only opinion that mattered to her. "As I told you before, I work for an organization that polices non-humans. Before the shifters went public, our number one goal was to keep the paranormals of the world secret. Since you have all announced your presence, we try to keep your kind safe while still hiding the others."

"And by others?" Alpha Shawn questioned.

She clenched her fist, bracing for the reaction. "Justin and I are Day Walkers."

"What does that mean exactly?" Max asked after several moments of silence.

Angel jerked in surprise when Alex covered her hand with his. Grateful, she smiled slightly at him before addressing the Alpha in training. "A Day Walker is the closest thing to what mythology calls the vampire."

The gasps were expected.

"I'm sorry, did you just say vampire?" Cassie Wilson demanded as she jumped to her feet.

Angel wasn't afraid of the pretty wolf shifter but since she was Alex's sister, Angel really wanted Cassie to accept their bond. "I can tell you that almost everything people believe about our kind is untrue."

"Do you drink blood?" Cassie challenged.

Since Alex stiffened next to her Angel knew her desire for a calm conversation wasn't going to happen. "We do."

The room exploded. Questions were shouted out as several of the shifters moved quickly to place their mates behind them. Looking up, Angel tried not to let her hurt show.

The Alpha of the Pack was closest to her, standing in the middle of the room and trying to calm everyone down. Max had pushed Cassie against one wall while using his body as a shield. Chase and Kayla warily looked around while Alex was now up from the couch with the entire length of it between them.

Raising her gaze to the most powerful man in the room, she met Shawn eye to eye. He turned to his Pack members. "We need to hear her out," he insisted.

"You knew about this!" Max accused.

It was a good thing she wasn't a shifter when Shawn let out a low, spine-tingling growl. All shifters in the room dropped their gazes and she could even feel the power radiating from the Alpha.

"I'm sorry, Alpha" — Max dropped down to one knee — "I was out of line."

"Raise, my son," Shawn ordered gently. "Everyone sit back down and listen."

As they moved to follow the Alpha's direction, Angel's heart broke with the distance Alex put between the two of them as he returned to the couch.

"Yes, I am aware of what Angel and Justin are. I have been since Marcus came to live with the Pack and informed me of his previous profession. This information is to be kept as a Pack secret. You're complete obedience is required or you will deal with me," Shawn stated firmly. He peered back at Angel. "Please continue."

"Because of what history has twisted about Day Walkers," Angel told them, "it is impossible for our kind to be revealed. We would be wiped out of existence without thought. That's why the Guardians were originally founded. At first our ranks were only made up of Day Walkers but over the years we've added other shifters, and even humans, to our goal of protecting those who don't know the real dangers out there."

"Kind of like the Wolf Council?" Max commented.

Nodding, she agreed. "We work closely with your council on matters that have to do with wolf shifters. The newly founded Shifter Coalition has also given us more options to expand our help."

She chanced a peek in Alex's direction but his entire posture was closed off to her. He sat hunched into himself with his jaw clenched.

"I can't believe you never told me." Kayla pointed at Angel's brother.

"I couldn't!" Justin exclaimed. "It's against the rules."

"So why are you telling us now?" Max inquired, suspicion tainting his tone.

Since Angel didn't think Alex would appreciate her revealing their destiny to everyone, she went with a second truth. "My boss and a few others are on their way to pick up Emilio. I've reported in everything that has happened and was given permission for you all to be brought up to speed. Working with Alpha Shawn, we hope to be able to prevent your Pack from being harmed because of a few rogue agents. They've targeted your family and we have to stop them."

She didn't mention the only reason Caspar had allowed her to share the information so soon was because she'd claimed Alex. Since they were close to her mate they'd benefit from Alex's connection to her.

"The first thing we need to do is send out the guards we have available into town and have them start patrolling. We don't want to cause a panic," Max spoke up.

"Why don't you call Jacob and the two of you work out rotations?" Shawn asked Max. "Chase, I need you to contact Kurt Moore with the council. They need to be aware of our situation. I don't know if he had any knowledge of the Guardians so for now, keep that under wraps."

"Yes, sir." Chase rose. "Are we to remain here?"

Shawn nodded. "At least until the other Guardians arrive and I get to speak with them."

"What about me?" Alex asked from where he still sat.

"I hate to impose on you further, but can you make up a few more guest rooms? The Guardians will have traveled far in a short amount of time and will probably appreciate some time to rest."

Alex nodded sharply before fleeing the room.

There was no doubt that he was trying to put as much distance between the two of them as possible. Tears threatened to fall as a feeling of devastation overwhelmed her.

"Thank you for trusting us." Shawn stood in front of her, pulling her attention to the large man.

"I only did what I thought was best for everyone," she responded sincerely.

"I know it's not easy."

Angel rose. "I didn't expect any other reaction. If you'll excuse me, I'd like some air."

She didn't even wait for the Alpha to agree. She quickly made her way over to the sliding glass doors and pulled one open. Stepping out onto the beautiful wood deck, Angel stopped to appreciate the large space. She didn't have an area like this at her residence. It reminded her of television shows and movies were family gathered. A spike of jealousy shot through her. Alex had family and friends that surrounded him. She ached to be part of his world there.

The dark color of the deck flowed from one beam to another while the entire surface gleamed in the sunlight. A huge barbeque pit was located on one side while a long picnic table dominated the middle. Closest to her she could see a stack of toys inside a box that must belong to the children of Alex's brother Jacob.

She stepped out, before closing the door behind her. The Texas heat had already warmed the area. Lifting her face to the sky, she soaked in the rays. The day before, she'd gotten to see the entire Wilson ranch while they'd been searching for Emilio.

It was a lovely piece of land located on the edge and inside the canyon. Angel had never seen such a beautiful property and would have loved to get a personal tour from Alex.

All she could do was give Alex time while praying he'd eventually want a relationship with her. If Alex rejected her she would move on and be alone for the rest of her life. She was used to being on her own but in the back of her mind she'd always held on to the fact that she could meet her mate.

Alex was everything she could have dreamed up. With him being a couple inches taller, she'd loved it when he'd pinned her to the wall and their bodies had fit together. His expressive deep-brown eyes flickered with gold when arousal hit him.

It was his body, though, that had filled her fantasies for the last several nights. Since she worked with heavily muscled, military-trained men, she truly appreciated Alex's compact, athletic build.

A warm breeze carrying the scent of horses lifted her hair from her back. Angel wasn't used to be around the big creatures but she'd had the urge to visit them since she'd arrived. *Well, no time like the present.*

After slowly walking down the wide steps, she felt the first touch of grass under her feet and smiled. If Angel ever got a home of her own she wanted acres and acres of grass. She still remembered the garden that had been one of her favorite spots in her parents' house.

Even though she hardly ever visited anymore, Angel would always cherish the few short years that she'd lived in the big rambling house.

Taken for training at seven years of age, most of Angel's earliest memories were of the compound. Almost thirty years she'd stayed in the same small one-bedroom, one-bathroom apartment located in the large structure claimed by the Guardians.

She'd never had a real home. Even her family treated her differently than they did one another. While her parents remained close with her brother, grandparents, aunts, uncles and cousins, there was a noticeable distance with her as the oldest Salvatore child.

Even though Angel knew her parents loved her, she had grown so far apart from them. Being on the Wilson ranch, and seeing the affection and loyalty that the entire Pack had for one another, was a reminder that she'd never belonged anywhere like that.

Pushing the longing aside, she strode toward the large barn. The doors stood open already so she was able to slip inside unnoticed. She scented two shifters close by but managed to avoid coming in contact with them.

A *neigh* had her popping her head up from where she was pressed against one of the stables. She peered over the door with caution, unsure what she'd find. Her breath caught as she stared in amazement.

The beast was magnificent. Dark brown hair gleamed in the light that came in through a small window. Looking up at the huge brown eyes, Angel felt the power radiating from the animal.

Holding up a hand, she called softly to the horse. *Wow!* Barely able to keep standing still she waited in excitement until the mare had brushed up against her palm.

She jerked her hand back before reaching out once again. Cautiously, she patted the neck of the large animal.

There was no way she'd step inside the enclosure, although she really wanted to. Leaning forward, Angel watched as the horse sniffed her. Before she knew what was happening, the mare had her nose buried in Angel's chest.

"Uh—" She froze in her spot. "Easy there."

"She's looking for treats."

"Ugh!" Angel turned and jumped back, getting her feet tangled. She hit the side of the stable before going down hard.

"You okay?" Alex stood in front of her with a hand out to help her up.

Shit! This really wasn't how she'd wanted to see the man again. Accepting his help, she allowed Alex to pull her back onto her feet. She expected him to release her immediately, but instead, he actually hauled her closer.

Stiffening against him, she prepared for rejection.

"I'm sorry," he told her quietly.

Sure that she hadn't heard him correctly, she just blinked up at him.

"I don't know what I started to freak out about. I think everything just caught up to me and I panicked."

"I understand," she replied, unsure what else to say.

"I hurt you," he said as he placed two fingers under her chin to make her look up at him.

She started to shake her head.

"I hurt you and I am sorry," he repeated.

Finally Angel lifted her gaze to meet Alex's. Right away she could see the sincerity in the chocolate-colored depths.

"I know I don't deserve it but I would like to learn more about you."

Shrugging, Angel wasn't going to deny her mate anything. If the shoe were on the other foot then she would want to know about his kind. "I'll answer any questions you have."

"No." He drew her closer, and Angel was powerless to resist.

Settling her hands against his chest, she could feel the muscles in his pecs moving.

"I want to get to know you. Not just what you are but who you are."

Overcome with emotion and relief, Angel wrapped her arms around Alex's back, burying her face in his chest. Feeling Alex's hands on the back of her head relaxed her even more. When she was sure that she once again had control, she pulled away and peered up at him.

He smiled. "First let me introduce you to Rebel Princess."

Confused, she looked around until she heard the horse behind her snort. "Rebel Princess?"

"Cassie named her but it fits. I call her Reba," he explained with a wide grin.

"She is so beautiful," she told Alex. He came back around, standing close.

"I've always thought so. I was driving Cassie out to college and on the west side of the highway there was this horse ranch. This one ran up and down the fence line over and over. I couldn't get the picture of her out of my head. She was just a little one back then. After the weekend I drove back by myself and pulled over to the side when I saw her playing again."

"Wow!"

"I knew I had to have her. I spun around and drove straight to the office. Two weeks later she was mine."

Once again she raised a hand toward Reba. The horse pawed the ground but came closer. This time the animal didn't hesitate to sniff her.

"I think she likes you," Alex commented with a chuckle.

"The feeling is mutual," Angel whispered back in awe.

"Have you ever ridden?"

"No, no, this is the closest that I've ever come to one."

"We have a tradition of taking the horses on a sunset ride down the canyon. I'd love for you to join us sometime."

"Really?" she asked, glancing over her shoulder.

"Yes, like I said, I want to get to know you."

"I want that too," she agreed.

Reba backed away, so Angel spun back to Alex. "What now?"

"I want to show you something," he told her as he held out his hand.

Linking her fingers with his, Angel followed behind her mate. She was counting her blessings that somehow he had overcome his fear and was at least open to the possibilities of learning more about her.

He led her farther back into the barn where she caught the faint sound of something rustling around. Alex winked over his shoulder before pausing in front of one of the half doors.

"Oh my," Angel exclaimed softly. Right in front of her eyes, a tiny colt was leaning against a much larger mare.

"He's only three weeks old," Alex told her.

"He's so little."

"The best part of having the ranch with the horses is watching the young ones grow up," he confided.

That sounded good to Angel. Alex had such a great life that she wasn't certain she would be able to fit in. Had fate made a mistake matching the two of them together? She didn't want to believe that Alex wouldn't be able to accept her.

But he was willing to try, so she would give him the benefit of doubt. She at least had to show him that even though she was infected as a Day Walker, she would never harm him.

"Will you come with me to see something else?" he asked softly.

Turning back to him, she smiled. "Yes."

Chapter Three

Alex was embarrassed and ashamed about his reaction earlier. Luckily his Alpha was very direct and wouldn't let Alex continue to act like an ass.

Shawn had demanded to know what his problem was, and when Alex hadn't been able to explain his behavior, he'd known how much he'd fucked up. Cassie had agreed to take over getting the rooms ready so Alex could find Angel.

His mate. That's what she had said. He wanted to talk to her about that claim but first he had some damage control to do. He'd wanted Angel for days and he had to fight his body demands to go slow with her.

Getting her to accept his offer to show her his favorite spot had been easier than he'd expected, but he wasn't going to complain. The ranch was big enough that they didn't have to worry about running into anyone else.

He was thankful since he really wanted to try to make up for his earlier behavior. Out of the corner of his eye, he could see Angel trying to take in all the sights. She'd get a better view on the back of a horse so he'd make sure they enjoyed that adventure together soon.

"This place is so big," she said.

"I love it here," he confided. "There is always something that needs to be done so I'm never bored, but I have enough staff that I can enjoy just being part of the ranch."

"The canyon must be beautiful at night too."

"Yes, watching the sun rise or fall can make any bad day just melt away. It's Mother Nature at her best."

Angel hummed a little, and a sharp catch in his chest surprised him. It was important that she loved the place as much as he did. That was one of the reasons he wanted to take her to the small lookout spot.

"Where are we going?" she asked after they'd been walking for a good five minutes.

"Just wait," he said. "I promise it's worth it."

She squeezed his hand. "I'm with you so I'm sure it is."

He paused to turn and look at her. Her face flushed as she peered at the ground.

"Hey," he said, cupping her face.

"I didn't mean to say that out loud."

"I'm glad you did." He bent and placed a gentle kiss against her lips.

She reached for him, but he shook his head while backing away.

"If I kiss you like I really want to we'll never get to where we're going. But I promise to kiss you again once we get there."

"You'd better," she playfully threatened.

Walking hand in hand with Angel again, he picked up the pace a little more. Now he had an even better incentive to get Angel alone. Seeing the trees that marked the entrance, Alex pulled Angel off the path.

"Uh." She licked her lips. "Are you sure you won't tell me where we're going?"

Chuckling, he only shook his head. He had to duck a little to pass through the small opening in the trees but Angel fit perfectly being shorter. Their view was blocked by leaves and branches hanging low. With a smile on his face, he led Angel around to stand in front of him. He could barely contain his excitement as he swept the branches aside to reveal the most gorgeous sight of the canyon.

"Oh wow!" Angel whispered.

He knew how she felt. The first time he'd seen the wide expanse of the canyon opening he'd been speechless. Even as a kid he'd recognized that it was such an amazing experience to be so blessed with a landscape of colors and texture. The canyon spread out in an array of shades that glowed in the sun. Crystal-blue waters. Green foliage scattered around brown stumps. The rocks and caves had colored over time, turning the ground around them white in some areas.

The light breeze brought with it the scent of water, brush and animals. Above them the sounds of birds echoed faintly.

They stood there in silence for several moments without speaking or moving. Finally he tore his eyes away from the canyon to peer down at Angel. She stood in front of him with her hand up to her chest. If he'd ever seen anyone so stunning, he couldn't remember. Her stature and features were small and delicate but he knew the truth. She was a tough and strong woman who spent her life protecting others. There was a sort of innocence about her that had drawn him in from the very beginning. He couldn't stop himself from laying his hand on her hip to pull her back against him.

Glancing over her shoulder as her back hit his chest, she smiled shyly before she licked her lips. Following the movement of her tongue, he hardened so fast that he had to take a deep breath.

She'd probably feel his erection against her leg but he didn't have a problem with her knowing how much he wanted her.

She leaned back into him slightly. Oh, he liked that.

Bending his head, he licked at her bottom lip. She gasped in response before turning into his embrace. His fingers itched to touch her hair so he didn't deny himself the opportunity. Wrapping his fingers in the silky strands, he pulled her head back as he dove down to steal another kiss. This time he left his lips pressed to hers and nipped silently asking her to open for him, and she did.

She tasted like his favorite dark brew of coffee. Groaning, he deepened their lip lock until she was grabbing at his shoulders, trying to get him even closer. He wasn't sure he could, though, without actually being inside her. That thought was almost enough to push him over the edge. He yanked his head back with a curse. She was panting right along with him.

"I want you so bad," he confessed.

"Yes," she agreed while running her palm down his side to the front of his jeans. He pushed his hips hard into her hand when she cupped his package.

"We can't...do this here," he said, trying to be convincing even though he knew it was much too late.

The first time he made love to Angel, he wanted it to be in his big soft bed, however, that didn't mean that he couldn't give them a taste of what was in store. He dropped to his knees, bringing her with him.

Laying her back, he made sure she was comfortable before he caught her hand and brought it to his mouth. He gently ran his tongue over her wrist and up to the center of her palm. She shivered.

"Tell me you want his," he ordered.

"I do," she answered. "I want to feel you."

That's what he needed. Covering her body with his, Alex was lightheaded as their lips met. He lost himself in the rhythm of their tongues rubbing against each other. He ran his hand across her ass to hold her body closer to his. His cock was so hard that Alex didn't know how long he would be able to hold himself back. Angel wasn't helping him with his control as she wrapped her legs around his waist.

The movement caused his erection to fit snug against her pussy. He snapped his hips while he continued to devour her mouth. He didn't think he would ever tire of her intoxicating flavor. Dragging his cock against her, he had to pull back for a minute. The tingling at the base of his spine was a warning that he was just too close. Angel was still rocking against him. Pushing back so he was on his knees, he lifted her T-shirt up. Luckily the soft grass under her back was enough cushion that he didn't feel bad about laying her out flat. The black silk material that covered her firm breasts was easily unsnapped, so he had access to her beautiful flesh. Lowering his head, he took one hard nipple into his mouth and sucked.

She cried out, grasping at the back of his head. He trailed wet kisses between her mounds as he went to tease her other nipple. Each time he pressed into her skin her hips rose. There was no doubt that she wanted him just as much as he wanted her.

Dragging his fingers lower until he reached the waistband of her pants, he watched her face. She was flushed, so damn pretty, caught up in pleasure. While undoing her pants, he lifted his chin to lay his mouth back on hers. He slipped his hand into her panties and she strained to spread her legs farther apart but was hampered by the material still around her legs.

Grinning against her lips, he rubbed one long digit between her wet folds. Angel's moan was long and low as he speared her with his finger. After a few moments, he added a second.

"Alex! Alex!" Angel called.

Someone could come up on them at any minute. He knew they needed to hurry. He couldn't help himself from pleasuring her though. The thrill of being caught added to the desire that coursed through him.

With his free hand, he quickly yanked on the buttons of his jeans to get them loose enough to tug down the material so he could palm his cock.

"We're going to come together," he ordered her.

She reached for him. "Let me feel you," she pleaded.

He moved to kneel at her side so she had enough room to grasp his cock. Still fingering her, he had to concentrate on his task as she started to jerk his cock with a firm grip.

Rocking his hips into her hold, Alex couldn't stand it anymore. He speared three fingers deep inside her pussy, and she screamed as she climaxed. Grabbing a hold of her hand, he continued to stroke himself until his seed pumped out.

"Damn," he murmured, collapsing beside her on the ground.

Angel huffed before she started to laugh. "That was awesome."

"Yeah," he agreed. Okay, so he hadn't meant to get so carried away. The connection between the two of them was just so hot and he couldn't seem to keep his hands off her. He turned over to convince her to return to the house for a shower when he heard soft footsteps coming up to their hideaway spot.

"Someone's coming," he told her, rolling onto his knees. He yanked his pants back over his hips and started to straighten his clothing while Angel groaned. Chuckling, he reached down to kiss her quickly. "You'd better get dressed before someone else sees this amazing body. I don't share."

Her eyes widened before she quickly started to scramble around to right herself. They'd just gotten up on their feet and were still leaning on each other when a voice called out to them, "Are you done fucking? It's too hot out here to be hiking in the middle of fucking nowhere."

"Ah shit," Angel cursed.

Alex stiffened, pulling Angel behind him. Two men stepped into view and Alex bared his teeth, letting a growl roll though him.

"Hey at least we waited until you were done!" the taller one said with a smirk. Alex already didn't like the asshole. He had no business interrupting them. The man by his side was short and stocky.

"Who the hell are you and why are you on my property?" Alex demanded.

"Easy there, wolfie," the same man replied. "We were invited."

"Wolfie?" Alex fumed.

"Shut the fuck up, Kieran!" Angel yelled. "Alex, wait."

"You know these guys?" Alex demanded. The only reason that he held back was because Angel had grabbed a hold of his arm and he didn't want to hurt her by ripping himself free.

"I'm sorry." The shorter one lifted his hand in a placating manner before holding his neck slightly to the side in a sign of submission. "We don't let K out much. He doesn't have any manners.

Kieran huffed before throwing Stocky a dirty look.

Breathing deep, Alex took in the strange wolf shifter's scent. Asshole had no smell so he could guess that he was a vampire or Day Walker like Angel.

He nodded back to the shifter before glaring at the man who'd insulted him.

"Alex, these two guys are my partners at the agency. The blond is Remy and the rude one is Kieran."

"Hey!" Kieran protested.

"She's right. And Caspar just told you to behave," Remy stated as he walked past Kieran to shake Alex's hand.

Alex shook before turning back to Angel. "Caspar?"

"My boss," she explained.

"He's talking to your Alpha," Remy told him. "You're Alpha sent us to find you. He wants you back at the house. "

"And boy did we find you," Kieran sneered. "Any sooner and we'd really have gotten a show."

"Shut up, K!" Angel shouted at the same time Alex growled again.

"Damn, man, you don't know when to stop," Remy said, turning toward Kieran. "Now, we've delivered our message so we can go."

"I don't know," Kieran hedged. "I like it out here. All kinds of interesting sounds."

Alex knew that Kieran was talking about hearing him and Angel. Partner or not, Alex was going to teach the asshole some manners. He started forward and Kieran grinned at him.

"We don't have time for this," Remy blocked Kieran from Alex. "Caspar is getting the information on what your Alpha wants us to do. We should go see how we can help."

Kieran snorted. "Like I'm going to follow some *beast's* order."

Alex saw red he was so pissed. "You don't disrespect my Alpha!" he roared.

Chapter Four

Out of everyone her boss could bring with him, Angel had been hoping Kieran wouldn't be chosen. Instead of her wish, she now stood between Alex and Kieran, trying to keep the Guardian and wolf shifter from tearing out each other's throats.

"Kieran," she warned.

"What?" he snapped back. "You're telling me you're okay with giving the wolves the lead on this?"

"That's what Caspar said, plus the Pack are the ones in danger."

"Figures you'd side with them," Kieran accused. "You always did have a soft spot for animals."

Alex growled as he started taking a step forward. If she didn't know Kieran's history with shifters, she'd be the first one to punch him. But she did know what had happened when he'd been captured by a rogue Pack right after turning eighteen. Years of abuse at the hands of his tormentors had left a lasting impression on Kieran. The only shifter Kieran could stand being around was Remy. And that was only after years of working side by side.

"Bring it on, dog!" Kieran taunted.

"Knock it off, K." She pushed him back before turning to Alex. "Please don't."

Kieran stumbled a few steps, but easily caught his balance, glaring at her. It took a few more moments until Alex glanced over at her.

"I know he's an ass but he is my partner," she explained to her mate.

Rolling his shoulders, Alex relaxed his stance, although Angel could still detect the need inside him to defend his home and people.

"You don't have to explain yourself to him." Kieran spoke to her, but his words were no doubt for Alex.

Shaking her head, she tried to hold on to her patience. "While Caspar is talking with the Alpha why don't I take you to see Emilio," she offered, instead of continuing the fight Kieran wanted.

Kieran hissed at the mention of Emilio. They'd never gotten along either. Of course the one thing they had in common was their dislike for shifters, but Kieran was a Guardian through and through. He would never have allowed anyone to hurt an innocent. Even if they were a shifter.

Slipping her hand in Alex's, she tried to make a statement without having to spell it out for Kieran. Alex was hers. She would fight to defend him and his people. Not that she really thought he'd let her, but she knew how to handle her partner. Kieran wouldn't try to attack Alex again. Putting Kieran in the same room with Emilio meant that for the first time they might get an answer. Kieran could be one scary fucker when he wanted to be.

Dropping his eyes to her and Alex's intertwined fingers, Kieran lifted the corner of his mouth but remained silent. He spun on his heel so Angel tugged

Alex to follow. They might not have shared blood yet but there was a connection between the two of them. Through that link, she knew Alex remained wary of Kieran, but was also curious as to how the Guardian would handle Emilio. Once the mating was complete, she'd be able to pick up pieces of what Alex was feeling. That's what she'd been told anyway. The sacred bond that formed between Day Walkers and their intended kept her excitement at the forefront while they made their way to the house.

Entering from the patio door that led into the den, Kieran paused at the entry. Angel knew exactly what had stopped Kieran. The first feeling when she'd entered the large den was the noticeable homey atmosphere. The dark walls were broken up by large painted canvases and numerous framed photos. Family and friends were obviously important to Alex. He showcased where his heart belonged by the art he hung on the walls.

Furniture filled the room. To Angel's way of thinking, Alex's home must have been used often for family gatherings. She knew that his siblings lived at the ranch also in their own houses, but it looked as if Alex's place was the meeting point.

There was a large-screen television, fully stocked bar with bottles lined up on a shelf, and the most expensive stereo system she'd ever seen. The first time she'd entered, her breath had caught and the overwhelming feeling of comfort had spread over her.

Kieran would have recognized the same ambiance she had. Her friend recovered from his surprise quickly and his stance relaxed for the first time since he'd been introduced to Alex. Kieran was a creature of comfort and owned just as many gadgets while attempting the same domestic sense in his own place.

Even though Angel never settled herself, Kieran was different from her. Angel felt hope at the first spark of something for Alex and Kieran to share. She wanted the two men to get along. Sure Kieran was hard to care for, but she did.

"Nice," Kieran said very quietly before stalking through the room.

She glanced at Alex, noting his confused expression. Later she had more to tell her mate. The amount of information he needed to know kept growing. She should probably start writing down a list. If she was being honest with herself, she could admit to being reluctant to get into all of the secrets she held. If Alex wasn't ready for the strange world she lived in, would he run?

Day Walkers didn't recover easily from their mates rejecting them. Due to the illness that ran though her body, Angel needed someone who'd anchor her.

"Where is he?" Kieran questioned as they reached the hall.

Snapping out of her thoughts and worries, Angel pushed down what was going on with herself to concentrate on why the other Guardians had come in the first place.

"Upstairs, last door on the right," Alex answered before she could.

As Kieran stalked in that direction, with Remy at his heels, Alex held Angel back. "You okay?"

Trying for her most sincere smile, she looked up at him. "Yes, sorry, Kieran takes a little to get used to."

"That's not what I'm talking about," he said, drawing her closer. "I felt waves of worry coming from you."

In response she simply lifted an eyebrow in question.

"Shifters can pick up strong emotions. You knew that, didn't you?"

She did, but that meant Alex had to have been paying pretty close attention to her. "Sure."

"So...?" he pressed. Alex didn't seem like the type of man who would easily be put off.

"I guess I'm just concerned with so much happening at once," she tried to explain. "Me and the Day Walkers, the threat to the Pack, and all these strangers. It's a lot to take in."

He pulled her until their upper bodies brushed together. She could smell their earlier activities still on them. Of course that also meant that everyone else could too. They should probably clean up but Angel didn't want to. She liked that her claim was still clinging to Alex. *Mine,* her scent screamed to anyone who might wish to steal Alex away. Even though she was fully aware that Alex was surrounded by the same people who had always been in his life, she didn't know the shifters well. Her instinct was to assert that he belonged to her.

Burying her face in his chest, she breathed deeply. The entire day had been screwed up one way or another. Stating that Alex was her mate in the kitchen hadn't been smart. Especially with other wolf shifters around, but she hadn't been able to hold back any longer. Now that her boss and the other Guardians had arrived, they didn't have the time to sit back getting to know one another forming the bond she wanted.

"Hey," he said gently, his hand resting at the back of her head. "I might not know everything that is going on but I can help. This is my Pack. We'll gladly accept the assistance. Besides, that gives us more time to get to know each other."

While her worry didn't exactly disappear, Angel did feel better.

Above them, she heard a door slam against a wall and she jumped. "We'd better get up there before Kieran kills Emilio."

"I don't get why Kieran would be willing to help when he obviously feels the same about shifters," Alex commented.

"Trust me," she assured him, "Kieran is on our side."

They rushed up the wide stairs before jogging down the hall. The bedroom door stood open and as they reached the entry they skidded to a stop.

Kieran stood in front of a tied-up Emilio. Her partner's arms were crossed against his chest while he glared down at Emilio. The two shifters in the room were braced for an attack—crouched low and ready to either defend themselves or shift to keep their charge safe.

"It's okay, guys," Alex said to the guards, pulling Angel into the room. "I got this. Why don't you go downstairs and get some coffee?"

The guards straightened and nodded to Alex. Once they'd exited, Alex reached back and gently closed the door.

Emilio was tied by his arms, chest and feet to a sturdy wood chair. He'd been stripped down to only his dirty pants. If would be difficult for him to get loose, but it was possible. That was the reason there had been two guards stationed inside the room with him. He was a trained weapon and if he'd been at full strength, Emilio would be fighting. She'd suggested to the Pack doctor to inject Emilio with enough sedative that he'd sleep through the night. It seemed to have been a good idea.

Looking into Emilio's clear gaze, Angel was certain the drugs had worn off.

Emilio was glaring at Kieran, not even bothering to acknowledge Remy, Alex or her. Of course Kieran was the biggest threat to him at the moment.

"You broke your oath," Kieran said to their prisoner.

The words sent a shiver down her spine. Anyone who knew Kieran knew that was the worst betrayal to him.

"Did I?" Emilio challenged.

Angel gripped Alex's hand and dragged him to the far wall. Caspar wouldn't have sent Kieran if he hadn't wanted her partner to interrogate Emilio. It wouldn't be a pretty sight. Both Kieran and Emilio knew that but Alex didn't.

"You vowed to protect those who couldn't protect themselves," Kieran said coolly.

"I didn't agree to become a trained pet on a leash," Emilio threw back. "Admit it, K" — Emilio smiled — "wouldn't it feel good to get your revenge on the animals that tortured you?"

Kieran snarled and leaped forward. Emilio's chair tipped back as Kieran gripped the top of it in his hands. "You don't know me. Don't pretend."

Face pale, Emilio was shaking his head, showing fear for the first time. Still he didn't shut his damn mouth. "I know how it feels to take down one of those dogs," Emilio said. "To feel their blood in my hands. To watch the life drain out of their eyes."

Alex had started to growl as Emilio continued to taunt Kieran. She dug her nails into his hand to hold him back. She didn't need both Kieran and Alex going after Emilio. They didn't want him dead, yet.

Kieran straightened, letting the chair fall back down. Emilio's head snapped forward at the unexpected move. Kieran was grinning, flashing his fangs. "How many?" he asked quietly.

A spark of triumph entered Emilio's gaze. "Six, but we've just gotten started," he claimed.

"How many of you are there?" Kieran inquired, seeming more relaxed.

Emilio cut his gaze to where she and Alex stood.

"Don't worry about them." Kieran waved off their presence, but Emilio was shaking his head.

"I know how you feel about your partner," Emilio told him. "Get rid of them."

Hands clasped together, Kieran turned his head. Angel knew what he was doing. Trying to let Emilio think he'd be interested in joining the rogue ranks. She knew it wouldn't work, and, from the expression on his face, Kieran agreed. He turned back to their prisoner. "Nah, I like them here," Kieran stated cheerfully.

This time it was Emilio who snarled. "You were always weak!"

The grin slowly drained from Kieran's face until the mask of no emotion was in place. Bracing herself, Angel knew things were about to get worse for Emilio.

Kieran grabbed Emilio's throat. It was just a blur of movement her eyes couldn't follow. He was the fastest of all the Guardians. Trying to pull his head back, Emilio was no match for Kieran, especially tied down. Emilio's feet scraped at the floor but he couldn't get any push with his ankles secured.

"Who is the weak one here?" Kieran asked, tightening his hand.

It was a myth that their kind didn't need to breathe. Of course they did. Her heart pumped the same as every other living creature. Blood flowed through her veins just like humans. Cutting off his air supply could kill him, but just as his face turned a faint shade of red, Kieran released Emilio. Emilio sucked in a deep breath only to have it whoosh back out when Kieran punched his chest. The strike echoed around the room with a thud. Emilio was gasping as Kieran knelt in front of him.

"Now, you know I can do this all day," he told Emilio. "How about you?"

Tears ran down Emilio's face but he didn't respond. "You knew the minute you were captured that it would come to this. You betrayed the organization for your own agenda. You're going to tell us everything you know," Kieran declared.

Every hit, cut and pound of flesh that Kieran gave Emilio, Angel and Alex stood and watched. Day Walkers didn't heal like shifters. Especially without blood.

After the first half hour, Caspar and the Pack Alpha joined them. Caspar walked around to stand behind Kieran. Shawn and Remy remained close to the door to stop an attempted escape or someone from entering. That's what Angel thought anyway. None of them spoke so she didn't know for sure.

Kieran had barely paused when they'd entered. For fifteen more minutes the beatings went on and Angel found herself struggling with control. The scent of blood in the room was strong. It'd been several days since she'd fed. When Caspar held up a hand to Kieran, Angel relaxed with relief. Power radiated off Caspar like no one else she'd ever been around. Not even Pack Alphas had the same level of authority that Caspar surrounded himself in. Kieran stepped back. He brought up his hand to lick at the blood that coated it.

Angel's gums tingled with the need to let down her own fangs. Kieran was playing with the shifters in the room, trying to scare them by using the vampire myths against them. She'd seen him do it before. Most people believed all vampires or Day Walkers to be slaves to blood. While Remy showed no reaction, beside her Alex stiffened. Since she was pretty sure that her own needs would be evident to her mate, Angel kept her head bowed. She could still see Caspar kneel in front of Emilio.

"We have most of the others," Caspar said. "We know who we are after. All you have to do is tell us where they are."

Emilio lifted his head. "I wouldn't worry about it. They'll find you. All of you."

Shaking his head, Caspar rose. He glanced around the room before motioning with his head toward the door. Remy reached over and opened it before stepping out. Angel hurried to follow. It would be better to get outside in the fresh air, but at least escaping the strong scent of blood would help her gain control.

Two large men—shifters—stood in the hall.

"I don't think he'll give you any trouble but watch him closely," Alpha Shawn told the two men. They nodded before entering the room.

Remy led them away from Emilio. She knew Alex was right behind her as the others fell in step after him.

"You okay?" Alex's hand came down on her shoulder.

She didn't stop but nodded. His hand tightened briefly before patting her shoulder then falling away. Everyone was quiet while they descended the stairs toward the kitchen. Angel went immediately to the sink and turned on the cold water. Grabbing the hand towel from a hook, she wet the fabric and used it to cool down her face and neck. She could hear the others moving around.

"I'll make some coffee," Alex suggested.

She turned off the water before bracing both hands on the sink. She gazed out of the kitchen window, which was opened slightly. A small breeze floating through brought with it the aroma of fresh grass and Packed dirt. The whiff calmed her so she could pay attention to the Guardians and shifters in the room. Her gaze landed on Alex after she'd turned around. He'd just poured water into the large coffee machine but was watching her. She smiled before stepping closer. Brushing her hand down his arm, she hoped to tell him that she was indeed fine.

When his gaze dropped to her lips she knew he wanted to lean down and kiss her. They weren't alone, though. Winking as a promise for later, she strolled away from her mate.

Alpha Shawn and Remy were speaking quietly, but Caspar's intense stare was right on her. She dipped her head with respect before sitting beside him.

"You need to feed," he whispered with his mouth right next to her ear.

Before she could respond, a low growl filled the room. She jerked away from Caspar as Alex stalked forward, eyes on her boss.

"Alex." Shawn stood blocking his way.

Angel jumped up from her seat and rushed forward but she couldn't reach her mate since Shawn's huge body was between them.

The rumble was still coming from Alex. Shawn responded with a low snarl while gripping Alex's shoulders. Angel squeaked in protest but Remy, out of nowhere, put himself between her and the other two shifters.

"Let his Alpha handle this," Remy said softly.

She wanted to protest, but Caspar's grip on the back of her neck had her submitting. She watched as Shawn pushed Alex down, the Alpha taking Alex all the way down to the floor. Shawn was crouched in front of Alex murmuring to him.

With adrenaline spiking through her body, it took several minutes before she could make out what Shawn was saying to Alex. She raised her shaking hands to grip the front of Remy's shirt. She wanted to comfort her mate but instead didn't know how to help.

Chapter Five

The wolf had been so close to the surface that Alex wasn't surprised to find himself on the kitchen floor with his Alpha looming over him.

It had started during the interrogation. Each time Emilio had taunted Kieran with how he'd killed shifters, he'd wanted to step in and pound the evil man himself. Even though he wasn't the most dominant wolf in the Pack, he still couldn't stomach the fact that his fellow shifters had been tortured and murdered for no other reason than what they were.

He'd been relieved being able to exit that horrible room. The scent of blood kept his animal too interested in his surroundings. Alex normally had no problem controlling himself. In fact, he actually shifted a lot less than some of the others in his Pack. He'd always thought of himself as mostly human with only partial animal instincts.

He wasn't so sure now.

Something was obviously bothering Angel since they'd entered the kitchen. She tried to smile and act as if she was fine but he could see it in her tight features and uneven breathing.

The last straw was seeing another man, a stranger, touching and speaking into her ear. Without even realizing what he'd been doing he'd almost pounced, only to be stopped by his Alpha.

Now, shaking and sweating from where Shawn pinned him, Alex had to struggle not to fight. Emotions still swamped him and he couldn't see reason. His wolf wanted to get to Angel and claim her in front of the others. To let the men in the room know that she belonged to him and only him.

"That's it," Shawn crooned in his ear. "Let it go. Get control once again."

His vision, which at some point had grayed, cleared. He peered up at his leader, trying to tell him how sorry he was for snapping.

"It's fine," Shawn replied to his silent plea. "Everyone here understands."

Did they? They weren't shifters. Plus, he wasn't even certain he knew exactly what had happened. *Shit! What must Angel think?* He closed his eyes in embarrassment.

"Ready to get up?" Shawn asked gently.

Better face the music. He nodded and accepted the hand that his Alpha had offered. Once on his feet, Alex raised his head to see Angel close by. The two Guardians stepped away at the same time Shawn's bulk disappeared.

Angel's gaze met his. Alex wasn't sure what he'd been expecting but the compassion visible was a shock. He held out his hand and she leaped to take it within hers. He pulled her against his body, wrapping his arms around her. Burying his nose into her neck, peace settled through him.

She was rubbing his back while peppering kisses against his neck. Clarity back, he squeezed her once more, easing his hold. He didn't let her go but instead tucked her into his side.

"I apologize for my behavior," he told Caspar.

"As do I." Caspar held out his hand. "I know better than to be so close to a shifter's mate when the claiming hasn't been completed. I was worried about Angel and wasn't thinking clearly."

Alex shook his hand. It rankled that he had to show any sort of submission to a stranger in his home but Caspar's dominance was even stronger than his Alpha's. Plus, he could easily pick up Angel's respect and care for the man. After the tension with Kieran, he didn't want that to extend to the rest of Angel's team.

"I'll grab the coffee," Remy offered. Alex glanced up at Remy, receiving a nod of approval.

He flushed slightly. He'd lost control not only in front of his Alpha and his mate but Remy, a strange shifter in his territory.

Angel was tugging him to the table so he couldn't worry about it just then. Angel slipped into one of the chairs against the wall. He scooted his chair closer to hers before settling on the sturdy seat. He placed his arm around her shoulder as she instantly cuddled into his embrace. Having her acknowledge his claim calmed his wolf, until, inside, he actually felt his animal stretch in contentment.

Remy arrived at the table with mugs and containers of sugar and milk. He hurried back, grabbing the coffee pot while they shuffled around cups. Once he had a full mug he took a strong whiff. He'd used his favorite southern blend that included pecans. The rich aroma drifted to his nose, making him smell home.

Beside him, Angel took a small sip of the hot drink and moaned. "This is good," she told him.

Instead of commenting, Alex had to shift slightly in his chair as his body came alive at the sound she'd made. His hard cock pressed against the zipper of his jeans. Since he was in a room with others like him he needed to contain his arousal. The scent would be too easy to recognize.

Kieran grunted across from him, drawing his attention. He had his nose buried in his cup. He glanced up and grinned. "I need to take some of this with me."

Alex laughed. "It's a local company. I'll get you a pound or two."

The transformation that overtook Kieran was startling. Instead of the dangerous being that had pounded on someone not less than ten minutes ago, he was practically bouncing in his spot.

Angel giggled softly while Caspar appeared used to the change in Kieran and looked at him like an amused parent.

"You've just found the secret to getting along with K," Remy told him with a wink.

Shawn cleared his throat. "Shall we discuss our next move?" he asked, pulling them back to the reason they were all there.

"I don't think we'll get anything more from Emilio here," Caspar commented. "I'd like to take him back to our home base. The others are already locked up."

"I agree." Shawn nodded.

"What about the other three?" Remy questioned. "We sent people to Lubbock but they couldn't come up with anything."

Marcus' daughter Kayla had barely escaped a kidnapping attempt while Marcus had been shot.

Kayla lived in Lubbock and had hurried to her father's aid even with someone after her. It took less than two hours to drive from Lubbock to Canyon so they'd been working on the assumption that the attack on Marcus was connected to Kayla's attempted kidnapping. Turned out they were right.

"Remy and I could go check it out," Kieran spoke up. "We know more now."

"That might be a good idea," Shawn agreed. "I could send a few of my wolves with you."

"Nah." Kieran waved the offer aside. "We know what we're up against. Plus I don't think we can count on them still being there. Your Pack should still be on guard here."

"Yes, I'd say the rogue agents are going to make a statement soon. They'll either try to finish things here or hit us at home. We've captured most of the Guardians that had gone off on their own but we also picked up two men who weren't connected to us. Hopefully, once we get Emilio secured, he'll feel a little more…talkative," Caspar told them.

Alex could read between the lines. Once Emilio was at the Guardians' facility they would find one way or another to get what they needed out of him. The small display upstairs had really been nothing. He shivered knowing just how damn dangerous this group was. Peering down at Angel, he wondered how she faired with the organization.

"I'd like to leave Angel here. She can set up a secure network between the Pack and our people." Caspar looked over at where Angel was ticked up against him. "Plus I believe she has some unfinished business here."

"I'm in the room," Angel teased.

Caspar laughed.

"I think this sounds good to me. We appreciate any help we can get," Shawn said. "Marcus returned home this morning, taking Kayla and Chase with him. They were going to shift and run in the area around the canyon to see if they could pick up anything else. I also have my Alpha-in-training, Max, speaking with the Wolf Council," Shawn told them.

"We'll drive to Lubbock, but if we don't find anything we'll head back up here just in case," Remy added.

"After lunch," Kieran stated firmly. "And more of this coffee."

* * * *

Alex led Angel up the stairs, away from the guest rooms to where the master suite was located. Remy had volunteered to make lunch just as Max and Cassie had arrived from her house next door. Cassie had suggested they grill out so plans had been made quickly.

He was still shaky from losing control earlier so he'd stolen away with Angel to have a few minutes alone. Angel was quiet as they walked slowly to his room. While he always kept guest rooms available for the Pack, his own space was at the back of the house and farthest away from the other bedrooms.

No one came into his private space. Not even his brother and sister. Because he shared his home with so many members of the Pack when they needed him, Alex had found that he craved solace once in a while. Cassie had suggested he make the master suite his own.

At the time Alex hadn't taken her seriously, but over the years he and his wolf had become more in need of separation from the demands of the Pack. He held his breath as he opened the bedroom door, allowing Angel to enter before him.

She gasped when stepping inside. Grinning, he closed the door before wrapping his arms around her from behind.

He'd knocked out a wall, making two rooms into one large space. Closest to the door, on the left side, was a soft brown fabric couch with matching reclining chair. The walls were floor-to-ceiling bookcases that held his favorite books.

Across the room the king-size bed was on a platform with a huge bay window. The dark chocolate bedspread matched the rest of the décor. Tucked in a corner was a small mini fridge and counter for snacks. Angel wouldn't be able to see the bathroom and Alex had to fight the urge to take her in to wow her even more.

"This is awesome," Angel said, turning in his arms. She looked up at him. "I love how warm it is."

He grinned back at her. That's what he wanted her to feel. To their right stood the rock mantle for the fireplace. During the winter, when snow covered the ground, he could see himself wrapped around Angel in front of the roaring fire. "I'm glad you like it."

She rose onto the tips of her toes. "Is this all you wanted to show me?" she asked suggestively.

Just like that, in less than a minute, his cock was hard and straining for release. Bending his head down, he brushed his lips over hers. "No," he confessed.

"Good," she told him before burying her fingers in his hair and holding his head still.

He moaned as Angel licked at his closed lips. Opening for her, he tasted coffee and woman as their tongues grazed against each other and played. He tightened the hold he had on her back, pulling her even closer.

Sparks sizzled down his spine all the way to his toes. Need, almost overwhelming, welled up until Alex had to jerk back his head.

"I still don't have full control over myself," he admitted shamefully.

She was already shaking her head. She tugged his tucked-in shirt from his jeans. "I don't want control."

He allowed her to raise the shirt over his head. Once his chest was bare, Alex was impatient to get Angel's clothes off. Kissing her deeply, he went to work on the button of her pants while pushing up her blouse. Only when they had to stop to catch their breaths did they pull back. At that time Angel let her top fall to the floor.

Angel's body was gorgeous. Her breasts were full and round, encased inside black silk. Alex cupped her mounds, causing her head to fall back. Her sighing while he brought his lips to the soft garment spurred him on. He used his teeth to nip just above her clothing until she reached behind her and unhooked her bra. As her smooth skin was revealed, he dropped to his knees. He ran his hands down to her hips and took one pert nipple between his lips. He sucked while she started to tremble with need. He could smell her excitement and already loved the scent. He was a man who depended on his nose to tell him things. He didn't actually need his extra senses, though, as Angel was vocal enough. She hissed, gripping the back of his head as he trailed his tongue from one breast to another.

Tracing the top of her pants with his fingers, he teased with what was to come.

"Alex," she pleaded hoarsely.

He lowered his mouth to her stomach and kissed her skin while tugging down her pants, making sure to snatch her panties also. She had to lift her feet so he could slip off her shoes and socks, but before long she was naked in front of him.

His cock was still stiffer than he could ever remember it being but first he needed to take care of Angel. So ignoring his own need, he gained his feet, picking her up with him. Her quick intake of breath gave away her surprise. He nipped her chin playfully as he strolled to the bed. Giggling, she squirmed in his hold, brushing her chest against his.

He laid her down on top of the light tan sheets after pulling back the heavy brown comforter. Her dark complexion seemed to glow above the lighter bedding. She reached out a hand but he caught it in his. He placed a kiss on her wrist, as he raised an eyebrow.

Lifting her face, she narrowed her eyes. "Don't tease," she complained.

He took a step back as he dropped her hand. He bent to remove his boots, hopping from one foot to another. It would have been much easier to sit on the bed but he was worried that once he was down he wouldn't be able to resist Angel's tempting body. Instead he struggled with his boots and socks before finally pulling down his zipper. He almost went lightheaded with the release of his erection from the confine of his pants.

He quickly shucked the rest of his clothes. While watching him, Angel had been running her palms down her stomach and up to cup her breasts. Watching her touch herself, Alex could think of a lot more fun they could have next time. He needed her too much right then to watch her pleasure herself. Damn it was a turn on, though. Hopefully soon he could talk her into giving him a show.

He grasped his cock, giving himself a few tugs while her eyes roamed over him. As soon as she licked her lips he knew he'd made them both wait as long as they'd be able. Alex climbed on the bed between her legs, circling her ankles with his palms. Slowly he ran his hand up her legs, forcing her to spread for him. Yes, he could smell her need and arousal.

Barely brushing his thumbs over the wet folds that covered her pussy had her lifting her hips. With his elbows down between her legs to hold her in place, Alex opened her up to lick at her entrance.

"Please," she begged so sweetly.

He buried his face and feasted while she squirmed under him. He added his fingers and started to prepare her to take his cock. He couldn't wait to be inside. First he wanted to blow her mind. Plunging two fingers in and out, he brought his lips down to her clit and sucked hard.

She cried out as she crested over the edge, Angel found her climax, arching and clawing at the bed. Alex worked her through her orgasm until she was panting and flat on the sheets. He climbed up her body before using his knees to keep her open. He sought her mouth so he could share her unique flavor. Diving into the kiss, he moved his hips to drag his hard-on against her leg.

Angel's nails dug into his lower back while their tongues battled for dominance. Finally she relented and let him control the speed and pressure of the kiss. Once she'd given in, he lifted his head. He positioned his cock at her entrance. With her heels planted on the bed, Angel lifted up to accept him.

Slowly he pushed in.

Fuck, yeah. It felt good to have his cock sliding into her slick, sweet pussy.

Before he'd filled her completely he withdrew only to snap his hips then thrust deeply. This time he plunged fully. Angel was already moving in rhythm with him. They clung together as he drove them closer to the edge. Sweat covered their bodies with the force of their coupling. Angel had her chin tilted back and eyes clenched, urging him on with moans and huffs of breath.

He'd known it wouldn't take him long to come once he'd gotten inside her, but he had to take her with him in pleasure. He braced his knees firmly on the soft mattress and sat back and lifted her ass in the palms of his hands. He held her hips off the bed, driving himself faster and harder.

Her cries grew in volume as he sped up the pace.

"Alex!" she screamed at the same time her inner muscles clamped down on his cock.

With one hand beside her head, he drove in one more time before he lost it. Vision blurry, his climax hit him and he came, empting his seed deep inside his mate.

"Holy shit!" He managed to get out the words.

Angel collapsed back, gazing up at him. The blue of hers eyes were even more amazing than before. The color was bright with the sparkle from earlier, but now they actually glowed, showing her arousal. Still blue, her eyes could probably light up an entire room when they looked like that. He'd only seen them glow once before, but it caused shivers of anticipation that he could draw that reaction from her.

Day Walker—what Angel was hit him suddenly. She'd said she drank blood but she hadn't bitten him.

She was faster and stronger than a human, but that was the only evidence that she was different, if he didn't count her glowing eyes.

He stared down at her but she wasn't trying to hide this from him. He wondered if this was why she'd kept her face buried from view before.

Doesn't matter. She was allowing him to see her now.

With their gazes locked, he bent his head. Raising her face, she smiled so trustingly that Alex knew he'd just met his match in every way.

Chapter Six

Angel knew she couldn't hide her reaction to Alex's and her mating. After what they had just shared, there was no going back now. Alex belonged to her.

With gentle hands, Alex cupped her face as he peppered kisses over her forehead and cheeks. She closed her eyes, enjoying the post-lovemaking attention.

"You are so beautiful," Alex told her quietly.

It was all too much. Tears of joy pooled in her eyes. She blinked rapidly, trying to hold them back. She didn't know what she'd done to deserve a man like Alex but she was going to appreciate every moment with him.

"I wonder how long we can hide out in here?" he asked while he finally settled down by her side.

Rolling onto her stomach so she could rest her chin on his chest, she peered up at him and just smiled. "I bet not long."

"I'm glad you're staying here."

"Me too," she admitted. But what about when this was over? She still had a job to do, and Alex's place was with his mate.

"Can I ask you something?"

The way his body had stiffened while he'd spoken had tension tightening her shoulders. "Sure."

"In the den, you said that you drink blood. I saw Kieran's fangs. Why didn't you bite me?" He sounded honestly confused.

"I wouldn't do that without your permission," she assured him. Curling her legs under her body, she slowly sat up.

Alex raised enough to lean his back against the headboard and they were facing each other. Time seemed to draw out as he reached for her hand. He never took his eyes off her, but he didn't speak either.

"Alex?" she asked. How had he really thought she would bite him during sex?

"But you do want to bite me?" he asked.

Unsure how to answer that, Angel had no choice but to be honest. She nodded.

"Okay."

"Okay?" she repeated.

"I thought maybe you didn't want to," he confessed.

Why wouldn't I want to drink from my mate? Have I done something to make Alex think I don't want him? Angel was trying to give Alex time to get used to what she was. Surely he'd seen movies where vampires bit... *Oh, oh!* She understood! She started to laugh. He frowned when she tipped to the side, not able to contain it.

"Sorry, sorry," she said, waving her hand but unable to stop giggling.

Waiting patiently for her to stop, he couldn't hide the twitch of his own lips.

"I just pictured what you must have been imagining," she told him.

"Not really seeing what's so funny," he commented, pulling her back toward him.

She went willingly. "While I might take a nip while we're making love I wouldn't actually drink from you," she explained. "There is too big a chance of taking too much blood, which would hurt me and kill you."

"What do you mean hurt you?"

"I do need to drink blood. But not because I'm dead or something like that."

"You said before that all the myths about vampires weren't true," he pressed.

"I have a blood disorder. It is heredity for my kind. I need to replace my tainted blood with fresh, good blood. The poisoned blood eats away at the good blood, so if I don't feed I will die."

"That's a lot different than most stories," Alex commented.

"Yes, our belief is our kind has evolved through many centuries and in the order to survive we've adapted." She tapped her teeth. "That's why we believe we have fangs that drop."

"I've seen you in the sun," he stated.

"There is no reason I can't be outside during the day. I have no problem entering a church. I eat garlic and am not burned by crosses."

"So just about everything is wrong."

She nodded.

"How much blood do you need?"

"Not a lot, and the older we get, the less we need. I can't turn someone into what I am either. You have to be born with this disease."

"That's amazing," Alex said. "I would never have imagined any of this was possible."

There was more that she needed to tell him but Alex was taking everything so well she didn't want to ruin anything.

"What about the increased strength and speed?"

"We get those benefits from the difference in our blood. The more we use it, the more good blood that gets eaten."

"So, since the fight yesterday, you should have fed?"

This was what she was afraid he'd figure out. "Yes."

"So how should we do this?"

"No, not yet," Angel told him.

"You need it," he argued.

"I can feed from Remy before he leaves," she replied easily.

"No!" His voice rose, surprising her. "Sorry, I didn't mean to shout. But my wolf isn't going to allow you to be that intimate with someone else."

"It's not like that. It's just like any other procedure. Fast and easy."

"Maybe, but with my wolf close to the surface, it wouldn't be a good idea. After the way I reacted to Caspar close to you, knowing that you were feeding from someone else wouldn't be good."

"Alex…" She couldn't do it.

"I never lose control like that," he said, gripping her hands. "Never."

Their bond had already started. She understood that but… Shit, she was going to have to confess.

Taking a deep breath, she prepared for the worst part. "Alex, when I feed from someone it makes them sick."

"What do you mean?"

"The poison that's involved transfers from me to my donor. It dangerous."

"How sick would I get?"

He still wants to do it? Angel was truly shocked by his offer. She knew other Day Walkers who'd had to wait years for what Alex was willing to give so freely.

"We belong together. You called me your mate."

"Yes but..."

"So how sick will I get?"

"I don't know," she replied honestly. "Remy usually gets a headache and sometimes sick to his stomach. Shifters seem to do okay, much better than a full human, but I really don't know. You should be okay."

He nodded.

She appreciated what he was willing to do but Angel knew Alex didn't know what he was actually offering.

"Hey." He kissed her lips gently. "I want to do this."

Angel had to get blood one way or another. If Alex didn't want her to get substance from Remy this was the only other alternative.

"Please be sure," she told him, but already her gums tingled in anticipation.

"I am," he promised.

Bringing his arm over her lap, she thumbed the inside of his elbow. "Close your eyes," she ordered softly.

He snorted but complied with her request. Her fangs breaking through hurt but she knew that wouldn't last long. She looked over her to mate to make sure he hadn't changed his mind.

But no, Alex remained relaxed, offering up himself. Powerless to resist her mate's blood due to both her need and the desire to taste him, she bent forward. As carefully as she could, she sliced her fangs into his soft flesh.

He hissed but didn't jerk away.

Sweet, precious blood flowed from her mate into her mouth, to coat her tongue. She took a deep pull, which was like liquid gold. The high from the exchange had her vision sharpening as a sense of peace overcame her. A couple more deep drinks and she extracted her fangs. She licked the cuts, although another myth was her being able to close the wounds.

She did it just to soothe him. Alex opened his eyes, and she tried to gauge how he was doing. He smiled at her and she relaxed. A box of tissues was on the nightstand beside the bed so she reached over to grab one.

Alex had already started to heal but she blotted at the small amount of blood.

"You okay?" she questioned.

"Fine," he replied, leaning forward.

A loud pounding on the door made them jerk apart before their lips could touch.

"Hey!" a female voice shouted. "Lunch is ready!"

"We'll be right there," Alex yelled back. He returned his attention to her. "I guess we should get dressed and go down before my sister barges in."

"Okay," she agreed even though she really didn't want to get up. But after they'd eaten, Remy and Kieran would be taking off and she needed to speak with them first.

"I wish we could stay right here." Alex's words corresponded with her feelings. "After we eat, maybe we can sneak away again."

Angel was in full agreement.

Alex's head ached with what he would call a very mild headache but he'd expected a lot worse with how worried Angel had been. Watching her dress, it was all he could do not to wrestle her back onto the bed.

"I know what you're thinking and we don't have time," Angel told him without even looking up. "It's *your* sister that will barge in here."

He didn't really think Cassie would burst into the room. In fact, he was certain she would be more than happy to make excuses for them. But they had responsibilities and couldn't put them off. The safety of the Pack wouldn't suffer because he wanted to get laid. However, once this was all over, he was locking Angel in his room for at least twenty-four hours—maybe forty-eight, he amended.

After yanking back on his jeans he strolled to the closet to get a clean T-shirt. Passing Angel, he stopped for a quick kiss. She grinned up at him with a dazzling smile. He hadn't noticed before how pale she'd gotten from when she'd first arrived. Now that her face had regained some color, he worried that she'd not let him know what she'd needed.

As her mate he should provide for her. That brought up another question.

"You said we're mates," he said while reaching into the closet to grab a top. "How did you know?" he asked, turning back to her.

She was done dressing and sat on the bed. "I know that shifters choose their mates and you don't believe in destiny," she started.

He held up a hand. "Actually there have been stories about fated mates. It's very rare but a few years ago there was a couple not far from here in southern Oklahoma who were believed to have been fated. Cain and Emily are mated now, and from the stories I've heard they are one of the strongest bonded mates ever," he shared. He'd never met the couple but their story was told from Pack to Pack as a sort of fairy tale. Everyone wanted to find that special person who completed them.

"Good," Angel replied. "So you may understand better than I thought. A Day Walker can only feed from someone a few times before they get too sick to be used any longer. Because of this we have to be very careful who we get substance from. Our mate, or bonded, can feed us for all our days without getting poisoned. You'll get sick, but unless I drink all your blood you won't die."

"That's good to know."

"How are you feeling?" she asked, and he could hear the concern.

"Actually I feel fine."

She looked skeptical, which he guessed he shouldn't be too surprised about.

"I had a small headache at first, but I've started moving around, I really do feel fine. It didn't seem like you took too much today? Is that a normal amount?" he asked since he still wasn't sure that Angel would tell him what she needed. He wanted to understand everything about her so he knew how to take care of his mate.

He had no doubt that Angel was his. He'd been feeling the connection from the very beginning. It hadn't really hit him yet that he'd found his mate. Sure he was excited, but there just hadn't been time to think about it. Alex always thought about everything. Cassie accused him of overthinking too often, but Alex didn't take that as an insult. "Ready?" He extended his hand to Angel.

Leading the way from the bedroom, Alex kept Angel's hand between his two so she practically had to walk against him. He was playing with her, but the smell of her amusement and happiness told him she didn't mind.

They cut through the den to exit the house directly onto the porch. He smiled as he stopped and just looked around. He brought their hands up to his heart as the scene in front of him surprised him.

Max and Remy were leaning back against the rail with cold beers in their hands. They had big smiles on their faces and they spoke animatedly. Shawn and Casper were seated at the picnic table and had their heads together, talking quietly.

The biggest surprise was Kieran, who stood at the work cabinet mixing something in a large bowel, laughing with Cassie.

"They look like one big happy family," Angel stated in awe at his side.

That was exactly what he'd been thinking.

"Hey!" Remy noticed them first.

As everyone turned toward them with smiles and sly looks he refused to be embarrassed that they knew what he and Angel had been up to.

The scent of burgers cooking drew his attention so he released Angel to head over to the grill. His mate stopped at the table to visit with Shawn and Caspar.

"Hey, brother," Cassie said as he walked behind her.

Since he'd played a role in getting Cassie together with her mate, Max, he knew she was going to tease him. "Cassie." He nodded to her.

"Glad you could join us," she continued while glancing over her shoulder with a huge smile.

"I couldn't let you make the burgers," he teased back. "We don't want charcoal meat."

Kieran snorted as Cassie tossed a piece of fruit at him.

He caught the apple slice before popping it in his mouth. As he lifted the lid to the barbeque, the scent drifted up. His stomach was already growling in hunger. After reaching for the spatula he flipped them all once. "Yeah, these are about done," he stated.

"I'll go grab the buns," Cassie offered without waiting for his acknowledgment.

"I got the platter," Kieran told her.

"Thanks," Alex told Kieran as he brought the large plate they used to stack the burgers on. He started to slide the meat from the grill onto the platter.

"You fed Angel," Kieran spoke softly.

He jerked up his head to meet Kieran's gaze. Kieran's features were soft and his normally hard eyes seemed lighter. "She wouldn't have asked so you must have offered. She's funny like that," Kieran told him. "I was worried, but I'm glad to see you're taking care of her needs."

At first he tensed thinking Kieran was being critical but his nose was telling him that Kieran was being sincere and was relieved.

"She's my mate," he said. "I'll do anything for her."

"Good," Kieran said simply before his expression returned to the same mask of no emotion that the man normally tried for.

It hit him that Kieran didn't want people to know how much he really cared about them. Angel had told him that Kieran was more than he appeared, and Alex was starting to see it. Alex wouldn't point out his findings to Kieran just yet. He had a feeling that the more he was with Angel he'd also be adding Kieran, Remy and Caspar into his circle of family and close friends.

With the burgers ready to serve, he nodded to Kieran to take them to the table. Closing the lid, he turned to the others. Everyone had started to take their seats and he noticed they'd left a spot open between Angel and Remy.

Strolling forward, Alex joined the others. As soon as he was sitting beside Angel she passed him a beer. He took a long drink before setting it down to accept a bowl of potato salad. He filled his plate as food was delivered to him then handed it over to Remy. No one really talked while they settled into eating except a few teasing words and grunts of compliments. Even with the new arrivals at the table, the meal was like any other he'd hosted in his yard. Smiling, he picked up his burger to take a big bite. A discussion on the horses was brought up by Caspar and they spoke about them for a while.

"So you gonna get on one?" Remy asked Angel.

"I think so," she responded although somewhat hesitant. "Alex thinks he has a mare that I could learn to ride on."

Kieran opened his mouth, but Caspar pointed his fork at him. "Don't even," Caspar ordered.

Although Kieran tried to shrug innocently they all knew a crude comment had been about to be added to the conversation. Angel glared over at Kieran before tipping her head to wink at Alex.

Heat from the promise in her eyes made sitting at the table more difficult. He didn't want to get an erection surrounded by so many people who could scent him. Angel wasn't helping when she slipped her hand under the table to rub it across his knee. It wasn't overly sexual but his body wasn't getting that message. Just a touch from Angel and he was as hard as nails.

He caught her hand in his as her fingers traveled up his thigh toward his crotch. *Oh, she wants to play huh?*

Grasping her hand gently, he brought her palm down on his erection to apply pressure. *God, that feels good!* Tightening her fingers, Angel delivered a prefect stroke. He sat straighter, realizing while he and Angel were occupied, the conversation had moved on to the trip to Lubbock for Remy and Kieran.

Placing his hand over Angel's, he had to admit defeat. She would have probably continued to rub him to release. She'd called his bluff.

"Justin and Randy are headed over," Remy mentioned. "Since Kayla is staying a few more days they agreed to show us where Kayla and Randy were chased from."

Angel jerked her hand away. "What?"

"Don't worry, we'll keep an eye on them," Remy promised. "Randy needs to get back to work and your brother wants to go home. He said he's had enough company for a while."

Alex was kind of sad that he wouldn't get to spend more time with Angel's brother. He hadn't gotten to know the quiet but intense man very well.

"You'd better not let anything happen to them," Angel ordered, deadly serious.

Both Guardians nodded.

She leaned into Alex a little so he put his arm around her shoulder. He knew Angel and Justin were pretty close. He'd make a call to the wolves in the area of Justin's place so they could also keep an eye out for trouble.

As Angel's brother, Justin now belonged to him too.

Chapter Seven

It was later than what she'd planned by the time Angel climbed up the stairs, heading toward Alex's bedroom. Before everyone had been able to take off she had got to spend some time with her brother. Justin and Alex seemed to get along as well.

"I don't know about you but I am exhausted," she said as they entered the main suite. She still couldn't believe what an amazing space Alex had made for himself. She loved every inch of it.

"How about a hot shower?" he asked while closing the door behind him.

She moaned because that sounded like heaven. Even better if Alex planned on joining her. "Yes please."

Alex's chuckle was rich and deep. He grabbed her from behind, spinning her to face him. "I want to hear you make that sound again," he said with a soft voice before dipping his head.

Leaning up, she met his lips with hers. The contact initiated sparks through her entire body. She held tight, clinging to his shoulders as he lifted her off her feet. "God, I love shifter strength," she praised against his mouth.

"You haven't seen anything yet," he promised, walking toward the bathroom.

Excitement filled her and already she couldn't wait to get her hands on him. Actually, she mused to herself, she didn't have to wait.

She was rewarded as a shudder racked through his body when she ran her tongue around the shell of his ear. He stumbled, bringing a small smile to her face. Since she was pretty sure he had a good hold on her she released his shoulders to run one hand down his back.

Under her palm, his muscles stretched. Alex had the kind of body that Angel could appreciate. He wasn't a gym rat but instead worked hard with the horses, keeping his body in prime shape.

They reached the doorframe so Angel glanced over her shoulder. Her breath caught at the elegance of the room. Squirming, she silently asked Alex to release her. He did.

"Wow!" Stepping away from him, she couldn't hold back her awe. The gray marble and rock that covered the walls was gorgeous. The bathroom was bigger than most people's living rooms.

"When I decided to remodel I wanted to make this comfortable and somewhere my mate would love."

"You did a fantastic job," she told him with honesty.

She ran her finger over the countertop to the his-and-hers sinks. Angel could see herself getting ready in this space every day. Would Alex want that with her? Though they'd discussed how Angel knew Alex was his mate, they hadn't made any plans about the future.

She knew they needed to get to know each other better. Alex had no idea what being mated to a Guardian meant.

"Here's my favorite part." Alex drew her from her own thoughts.

Alex grasped her hand, pulling her along. They passed the large Jacuzzi tub before standing in front of a huge, standing, shower stall with frosted glass doors. He pulled the door open, letting her peer inside. There were three wide shower heads pointed down at the tiles. The space was massive and just the perfect size for them. "Join me?" he inquired with a lifted eyebrow.

Angel was already pulling her shirt over her head. "Try to stop me," she replied back playfully.

He laughed while reaching in to turn on the knobs. He appeared relaxed and happy. She felt good just hearing the sound. Alex's mirth warmed a part of her that she hadn't realized had grown cold over the years. Angel still couldn't believe that coming to this small shifter town had resulted in the peace that she was now filled with. When her brother had first called her, asking for help for Kayla and Randy, she'd actually been annoyed. Returning from a long trip on the west coast, Angel had just wanted to sleep for days before burying herself in a good book. Instead, after only four hours of sleep, she'd climbed into her vehicle and made the long drive to Texas.

Not that she wouldn't have done anything for Justin but she'd been worn out and tired. While on the road she'd started to feel guilty about her feelings. Justin, being the only one in her immediate family who kept constant contact with her, made any request he had difficult to ignore.

Calling Caspar while driving and not before she'd set off had been a good idea. He would have insisted that she take Remy or Kieran along. She loved her partners, really she did, but meeting Alex had changed everything.

Now she owed her brother for dragging her into the shifter mess and introducing her to Alex.

"Hey," Alex said softly, reaching for her.

Realizing she'd stopped undressing and was staring at him, Angel flushed in embarrassment.

"Sorry," she said quietly. "Got lost in thought."

"Well let me bring you back to the present." He went to work unzipping her pants and helping her out of the rest of her clothing. He was still fully dressed so she returned the favor.

Steam had started to fill the air around them. Alex reached in to test the temperature before holding out a hand to her. He allowed her to enter the stall first but followed closely behind. As soon as the hot water hit her shoulders she moaned once again. It felt so damn good.

"That's what I wanted to hear," he said, wrapping himself around her.

Leaning against his strong body, she let the flow of the water hit her chest and stomach while Alex's soapy hands started at her throat and began to travel lower.

Tipping her head against his chest, Angel just accepted Alex's touch and let herself float. Turning when Alex directed her with his hands, she closed her eyes, and the aroma of soap and Alex drifted around her. Alex started to pepper her skin with gentle kisses. Reaching behind her, she gripped the back of his head making her body bow.

"I love the feel of you in my hands," Alex murmured.

"I like you touching me," she confessed.

Her words were rewarded with a groan and he twirled her quickly. Her shoulders hit the tiled wall with Alex immediately closing in on her. Their mouths connected desperately.

While Angel fed on the taste of Alex he wrapped his hands around her waist, lifting her up. Her legs being up around her waist left her open for him.

"Please," she pleaded.

His fingers entered her wet pussy.

"Yes!" Moving her hips forward, she encouraged him.

"I'm going to bury myself in you. Claim you," Alex told her as he added a second finger.

Words wouldn't come so she agreed with pants and cries. "Alex, now!"

"Yes now."

His cock replaced his fingers. She gripped his arms as Alex pinned her to the wall, his cock impaling her. He filled her completely, not giving her a chance to catch her breath before withdrawing then plunging back inside.

Angel could feel each thrust through her whole body. Her chest expanded in need of air. Her breasts were full and flushed. Her blood pumped rapidly as Alex pounded her with pleasure.

She wasn't going to last. But at least she could take Alex over the edge with her.

He held her hips firmly while he pistoned in and out of her. Angel leaned forward and, at the same time as he pressed inside, she clamped her mouth down on his shoulder.

Angel didn't break skin but instead sucked to pull up a mark.

"Yes!" Alex cried out when he started to come.

His seed spilling inside her was enough for her to reach her own climax. Angel had never been happier to be mated with a shifter right then. To feel his release inside her was something that she wouldn't be able to describe if asked. Since shifters didn't transmit diseases to other species and mates very rarely ever used contraception, Angel felt claimed both inside and out.

"We might just have to stay in here all night." Alex sounded exhausted.

Laughing, Angel pushed at Alex's chest. He slowly withdrew from her before gently helping her to stand on her feet. Grabbing a washcloth from the shelf, she lathered it with soap before running the fabric quickly over Alex.

Doing the same to herself, she decided they were clean enough. She peered up at Alex before twisting off the water. He remained leaning, one shoulder against the wall, looking at her with amusement.

"Come on," she urged, spotting two fluffy towels hanging on a bar close by. She wrapped the first around her body before grabbing the second to start wiping down Alex.

"You don't have to," he told her but made no move to interrupt as she crouched to run the material down his legs.

"You took care of me so now it's my turn," she replied with a smile.

As she rubbed him down she couldn't help but notice his cock start to harden. Placing a soft kiss on the tip, she glanced up at him. He was biting his lower lip while looking at her through half-closed eyes.

Closing her lips around the head of his erection, she sucked.

"Jeez," he shouted.

Sitting back on her heels, she grinned. "Race you to bed?"

He yanked her forward with his fingers holding her chin, for a wet and messy kiss. "Now," he said when they parted.

As fast as Angel could, she wiped away the water still on her skin. Tossing the towel on the counter, she rushed to catch up with her mate.

* * * *

Heat covered her back, waking Angel up in the early morning darkness. She tried to roll over but the weight against her held her still. Smiling, she realized that Alex had effectively pinned her in his sleep.

The amount of warmth that was radiating off him was enough for her to not need blankets. If they were going to sleep together often she'd have to make sure to lower the thermostat before climbing into bed.

Taking a breath, she took in the scent of her mate.

She cuddled into his hold still smelling the soap they'd used earlier.

It was too early for her to be awake but she didn't mind. Getting to lie in Alex's arms while he slept had its own rewards. She could hear the noise of the ranch from the open window above her head.

It was a comforting sound that Angel could see herself getting used to.

Marcus Webb had retired from the organization and moved to Canyon, close to Alex's home. Since she hadn't finished her commitment there was no way that she'd be able to do the same. However, even though she currently resided with the other Guardians, she wasn't required to do so. If she could find a way to work out moving close by she'd continue to see Alex when she wasn't traveling for the organization. She'd call her brother after breakfast and see if he minded having a house guest until she made a decision. Lubbock wasn't too far away and she'd probably be able to see Alex several times a week unless on a mission.

As she started to make plans in her mind she became aware of the horses starting to make sounds.

In the few days she'd been at the ranch they'd never been so loud.

Picking up her head, she concentrated on just what was different. The noise was growing in volume and dread hit her hard. The Pack was still a target. Remy and Kieran were searching for the three missing rogue Guardians, but there was a better chance that the rogues had followed Emilio rather than staying in Lubbock.

Trying to keep from waking Alex, she wiggled out of his hold. Up on her knees, she peered out of the window. The angle was all wrong for her to get a good view.

Another loud bang from the stables and Angel knew trouble had reached the ranch.

"Alex." She shook her mate. While she could take one or two of the trained agents, trying to capture them all was too big a feat.

"Come here, baby," Alex murmured reaching for her.

"Alex. Wake up!"

He lifted his head while squinting at her. "What's wrong? It's still dark out."

"There something in with the horses. We need to get out there and see what it is," she told him.

Alex stilled completely, and she could see him straining to hear what she had. Again a noise echoed around the empty land.

"Shit!" He jumped up, stumbling off the bed.

She hit the floor on her two feet while grabbing up her bag that Alex had moved into his suite earlier the day before. After pulling out panties, a bra, socks, jeans and a long-sleeve shirt she then dressed quickly. Her boots were by the door so she rushed to grab them and slip them on.

By the time she was done Alex already had a hand on the knob. "Are you sure you want to come?" he asked quietly. "I can go get Max."

After shaking her hand she waved toward the door. "No, let's go. It might be nothing."

"You don't believe that."

"No, I don't," she admitted. "But I'm in this. These are my people who are threatening you. We can grab Max if you want but I'm going down there with you."

"I'll call him and ask him to meet us there," Alex conceded.

The large house was dark and silent as they made their way through the halls and down the stairs. Kayla and Chase were staying with Kayla's dad deeper in the canyon at Marcus' house. Chase, Justin and Randy had gone back to Lubbock with Kieran and Remy.

Luckily Max and Cassie's house was only a few steps from Alex's. Alex was speaking softly in the phone but hung up as they reached the back door located in the kitchen.

"Max is going to come in the back while we take the front," Alex whispered to her.

"They'll be expecting us," she relayed. "Remember, they move fast. Your eyes won't be able to follow so use your other senses."

Alex sent her a confused look.

"I helped train Remy so I have a good idea how you'll be able to fight any Day Walker," she told him.

He nodded before squeezing her hand. "Let's go."

As they stepped out in the darkness the sounds in the stable had quieted down. Angel knew how to walk without a sound and was pleased that Alex also moved silently.

The stables weren't far from the house but it still took several minutes for them to see clearly. The doors were closed.

"If they can't see out they won't see us coming," Alex murmured.

"They'll sense us," she reminded him.

"Well if they're waiting, then let's not keep them," Alex said with humor.

Angel couldn't see his face but she just knew he was grinning. She'd always thought that the shifters were a little nuts and he was just proving her point. The animal in them actually enjoyed the fight.

They'd reached the door and while Angel took the left side Alex stood on the right. He held up three fingers. Nodding, she braced herself. Slowly he counted down until he held up a fist and yanked the door open with his other hand. Angel used her speed to rush inside. Her vision blurred, not being able to keep up with her body.

She was halfway in the stables before Alex followed.

Pressing her back against one of the stalls, she listened, trying to pinpoint what had caused the horses to act up. From farther down, near the horse she'd met before, she could hear the *snort* and *neigh*.

Leaping, she pushed off the wall.

Her jump was interrupted as she collided with another body. The sound of bodies crashing into each other was loud in the previously silent space. Hitting the ground, she rolled just in time to miss a boot to her head.

Bounding up, she crouched and prepared for the next attempt. They were dealing with the rogue agents without a doubt. She caught a punch aimed at her face and spun around. Losing her grip, she hopped back and away.

A low growl reached her and she wondered when Alex had shifted. The distraction of her mate was enough for her opponent to land a hard kick to her stomach. Angel soared back, slamming into the wall with the force of the strike.

She grunted, falling.

Desperately clawing at the ground, she picked up a handful of dirt before throwing it where she suspected her enemy would be. Her toss slowed down her opponent. Scrambling back up and taking advantage, she kicked out with her own roundhouse, connecting with a chest.

Before she could celebrate, arms came around her back and lifted her feet.

The slamming of the back door announced Max's arrival an instant before he howled. Max's appearance was enough for her to find an opening. She kicked back at the knee of the person who had a hold of her, using all her strength.

They went down together but she managed an elbow to his ribs, causing the arms around her to disappear as the man yelled.

She darted to the right as Max leaped over her to tackle her second opponent. There was a yelp from where Alex was but she couldn't look away from the younger man who circled her. Since Caspar had identified the three missing agents, Angel had received the files on each of them. Squaring off with her was Kyle Langley who was an expert in hand-to-hand combat. Fighting with him wasn't going to be to her benefit. She eyed the area around her and spotted a rope hanging from the ceiling. It looked like some sort of pulley system. Just as Kyle dove for her she jumped straight up. The rope brushed her left hand but she was able to wrap her right around the line. Swinging, she lashed out, knocking into Kyle's head.

He went down hard.

She landed next to him before throwing a punch. After hitting her mark, she tried to follow it up but found herself once again thrown through the air.

Chapter Eight

Alex saw Angel had landed hard and was slumped back. Fear rushed over him knowing she'd been hurt. He snapped his canines at his rival, hoping to catch him in a sensitive part.

He'd done pretty well so far. Angel had given him good advice in using his other senses. The rogue agents moved so fast that Alex could feel the wind against his fur just before contact was made.

His nose, however, alerted him whenever the rogue was close enough to strike.

Since Day Walkers, like Angel, had no scent, he couldn't smell the threat from them. Instead he concentrated on the disturbance around him. The odor of the dirt being kicked up. The sound of boots across the ground.

Spinning around, Alex bit down on the wrist of the person who tried to grab him. His opponent yelled but Alex clamped down tight. Tossing his head to the side, he could taste blood from the wound he'd managed. His enemy dropped to his knees, and Alex could see it was an older man. Samson or something like that, according to the file he'd seen. With a firm hold, he dragged the whimpering rogue closer to where Angel and Max were. He let go just as Max reached out and grabbed Samson. Max's rival was on the ground groaning but unable to move. It looked as if he had a broken leg and maybe even an arm. As soon as Max had Samson, Alex darted off to check on Angel.

Finding her crouched over a young man with her hand wrapped around his throat, her fangs flashing, he approached slowly. Angel looked over at him, still hissing.

Having not seen this part of her before, he wasn't sure what to do—or what not to do—to ensure she wouldn't think him a threat. He wasn't afraid of her, though. Actually the opposite was true. Seeing that she'd defeated the trespasser and protected his home, Alex thought she was sexy as hell.

Her shoulders relaxed but she didn't let up her hold. Alex whined at the back of his throat. He could smell blood and didn't know whether it was the man's or his mate's.

"I'm okay," she told him as if she knew what he was thinking.

Alex didn't really believe her though. Angel's shirt was torn and there was blood staining the knee of her jeans. He couldn't hold back a growl at the rogue who'd hurt her. "Angel?" Max spoke quietly as he approached.

She smiled, not taking her gaze off Alex. He crawled forward.

"I'm not hurt," she said again.

He didn't know if she was talking to him or Max. It didn't matter. He needed to check for himself.

"The other two are tied up. I'll grab this guy and let Alex check you over," Max offered.

Exchanging places, Max took over their prisoner while Angel hobbled closer to him. Alex stood on his four paws, walking to close the distance. The moment that her hand buried into his thick fur he grew lightheaded with relief.

He lifted his muzzle to lick at her free hand, causing her to laugh. He panted happily at the sound. Dropping down to join him on the ground, she buried her face in his neck. He could feel her taking deep breaths. Worry filled him. Taking a few steps away, he started his change back to his human form. Crouched down, naked, while drawing huge gulps of air, he shook his head to try to clear his vision. Angel was reaching for him as soon as he was fully human.

"You're such a beautiful wolf," she said in awe.

Bringing her into his embrace, he held her tight against his chest. "I know you're hurting."

She was already starting to shake her head. He growled softly, letting her know he wasn't buying it. "Do you need to feed?"

"I..." She pulled back. "Not here."

Understanding dawned on him. "Okay, let's get these guys secure and we'll go back to the house."

"I've got them tucked back into one of the empty stalls," Max told them as he walked up. He passed Alex the clothes that he'd quickly shed right inside the door.

"Thanks, man." Alex nodded in appreciation. "What should we do with them?"

"I'll call Kieran and see where he and Remy are," Angel offered.

"Sound good," he agreed.

Angel climbed out of his lap. Clenching his fist so he didn't yank her back down, Alex had to work on calming himself. The threat to the Pack was over but that didn't mean he wasn't still worried. He needed to get Angel back upstairs so he could check out her wounds. Standing, he redressed while Angel pulled out her cell phone from her boot. Alex glanced over at Max, seeing his brother-in-law grin.

"What?" he asked suspiciously.

"Your woman can kick ass," Max said while lifting his eyebrows.

"Yeah, she can," he agreed. Alex had known, hadn't he? She was a Guardian, which turned out to be a pretty bad-ass organization. While he was worrying about her injuries she was actually the most experienced of all of them.

"It'll be nice to have some extra help around here until things die down and we know everything's over," Max continued.

"We're… We haven't…" Alex trailed off in panic. He hadn't asked about Angel's plans after the rogues were captured. Would she be taking their prisoners back or was that why she was calling Kieran?

"Hey." Max's hand came down on his shoulder. "Don't worry—you have time to discuss things with her."

"I just didn't expect to have to think about her leaving yet," he confessed.

Angel was leaning against the wall with her cell phone to her ear. Long black hair that had been tied back fell in strands around her face. She was so beautiful. He didn't know how he was going to let her leave when the time came.

"If you're mates then it'll work out. I couldn't have left Cassie no matter what. The same will be true for you both."

Max was right. Angel had a dangerous job and if she wanted to keep her employment with the organization he would find a way to make it work. He spent most of his time on his ranch since he had a great staff that ran the businesses he owned in town. He didn't actually have to live there. He could move to wherever Angel called home.

How fucked up was it that he didn't even know where her house was? Sure it'd only been a couple of days as they'd gotten to know each other but he already had deep feelings for her. Hell, he was halfway in love. Angel was his mate and it was his job to make her happy.

He'd make damn sure he took that responsibility seriously. So he could go with Angel when she left. They could work out a schedule for him to return to the ranch and spend time with his family and Pack. It made him sick even to think about leaving the only home he'd ever known. Still Angel's needs were more important than his own.

"Kieran and Remy are on their way back. They'll be here in a couple of hours. Caspar is also flying in. He'll take care of these three when he gets here," Angel said as she strolled up to them.

"Good." Alex tried to sound normal but the frown on Angel's face told him he wasn't successful.

"What's wrong?" she questioned, stepping closer to him as she ran her gaze over his body. "Are you hurt?"

He laughed. Really, what else could he do? Angel was the one bleeding and limping yet she was concerned with him being injured. Damn, what a couple they made.

"I'm calling some of the guards to come and watch over these three while we wait on your men," Max said before Alex could respond to Angel's questions. "Why don't you two head inside and clean up. You'll be pretty busy when the others get here."

"If you're sure—" Angel started.

"Thanks, man," Alex spoke over her. He needed to get his mate in private. Putting his arm around her shoulder, he made certain that he was gentle enough that she could follow along without aggravating her knee.

"Are you sure you're okay?" she asked as they exited the stables.

He nodded, not trusting his voice just yet. The trek back to the house was a lot slower than when they'd left. Finally they reached the back door and he ushered her inside. After flipping on the kitchen light, he turned Angel to face him. He pushed back the hair that had fallen into her face, then leaned close enough to brush his lips against a bruise forming on her cheek.

She released a long breath.

"I hated seeing you fight but *damn* you're good," he confessed.

"You're pretty bad ass yourself. And your wolf is gorgeous," she said, cupping his face.

He was glad she thought so. His animal was such a big part of him. "Come up here." He lifted her to sit on the counter in front of him.

"I'm not hurting you, am I?" he asked while running his palms down her neck.

"No, your hands feel good on me."

Alex took that as permission and continued exploring her body, checking her over. Her T-shirt was easily removed since it was already ripped and hanging off her slim form. There were bruises on her stomach and arms so he bent down to place soft kisses on the small hurts.

Angel sucked in a breath while sliding her hands in his hair. He would have loved to comply with what she wanted but he had to finish inspecting her. Stepping back, he looked down at her leg. The tear in her jeans was open where the blood had been coming from. Taking the worn material between two hands, he tore it. She gasped out a laugh. The cut wasn't as bad as he'd thought. While the wound needed to be cleaned and bandaged, the bleeding had stopped. Satisfied she was really going to be okay, he smiled.

"Are you done?" she asked, amusement obvious.

"Yeah."

"Kiss me then," she ordered.

Moving in between her legs, he brought his mouth down on hers. Angel gripped his shoulders, bringing him closer as their tongues twined and rubbed against each other. His cock hardened, making him have to shift his stance to relieve some of the pressure.

"We should go upstairs and shower," he told her as he finally backed away.

Cupping his erection, she squeezed him while leaning forward to nip his chin. "After."

What fool would argue with that? Luckily the cabinet put Angel at the perfect level for what he wanted. Unsnapping her pants, he slowly removed the fabric. Once she was bared for him, he kissed her chin before pushing her back.

Angel spread her legs wide, giving him better access. Licking at her folds, he used his fingers to reveal her. She was already wet for him as he dove down to start pleasuring her. Each lick over her sweet pussy had her cries gaining in volume. It was music to his ears. He knew he was making her feel good. He was the one who could drown her in ecstasy until she couldn't hold back any longer.

Using his tongue, he devoured her. Spurred on by her moans, he took her closer and closer to the edge. Pushing two fingers deep inside, he mouthed her clit until she yelled and climaxed. She was still panting as he straightened, yanking off his own clothing. Grasping his hard cock, he jacked himself a few times before settling against her. Pushing just the head of his cock inside, he paused. "Look at me."

She blinked her blue eyes open to gaze up at him as he carefully pressed inside. *Fuck!* It felt so good to have her inner muscles clamp down on him.

"Yes," he hissed while withdrawing, before slamming back inside.

Crying out, she bowed her back, clawing at the cabinet under her.

Sliding through her juices over and over again, Alex was already too close to exploding.

Thrusting with long and deep plunges, he ran his hands over Angel's full breasts, enjoying touching what was his. With her head thrown up, Angel's orgasm rocked through her, causing her to arch and hold his cock tight. His pace grew erratic until he bent over and came. He sped up, yelling, coming and filling her with his seed.

His entire body shook as he tried to get himself under control. He couldn't give this up. They needed to shower and talk.

Chapter Nine

After a long, hot shower and applying bandages, Angel sat on Alex's bedroom couch in a pair of sweat pants and a tank top. She'd pulled on a thick pair of gray socks to keep her feet warm.

As soon as they'd finished cleaning up, Alex's phone started to ring. The Alpha, Chase, Marcus and even Caspar had all called to check on the situation.

Knowing something was on his mind, Angel waited until Alex had finished with answering questions. Alex had grown quiet while they'd bathed together. Unsure if it was just the excitement or if there was more bothering her mate, she was worried. She wanted to make things easier on Alex. Now that all the rogue Guardians had been captured, Alex's Pack should be able to get back to living their lives.

Clamping her hands together, she warily watched as Alex approached her.

"Everyone is excited that all this is over," he told her.

She nodded. "Aren't you?"

"I'm happy that my friends and family are safe."

"But?" She just knew there was more.

"But I don't have a reason to keep you here with me," he said, looking away.

Angel couldn't contain her gasp. Was Alex kicking her out? After all they'd been through in just a few short days—was he no longer interested in being with her?

Standing while trying to control her emotions, she wasn't sure what to do.

"I just..." Alex was still talking but she hadn't heard a word.

Instead of letting him break her heart any more, she jumped for the bedroom door just as her tears started to fall.

Strong arms gripped her around her waist. "Hey."

She struggled out of his hold but couldn't hide her face.

"Angel? What the hell?"

"Just let me go," she ordered. "I won't bother you anymore."

"You want to leave?"

"I promise you never have to see me again," she replied. Of course she never planned to come anywhere near the entire state of Texas.

"What are you...?"

Still attempting her escape, she sucked in a breath as she found herself lifted off her feet.

"Fuck this," Alex growled.

"I..." She didn't get any further before he tossed her onto his large dark bed before following to pin her.

"You're mine," he stated, peering down at her.

She tilted her head in a show of submission. "I'll always be yours," she confessed. "Even if you don't want me."

"Don't want you?" he repeated.

"You said you didn't have a reason to keep me here," she told him, trying her best to keep the hurt and anger out of her voice. Now that she'd started to calm, her hurt was taking a back seat to the fury swamping her.

"We need to communicate better," he demanded.

"Okay." What in the hell was she agreeing to?

His hands were gentle as he cupped her face while wiping away the traces of wetness. "How could you think I would want you to go?"

Blinking rapidly at the sudden turn of events, she opened her mouth to reply but no words came.

"My mate belongs by my side. I know you have a job to do. I've been thinking about how to make things between us work. I'll talk to my brother and sister today to see how much they can take over here at the ranch for me and what we'll need to hire out for."

"You're leaving the ranch?" She was missing something big. Damn it, why couldn't she think straight. Oh yeah, Alex had her pinned to the bed with his hard cock brushing her stomach. She couldn't concentrate because she wanted him so badly.

Wait, he had an erection. Shaking her head almost violently, she forced herself to really listen to his words. "Say that again."

"I said." He paused to smile. "That I go where you go. If you have to leave then I'll be at your side."

"Oh, oh!" She shoved up and wrapped her arms around his neck. "But we don't have to!" Her laughter released the ball of dread in her gut.

Alex was chuckling along with her. "Care to explain that?"

She pulled back enough to gaze into his eyes. "I live in one of the dorm rooms but I don't have to stay there. I've just never had a place of my own. I thought you'd want to wait and get to know each other better so I was going to stay with Justin in Lubbock until I found a place of my own. That way whenever I'm not working I'll be close by."

"See!" Alex barked. "We need to talk about these things. That's almost a perfect plan."

"Almost?" she teased.

"Other than you staying with Justin I totally agree with you. You'll stay here with me. I won't have my mate living two hours away."

"Are you sure you're ready for that?" she had to ask.

"Yes, are you? I'm kind of a bear to live with. I have to have my coffee before I can string together a full sentence."

"I can deal with that," she promised. "I might sleep some weird hours. Especially when I come back from an assignment."

"Lucky for me I work from home so I can take naps if you keep me up," he replied. "My sister and brother live in houses on the property. They're over here a lot."

"I like your family. But if I'm staying here you'll see a lot of Remy and Kieran."

"I like Remy and I guess Kieran will grow on me."

She punched his shoulder. "I can already tell you like Kieran too."

He held his hands up. "Fine, just don't tell him."

"It'll be our secret," she vowed. "Anything else you think you'll scare me off with?"

He scrunched his nose as he thought. "I'll have to have you…a lot. I don't think I'll ever get tired of touching you, being inside you."

Angel was already nodding. "If you don't, then I'll just jump you."

Grinning, he leaned forward. "I want you to stay. We'll figure everything else out."

She brushed her lips over his. "I want to stay."

Gripping his shoulders tightly, she tugged him to cover her body. As she slid her hand down his back the muscles beneath her palm moved while he rocked against her. It felt good to have his weight pinning her down.

"I want to feel your skin," he demanded, sitting back on his heels. He yanked off his shirt then reached for hers. She brushed away his hands so she could speed things along.

Alex refusing to stop touching her didn't help, but she was determined to get naked with him. By the time she unhooked her bra his hands where on her breasts, kneading.

Reaching for the button of his jeans, he lifted up but kissed her neck.

"We should have just stayed naked," she told him.

"I couldn't talk to you without clothes on," he confided.

Well, he had a point there. Wrapping herself around him, she pushed until he flipped back. Straddling his legs, she tugged off her pants before finishing removing his.

Already hot and hard for her, he moaned as she grasped his cock, pumping several times.

"Are you going to ride me?" he asked as his eyes gleamed in anticipation.

"Is that what you want?" she teased. "Or maybe..." Leaning forward, she licked at the head of his cock.

He moaned.

"That's what I thought," she said smugly, before taking him deeply into her mouth.

Wrapping her fist around the base of him, she set an easy pace that was sure to drive him wild. Alex pumped his hips, trying to get her to stop teasing, but Angel wasn't having any of that.

"Please! Angel, I need more."

Popping off, she grinned up at him. "What do you want?"

"You, always you."

He deserved a reward for that answer. She straddled his waist. As she reached back to position him at her entrance she locked gazes with him.

Sliding down, she didn't look away. "You're mine," she claimed him.

"Yes," he hissed.

That's all she wanted. Everything else would work itself out. Raising and falling, she took him hard and fast. With his nails digging into her hips, she knew she would have bruises but she didn't care.

All that mattered was the connection she felt as she made love to her mate.

* * * *

Sunlight was barely breaking over the horizon when everyone gathered in his den. Alex kept his arm around Angel's shoulder once they'd settled on the couch together.

Kieran and Remy had arrived from Lubbock to take over guarding the rogue Guardians. With his Alpha and Caspar speaking quietly about how'd they transfer their prisoners, Alex and content where he was.

"I take it you're staying here?" Caspar asked, glancing over at Angel.

"Unless you need me?"

"No, it should be fine. Keep your phone on just in case, but we can handle getting these three back," he told her.

"Then I'd like to stay." Angel peeked over at Alex. "We still have some things to work out but I'll return soon to get my stuff."

Caspar's wide grin lit up his entire face, making him look years younger. "So...?"

"He's my mate," she declared proudly.

Caspar laughed. "I figured, but you hadn't said anything. Take as much time as you need. Bring Alex with you when you come to collect your things so he can meet everyone," Caspar said as he rose.

Alex stood also as Caspar offered his hand.

"I'm very happy for you both," Caspar told him.

"Thank you," Alex replied sincerely. He knew from the way that Angel had spoken about her boss that she valued Caspar's opinion.

Alpha Shawn had also risen and was now hugging Angel. "Welcome to the family," Shawn said quietly to Angel.

His heart was full as he overheard those words.

"Thank you." Angel hugged Shawn back.

Caspar released him only for Shawn to wrap him in a bear hug, lifting him off his feet.

"Alpha!" he protested.

Shawn just laughed.

Once he was back on his feet, Alex reached for Angel. She came into his embrace immediately.

"Thank you both. We'll have a celebration once Angel gets settled in," Alex shared.

"That's great," Caspar replied. "We'll make sure to be around."

"You're always welcome," Alex told them.

"We'll have to work out a story about how you met Angel for the rest of the Pack but I'm sure they'll welcome her with open arms."

Alex had no doubt that everyone would love Angel as much as he did. But the other thing? "Story?"

"We still have to keep the Guardians a secret. It will be your job to help protect any of them who stay with Pack lands," Shawn explained.

"Of course!" He looked over the three Guardians there. "My entire family will safeguard you."

"We appreciate that. What we do is important. But it's better left in the dark. There are some things the humans are just not ready for. Now there is one thing we have to discuss," Caspar grew serious.

Angel stiffened against him. "What's that?"

"Who gets custody of Kieran?" Caspar asked gravely.

"What?" Alex asked confused.

"Not me!" Caspar and Angel shouted at the same time.

"I swear, I never get any love."

Alex glanced over his shoulder to see Kieran walk through the open sliding glass door.

"I thought you were helping guard?" Caspar asked, placing his hands on his hips.

"Too many puppies. I thought I'd see what was going on in here," Kieran answered with his usual smirk.

Now that Alex knew Kieran a little better he didn't get insulted. Instead he smacked Kieran in the back of the head as Kieran walked past him.

"Ow!" Kieran bitched.

"See, your man already knows how to handle K!" Caspar claimed.

"I don't know," Kieran said flopping on the couch. "I guess I like it here."

Alex knew they were joking. Okay, he hoped they were joking. They had better be joking! He tightened his hold on Angel, glancing at her. She shrugged.

"He does grow on you," she said, trying not to smile and failing miserably.

He groaned.

"Hey, look at it this way," Caspar told him, "you'll have help mucking out the stalls."

Alex turned an evil grin toward Kieran.

"Hey, I just remembered I need to finish some paper work," Kieran said jumping up.

"You don't do paper work." Angel stated laughing. "You pass it off to me and Remy."

"Shh," Kieran hissed at her.

Alex chuckled, glancing around his home at the additions to his family. The threat might be over but things were going to be far from boring.

About the Author

Crissy Smith lives in Texas with her husband, daughter, and three Labrador retrievers. The three dogs love to curl up under her computer desk and nap while she writes. It doesn't leave a lot of room for her but what's a woman to do?

When not writing or reading, she enjoys hunting, camping and shooting. But she has a girly side too and is addicted to pedicures and coffee.

She has been writing since she was a teenager and still loves everything to do with the paranormal. Her stories and characters all have a place in her heart. She loves the alpha male, the dominant werewolf, or the Master vampire which find their way in most of her books.

Learn more about the characters she has created at her website where they have their very own page. It will be updated from time to time to let you know what's going on with them. Also you can find out who will be in the next book.

Crissy Smith loves to hear from readers. You can find her contact information, website details and author profile page at http://www.totallybound.com

Totally Bound Publishing